Sorry? How could he explain that he didn't want her memory to come back because that would mean she would leave him?

How selfish did that make him? "Will you be okay up here?"

"Okay?" She tilted her head back, her eyes sparkling. "I can't wait to see this concert."

"It should be a good one. Khan is in fine form."

"I won't be watching Khan. I'll be looking at you." There was a husky note in Violet's voice.

And, because he couldn't help himself, Nate bent his head and kissed her. Fire spread through him as soon as his lips connected with hers, so hot he thought he might burn up with it. When his tongue probed the seam of her lips, they parted readily for him, and he probed the honeyed warmth of her mouth. Violet's hands bunched in the material of his T-shirt as though she was using him to stay upright. He groaned, kissing her harder, and she trembled, returning the caresses of his tongue eagerly.

She tasted like everything he had ever wanted and never knew he needed until now.

THE UNFORGETTABLE WOLF

JANE GODMAN

First Published in Great Britain 2017
By Mills & Boon, an imprint of HarperCollins*Publishers*
1 London Bridge Street, London, SE1 9GF

© 2017 Amanda Anders

ISBN: 978-0-263-93000-9

89-0317

Jane Godman writes in a variety of romance genres, including paranormal, gothic and romantic suspense. Jane lives in England and loves to travel to European cities that are steeped in history and romance—Venice, Dubrovnik and Vienna are among her favorites. Jane is married to a lovely man and is mum to two grown-up children.

This book is dedicated to my beautiful new daughter-in-law, Julia, who is already such a special part of our family. Congratulations on your wedding to my wonderful son, Mike. I am looking forward to sharing lots of amazing memories with you both.

Chapter 1

Just because he was no longer a werewolf didn't mean he wasn't big and bad. It just meant he had to be careful. Very, very careful.

Which was why, as the courier approached, Nate Zilar's every sense was on high alert. He had chosen this meeting place because of its deserted location and had checked the surrounding area carefully. There was no one around. The parking lot was empty, apart from his car and the truck in which the other guy had just pulled up.

"Do you have the merchandise?"

"In the back." The courier jerked his head.

Nate stepped forward. Another quick scan of his surroundings confirmed they were alone. Even now, after six years, he got flashbacks to that time. A reminder of that brief period when everything—his vision, hearing, scent and intuition—had all been so much more acute. When his body had been a raw mass of power and reaction. It wasn't welcome, but at times like this, that residual super-charging of his senses came in useful.

The courier stepped aside, allowing Nate to view the objects in the back of the truck through the open doors. Silver samurai sword. Three daggers in varying sizes. They were the real thing. Nate had seen enough imitations and alloys over the years to know pure silver when he saw .it. And he could smell it. It was another thing that had stayed with him. That crawling, gut-churning, nostril-burning stink of verdigris and death. When you'd been stabbed through the heart with a silver dagger, you never forgot the stench. It remained embedded in your pores, branded deep in your psyche.

Even though his shifting days were over, Nate remembered the damage silver could do. It was the only thing guaranteed to kill a werewolf. And he should know. He examined the guns. They were what he had ordered. His favorite Remington 700 and a couple of handguns.

"Bullets?"

"A dozen. Solid silver." The courier pointed to a box.

Nate shook his head. What if his quarry wasn't alone? "Not enough. I need at least twice that many."

He clenched his teeth hard, biting back his frustration. This was the problem with international travel. He couldn't carry his own kit on an airplane, so he was forced to rely on others to have things ready and waiting for him. At least here in America he could usually count on getting exactly what he wanted. In some places, like on his recent mission to a remote African state, it proved more of a problem.

"I was told a dozen." *Like hell you were.* For the first time, he looked the other man in the eye. The courier took a step back under the full force of Nate's glare. "I can get more, but it will cost you extra."

"Figures."

"I'll have them here in the morning."

Nate withdrew a roll of cash from the back pocket of his jeans and started counting. He knew from experience it was the only language that worked. "I'll be gone from here in the morning. I need them tonight."

The man's eyes fixed greedily on the hundred-dollar bills. "Anything you say." He paused. "Can I ask you something?"

"You can ask." *Doesn't mean you'll get an answer.*

"Can I get an autograph? It's for my daughter. She's a big fan..." Under Nate's steady gaze, his voice trailed off and he swallowed nervously.

When Nate didn't answer, the courier walked away, muttering an embarrassed curse under his breath as he climbed back into the truck.

So the day he'd dreaded had come at last. He'd been recognized. Had this guy already been to the press with the story, or would he have long enough to complete this mission before all hell broke over his head? The best headline he could hope for was something speculative like Why is Nate Zilar Stockpiling Illegal Weapons? The worst? Rock Star Turns Werewolf Hunter.

"My friends are not your business."

"I am the Wolf Leader. Everything you do is my business!"

They were the words her father had flung at her before Violet stormed out of his study in a rage.

He used the same words to end every argument. As the youngest daughter of Nevan, the ruler of the werewolves, Violet was tired of being expected to bend to his every demand.

Her father was a powerful figure in Otherworld politics. The Wolf Nation was one of the most influential dynasties in Otherworld, and many werewolves also lived alongside humans in the mortal realm. It meant the Wolf Leader was a dominant force in both worlds.

Their relationship had always been stormy. Violet's mother had died soon after she was born and, without the calming influence of the woman he had loved deeply, her father had become even more autocratic and domineering. Violet, the child many said resembled her mother more closely than any of her siblings, had borne the brunt of this.

Things had gone from bad to worse recently when her father had succeeded in his ambition to overthrow his sworn enemy, Anwyl, the former Wolf Leader. Now he was no longer Nevan the Rebel. He was in charge. His arrogance had swelled in proportion to his power and influence. Violet's defiance increased correspondingly. Their clashes became legendary. Confrontation was commonplace in the Wolf Nation, but when Nevan and his daughter fought, everyone else took cover.

Now Violet had reached adulthood, and she found her father's control stifling. She wanted to do something with her life, an ambition that horrified Nevan. No child of his was going to undertake any form of employment. Violet's suggestion that she should do voluntary work had also been met with scorn.

The vast series of rural islands that comprised the Wolf Nation was a difficult territory over which to keep control. Nevan wanted to maintain the appearance of a powerful leader with a dutiful family at his side. A daughter who went her own way did not fit that image.

Although Nevan had quickly consolidated his position with ruthless strikes against all those who had previously opposed him, a new resistance had soon sprung up. For so many years, Nevan had been the rebel leader. Now he had achieved his goal. Anwyl, the man he hated was dead, but the new rebel leader, Roko, was as determined as Violet to change the political landscape. The difference between them was that Roko was able to speak openly about his beliefs. Violet didn't dare.

It had been easier to pretend her closeness to Roko was friendship than to tell her father the truth. If he discovered she was working secretly with the resistance to help the refugees, those werewolves made homeless by Nevan's cruelty, the storm breaking over her head would have become a tempest.

Since becoming leader, Nevan's fury against Anwyl's followers had been boundless. The two main islands that comprised the Wolf Nation were Reznati and Urlati. Until recently, Reznati had been the base of Anwyl and his followers. Urlati had always been Nevan's home. Following Anwyl's defeat, Nevan had exacted terrible retribution upon the people of Reznati, burning villages and driving men, women and children out of their homes.

Violet drew a breath as she exited Nevan's study. In the most recent confrontation, her father had forbidden her from seeing Roko. He had forbidden her many things during her life, most of which she had disobeyed.

Leaving the house, the beautiful mansion known as the Voda Kuca that occupied a prominent position on the island of Urlati, she made her way to the nearby forest where she knew Roko would be waiting. Sure enough, he was lounging against a tree trunk.

Faced with her father's atrocities toward his enemies, Violet had no choice other than to turn to the resistance for help. But both Roko and her father made a huge assumption if they believed her interest in the rebel leader was romantic. *Maybe I haven't tried hard enough to convince either of them.* She experienced a pang of guilt as Roko's handsome features lit up with a smile when he saw her.

She had never given him any encouragement, but that look told her she might not have given him a clear enough signal that friendship and a working relationship were all she had to offer. Her conscience prodded her again. Maybe a part of her had enjoyed inflaming her father's anger even further by hinting that this was something more.

"Trouble?" Roko asked as he saw her expression.

"My father has issued an ultimatum. I am to stop working for the refugee movement or face banishment." The words came out in a rush. The tears she had tried so hard to suppress were close to the surface, but she didn't know Roko well enough to allow them to spill over in his presence. Her pride would not allow a display of that nature. She knew he would be only too happy to offer a sympathetic shoulder, but that would mean dismantling a boundary that she preferred to keep intact.

"Bastard." His features hardened. "What will you do?"

"What can I do?" Violet sighed. "I cannot accept my father's autocratic rule, not just over myself, but over the Wolf Nation. I've always known he is a cruel man. I've seen the evidence of that throughout my life. Even when I was younger, I tried to persuade him that there were other ways to secure the loyalty of his subjects." She laughed at the memory. "My efforts were always greeted with a sneer. When he finally defeated Anwyl and took over, his treatment of those who were loyal to the former leader was brutal."

Roko nodded. "I know. I see the evidence of it every day. Anwyl was a good man. He led our dynasty peaceably for many years until Nevan turned against him. I want a return to those days, a return to the werewolf traits of nobility and pack loyalty. We are not a nation that turns on its own."

Violet didn't point out to him that the resistance was

weak. Since Anwyl's defeat, Nevan had done everything he could to stamp out any opposition. The only reason Roko was still alive was that Nevan didn't view him as a real threat. Her father had made sure Roko had no real support. Anyone who might have considered joining the resistance was already in the refugee camp, fighting to stay alive.

"As I was growing up, my brothers and sisters tried to get me to follow their lead, to turn a blind eye to what my father was doing, but I couldn't. That this cruelty is going on in his name makes it so much worse, because I am associated with it through my relationship to him. He makes me stand at his side when there is a formal function. I must walk next to him when he goes on his triumphant journeys through the Wolf Nation. When he took over, I had to do something—anything—to make things better for the innocent werewolf packs caught in the crossfire of his revenge."

Violet shook her head. She hadn't answered Roko's question. What *was* she going to do? When your father was feared throughout Otherworld for violence, and within his own family for his temper, it was probably best not to openly defy him.

So why do I continue to do it? Violet wondered, not for the first time. *Why the hell don't I just accept defeat and bow down to his wishes?*

The answer was obvious. *Because if I give in this time, I'll do it every time. I would abandon my principles and let down all those people who are depending on me.*

Maybe this one time, I have to let go. It was a small, insidious voice at the back of her mind. She had been hearing it more and more frequently lately. No matter how hard she tried to shut it up, it refused to be silenced. She knew her father's threat to banish her was a serious one. She didn't have far to look for the proof that he meant what he said. After all, it had happened to one of her own brothers.

Roko cast a speculative glance in her direction. "Why don't you come with me to the mortal realm?"

Roko had boasted before that he had friends in the human world. It had seemed so exotic when he first told her about it. The mortal realm was a mystic place, somewhere Violet had heard of only in stories. She knew there were werewolves who lived alongside mortals without detection, but it sounded like the fairy tales she had read as a child. It was another world, one she had never thought to visit.

Even though the veil between the two worlds was a thin one, with Otherworld existing unseen alongside the mortal realm, there was very little overlap between them. All Violet knew was that access to the mortal realm could be gained through a series of portals. While some hardy adventurers used these as a means of traveling regularly between the two, most beings remained within their own worlds. Those in Otherworld had an awareness of the mortal realm, but mortals remained blissfully unaware of Otherworld.

She blinked at him. "Pardon?"

"There are werewolves there who can help the refugee cause. Wealthy businessmen and women who make their money in the mortal realm. They can provide the support we need for the camp of Anwyl supporters who have been displaced by your father's policies."

Violet's heart began to beat faster. "My father would never allow it."

"I wasn't suggesting we should tell him." Roko grinned delightedly at the look on her face. "Your father's beta werewolves, the goons he sends to sniff out a problem, are used to operating here in Otherworld. They'll never be smart enough to figure out where we've gone."

It all sounded so enticing, so brave, so spur-of-the-moment glamorous. There was just one problem.

"We are friends, right? Nothing more." She had to be sure Roko knew that before she embarked on any journey with him.

His grin deepened. "Sure thing, babe."

Babe? Had he listened to what she'd just said? Violet knew why Nevan was so opposed to her friendship with Roko. Apart from the fact that he was a rebel, her father saw her as a pawn to further his political ambitions. He wanted to marry her off to one of his powerful allies. Prospects were everything as far as her father was concerned. Prospects were something Roko lacked. He was not an alpha wolf, and his family was not noble.

Looking at Roko's smiling, handsome face, Violet finally understood what prospects really meant. It wasn't about whether the man she chose as her mate would further the werewolf cause with Otherworld dynasties. When the werewolves sat around the table at gatherings of the Otherworld Alliance, they met with faeries, elves, phantoms, and dryads, to name but a few of the many dynasties who made up the vast realm of Otherworld. Not to mention the age-old enemies of the werewolves. The vampire dynasty under its charismatic leader, Prince Tibor, was on the rise. Nevan wanted alliances that would make the werewolves a match for the vampires. That was what prospects meant to him.

But shouldn't prospects also mean her mate would be able to care for her, protect her and shelter her if they made a mad dash into the mortal realm? With Roko, the answer to all of those was a resounding no.

When she looked at Roko, Violet saw the opposite of

Nevan. She saw weakness instead of strength, but neither man had the true qualities needed to lead the Wolf Nation. Both were lacking the essential ingredients of compassion and empathy. It scared her that her people—her pack—were reliant on these warring individuals to provide the leadership they so desperately needed.

Oh, Roko could offer her fun…and fun had been one element that had been missing throughout Violet's life. Now and then, she had briefly wondered if it might be worth combining business with pleasure. But Violet had realized some time ago that fun might be all Roko had to offer. She wasn't sure what she wanted from her future mate, but it was a hell of a lot more than this.

Even though she had her doubts about the company, a proposed trip to the mortal realm offered her an escape from her father's threats and the chance to drum up some much-needed support for her cause.

"Very well." She nodded. "When do we leave?"

"How about right now?"

Nate jerked awake suddenly, aware that he was no longer alone in an anonymous motel room. Instinctively, his hand dived under the pillow for his gun.

"Relax. You don't need it." The voice of the man seated in the chair at the side of the bed was amused. The moonlight streaming through a gap in the curtains illuminated his face, and his eyes shone with a silver gleam that was unusual, but familiar.

"I wish you wouldn't do that. Can't you just arrange to meet in some seedy strip joint like other people do at—" Nate squinted at the digital clock on the bedside locker "—four in the morning?" He reached out a hand and flipped the switch on the lamp.

His uninvited visitor grinned. "Must I remind you that I'm a happily married man?"

Nate sat up against the pillows, tucking the bedcovers around his waist. "Looking good for it, Cal. Being a father obviously suits you."

It still felt strange to call Merlin Caledonius by his nickname. The greatest sorcerer the world had ever known, the man responsible for bringing the legendary King Arthur to the throne, should surely be accorded more respect. Nate reminded himself that Cal was the name the man himself preferred.

"You haven't seen me trying to change a diaper. It would do my reputation no good whatsoever if word of how bad I am at that simple task ever got out. Three children, and it doesn't get any easier. Stella sends her love, by the way."

Nate could never think of Cal's wife, Stella, without remembering *that* night six years ago. As far as he could recall it. Some of the details were a blur. The part where he had tried to rip Stella's throat out was pretty much lost in the mists of time. The voice in his head urging him on wasn't. Nate could still hear that voice. It haunted his dreams.

"Sending mine right back to her. And the twins? How are they? Nice touch on the names, by the way. Keeping the whole Merlin and Arthur theme going."

"We think so. And it's a tribute to one of my best friends, of course. Young Jethro and Arthur are thriving, thank you."

"It was certainly unexpected that your friend Jethro de Loix would turn out to be the reincarnation of King Arthur," Nate said.

"But useful when it came to naming our sons. We were able to name both twins after the same person." Cal cast a glance around the bland room. "Not up to your usual standard. Seeing this, no one would believe you were one of the most well-known men in Europe."

"The choice of location was yours. They don't exactly deal in luxury out here in the back of beyond. Anyway, I thought we agreed I wouldn't draw attention to myself. The band may only have made it big in the US recently, but people tend to sit up and take notice when I fly into town." Should he mention the courier? There was always a tendency to assume Cal knew everything. "Which reminds me, I was recognized yesterday."

Cal muttered a curse. "Give me the details and I'll sort it out."

Nate nodded. He knew the man assigned with the task of keeping the peace on the boundaries between Otherworld and the mortal realm was unlikely to mean anything sinister by those words. It was probable Cal would simply erase the courier's memory, or use some other sorcerer's trick on him.

Nate yawned and glanced at the clock again. He'd been asleep for four hours. It felt like less. "Who have you got for me this time?"

Cal produced a photograph from the pocket of his button-down shirt. It showed a young man, looking directly at the camera. There was a slight smile on his face as he raised a beer bottle in salute to whoever was taking the picture.

"He looks about the same age I was." Nate's voice was expressionless. This was always the hardest part.

"A bit younger." Cal's tone held a note of sympathy that Nate really didn't want to hear.

"How long?" He swallowed hard, fighting the emotions that were trying to rise up inside him. This was going to be difficult enough without feeling any sort of attachment.

"Three months."

"Just a novice."

"Hardly that." Cal produced another set of pictures, and Nate's resolve hardened. Blood, gore and the torn-apart bodies of innocent victims would do that every time.

"Where?" Nate became businesslike again.

"There is a thriving werewolf population in this part of the world. A peaceable one for the most part. They generally live alongside the humans without drawing attention to themselves, but there is a big party tonight. It's a fund-raiser of some kind." Cal tapped the photographs with one fingertip. "Our friend here is a feral werewolf, so he won't be invited. But he will be drawn to the other were-wolves. Pack instinct. He won't be able to help himself. It will be easier to hunt him and take him down out there, in the countryside, than in town."

Nate nodded. What Cal was saying made sense. Were-wolves were sociable. They liked to reinforce their pack status with regular parties and meetings. The rogues he hunted were cast out by the werewolves who lived along-side mortals. They gave werewolves a bad name. Even so, the feral ones, the ones who belonged to the legends of full moons and misty moors, still longed to be part of lycanthrope society and were drawn to their law-abiding counterparts without understanding why. It was just an-other facet to the curse they labored under. He remem-bered it well.

Nate drew a breath. The formalities might be over, but there was something else he needed to say. Even though he knew what Cal's response would be, he always had to raise the subject. It burned away inside him, ate him up. He needed to hear the words every time just in case, by some miracle, they might be different.

"You know which one I want you to send me after."

Cal shook his head. Like he always did. "You know it

can't be done. Nevan rarely enters the mortal realm, and it would be too dangerous for you to go after him on his home territory. Otherworld is not the place for humans."

"I'd risk it if it meant I could take that bastard out." Nate hated the tremor in his hands as he pressed his fingertips against his temple. "When I remember what he did to me. Having him inside my head…"

"Let it go, Nate." Cal's voice was gentle.

Nate leaned back on his pillows, breathing deep as he tilted his head to look at the ceiling. *Let it go?* Only a man who had never lived with the nightmare Nate had endured could utter those words. Six years ago, Nate had been attacked by a feral werewolf. Having survived, Nate had become a rogue werewolf himself, subject to the same bloodlust each time the moon was full. Even worse, his mind had been controlled by a powerful, manipulative werewolf called Nevan. This werewolf, one whom Nate had never met, had used an evil form of telepathy to try and force him to kill Stella.

Nate had a feeling he might be the only person who had lived through the horror of becoming a werewolf and coming through the other side as a human once more. That remarkable feat was due to the ingenuity of Cal and Stella. When Nate had attempted to kill Stella, Cal had stabbed him through the heart with a silver dagger, killing the werewolf within him. Stella, who was the greatest necromancer the world had ever known—so great that she was known throughout Otherworld as the "necromancer star"—had used her incredible powers to bring him back to life. Nate had survived the experience. He was intact, but not unscathed.

Cal regarded him steadily. "Although I've never questioned your commitment, I worry about what this does to you."

"It screws with my head, but I can't stop." Nate gave a shaky laugh. "And I don't see a queue of people lining up to take my place. So, worrying or not, I guess I'm the only werewolf hunter you have."

Cal nodded. "I know this is no consolation, but Nevan has his own set of problems right now. As well as struggling to maintain control after a bloody fight to take over as leader, his youngest daughter has gone missing."

"My heart bleeds for him." Nate managed a sarcastic snarl that was a little too wolfish for his own liking. "Just so we're clear…if the opportunity ever presents itself, I will do whatever it takes to make that bastard pay for what he did to me. With or without your approval."

The party was in full swing when they arrived. Held in a vast, ranch-style house deep in the heart of a Vermont forest, it was unlike any other Violet had ever attended. The dress code was casual; there were no formal introductions, and, since dinner seemed to consist of helping yourself to raw steak and beer, there wasn't a seating plan. The mortal realm was finally beginning to live up to its fairy-tale reputation.

Violet was conscious of the number of glances, both surreptitious and open, being cast her way as, with a proprietorial hand on the small of her back, Roko steered her out toward the backyard.

"Do these people know who I am?"

He shook his head. "No way. I haven't told anyone. Only Teo. One word in the wrong ear and your father's mongrels would find us and rip me apart."

"Then why are so many of them staring at me?"

Roko flashed his grin at her. He hadn't used it much since their arrival in the mortal realm, and somehow it had lost a lot of its impact. "Because you're gorgeous."

Teo, who'd overheard the remark, tilted his drink in her direction in an appreciative salute. Pack dynamics seemed to be off-kilter here in the mortal realm. In Otherworld, Teo would not have dared to cast a look in the direction of the daughter of the great Wolf Leader. Here it seemed to be okay to throw her a glance that blatantly told her he was picturing her human without any clothes…and her wolf self baring her belly in preparation for submission.

So far, the mortal realm had not lived up to Violet's expectations. From the moment they entered it, they had been in hiding. Her father controlled all werewolves, not just those in Otherworld. Nevan's word was absolute. From the minute they crossed the border from Otherworld, the search had been on. Violet was hunted, and Roko was a marked man. One or two narrow escapes had been enough to turn the swaggering, would-be alpha into a frightened, petulant cub.

Sunlight had become a distant memory. Hiding away indoors, staying cooped up inside for days on end, running scared: all of those things were alien to Violet's natural instincts. And the food? *Don't get me started on the food.* Prepackaged, tasteless and limited. It wasn't even fit for dogs. How mortals survived on this crap, she would never know. She needed to get out, to run, to hunt, to sink her teeth into her own kill. A kill that was still warm…

The backyard was predictably more crowded than the house. Like Violet, most wolves would rather be outdoors than inside. She tilted back her head, drinking in the velvety night sky and sniffing appreciatively at the loam and pine scent of the forest.

There was nothing she'd have liked more than to slip out of her clothes and let her wolf self run free through the trees. There was just one problem. She cast a sidelong glance in Roko's direction. She didn't want to give him the wrong idea. Violet almost laughed out loud. She didn't want to give him *any* ideas. Coming to the mortal realm in his company had been about the worst move she'd ever made. She wasn't going to compound it by letting him think she was ready to mate with him. She knew Roko was waiting for a signal from her. A signal that was never going to come.

Violet found herself in a new situation. Strong-willed, headstrong and determined, for the first time in her life, she didn't know what to do. Slink back to Otherworld with her tail between her legs, face her father's wrath and the subsequent humiliation? Or remain here in the mortal realm with a man who wanted more than she was prepared to give? So far, there was no sign of the support he'd promised for the refugees, and she needed to get back to the Wolf Nation and back to her role in helping them. It was a dilemma, and she found herself paying more attention to her thoughts than to her fellow partygoers. The only thing she knew for sure was that she was never going back to her role as the oppressed daughter of the Wolf Leader. She wanted to *do* something with her life. What that something might be, she had no idea. All she knew for sure was that it would involve helping the oppressed werewolves under her father's control…which meant she would be pitting her will against his.

After a few beers, Roko seemed to relax and was soon the center of a group of young males. Violet got the impression he was inviting their admiration because of her, in a look-what-I've-got way. It annoyed her, because it provided more evidence of her foolishness in being here with him. She drifted away from him slightly, following her instincts and allowing the woods and the night to call to her.

The moon was full, adding to her restlessness, and she walked deeper into the trees, leaving the sounds of revelry behind. She breathed deep, inhaling the darkness. Her inner wolf leaped at the scents and sounds around her. Damp earth, crackling leaves underfoot, scurrying creatures. Night sounds. A glance over her shoulder showed her the lights of the house, barely visible now through the dense tree trunks.

Why not?

What possible harm could there be? Violet's wolf self nudged insistently at her human. *Make it fast. No one will ever know.*

Slipping off her sneakers, she tugged her sweater over her head. Jeans and underwear followed. The cool breeze felt wonderful on her naked body. God, she had missed this. How had she gone so long without shifting?

Hiding her clothing in a neat pile inside a hollow at the base of a tree, she was just about to shift when a low growl made the hairs on the back of her neck stand on end. Looking up, she encountered the burning, yellow gaze of a feral werewolf.

Chapter 2

Using the photograph and information Cal had given him, Nate tracked down the young guy to a house in the town. He followed him as he left his home, and watched as he glanced furtively all around before making his way up to the woods. Nate observed in dismay as darkness fell and the fresh-faced young man shifted by the light of the full moon. The memories came flooding back. He saw the fear and confusion on this guy's face just before his body altered. His heart ached for the other man. Nate knew exactly what he was thinking. *I'm going out of my mind.* It was what Nate himself had believed six years ago.

Now, of course, he knew exactly what had been happening to him. Back then, he had been twenty-two-year-old Nathan Jones. Zilar was his mother's maiden name, and he'd been pushed into using it by his band's manager, who wanted to go sexier and catchier. A promising music student, months away from graduation, he'd had his life turned upside-down. He'd been scared, lonely and unable to talk to anyone about what was going on inside his head and, even more frighteningly, within his body.

He clearly remembered the werewolf bite that brought about his transformation. It was after a night out with friends. He didn't have the money for a cab, so he had walked home. Something or someone—he thought at the time it was a wild dog—had jumped out on him from a narrow side street in a quiet part of town. It went for his throat. He thought he was dead for sure, but a group of passersby disturbed the animal and it ran away.

Unconscious, Nate had been rushed to the hospital. He had bite marks to his throat and scratches on his chest and face. The police insisted they were looking for the same attacker who had brutally murdered a number of young men in the same area. He was lucky to be alive, they told him. It was only when the next full moon came around that Nate had known there was something very wrong. *Lucky to be alive?* He had lived with the irony of those words ever since.

Nate watched now as the werewolf crouched low, stealthily approaching the house through the trees. The backyard bordered the forest, and the businessman who lived here had chosen the location well. Privacy and country living combined to make this the perfect home for a werewolf blending into human society. He could hear the sounds of the party. The young werewolf sniffed the air, and Nate felt a fresh wave of pity wash over him. Acceptance and belonging were part of a wolf's makeup. Pack instincts. The parts that had been stripped away from this youngster by whoever bit him. This youth was an outcast. No longer human or wolf. He belonged in neither world and would be destined to walk on the darkest edges of both. When the moon was full, his lust for human blood would be out of control, and, out of his mind and out of control, he would satisfy that lust with wild attacks on people, leaving a trail of bodies in his wake. Until Nate put an end to his torment. *The way I begged Cal to do for me.*

And Cal had obliged. Because there was only one thing you could do for a feral werewolf. The final kindness you could do the poor, tormented scrap of humanity left behind after a werewolf attack was to kill it. But there would be no one to step in and rescue this guy the way Nate had been saved. No one was going to start his heart up again once the silver bullet had stopped it beating. *Lucky bastard.*

All werewolves, whether in the mystical realm of Otherworld, or here in the mortal realm, came under the rule of a single leader. The recent overthrow, and death, of the long-standing Wolf Leader, Anwyl, by his rival, Nevan, didn't change that. A different face at the top didn't alter tradition. Nevan was in charge. Just the mention of that name made Nate's blood run cold, but he forced himself to focus.

The problem for the Wolf Leader was that these feral werewolves—the true werewolves of ancient human legend—were not members of any pack. No group would accept a feral werewolf into its fold. They didn't obey the rules. They had no idea there were rules. The hierarchy that applied to wolves in the wild was equally important to werewolves. The social structure of an alpha male whose rule was absolute was unchanged. Anyone who was unwilling to accept that dynamic was cast out. Feral werewolves were not welcome in such a well-regulated society. They were the dirty secret of which werewolves didn't care to speak.

When in the grip of their wolf selves, feral werewolves were governed by uncontrollable rage and hunger for blood. They were driven to kill everyone they encountered, regardless of their human part. Once they returned to their human form, they remembered nothing or very little of what they had done. The condition was transferred through a bite, assuming the bitten person survived the attack the way Nate had done.

Over time, werewolves had mutated, achieving a remarkable feat. They were able to gain control over their bloodlust, although their other lupine instincts remained intact. Gradually, the werewolf world had split into two packs. One dwelt in Otherworld, while the other chose to reside in the mortal realm. With strong leadership, they could have been an imposing force. As it was, they warred among themselves and more closely resembled a pack of rabid dogs.

Although they were becoming rarer, feral werewolves remained a problem. Six years ago, when Nate had been feral, he had been cruelly used as a weapon by Nevan in his attempt to destroy Stella. When Nevan had gotten inside Nate's head he had urged him to rip out Stella's heart. That sort of mind control over feral wolves wasn't used often, but it wasn't unknown. Often, they ended up in prison cells and mental institutions in the mortal realm, unaware of the terrible deeds they had committed when the moon was full.

That was where Cal, in his role as Otherworld peacekeeper, stepped in. He and Stella couldn't save all feral werewolves the way they had helped Nate. That would have been an impossible task. The best Cal could hope for was to find a werewolf hunter who would destroy feral werewolves in a way that was as painless and humane as possible.

That was why Nate was here now, lining up this young wolf in his sights, preparing to fire a silver bullet into his heart before finishing him off by decapitating him with a samurai sword.

His finger tightened on the trigger. This part was never easy. There was always a temptation to walk away, to tell himself he'd done his share of these kills. To let someone else take over now. Except, as he'd pointed out to Cal in the early hours of this morning, there was no one else. And he couldn't stop, even if he wanted to. He owed it to the poor bastards locked in this torment.

Just before Nate could pull the trigger, the werewolf's lips drew back in a snarl and he crouched low, his eyes fixed on something a few feet away. Nate breathed a soft curse and turned to look at whatever it was that had caught the werewolf's attention. A dog? Maybe a deer? There was enough light from the full moon through the tree canopy to illuminate the scene. Even so, he thought he must be imagining things. There, standing stock-still like a marble statue, her long, dark hair hanging loose about her shoulders, was the most beautiful young woman he had ever seen. He did a double take. The most beautiful *naked* woman he had ever seen.

The werewolf sprang, closing the distance between himself and the woman. His eyes glowed toxic yellow, and his huge fangs were bared. Frozen out of her immobility at the sight, the woman stumbled back. With not a second to lose, Nate fired while the werewolf was in midlunge.

The huge beast shuddered as the bullet caught him in the chest. At the same time, the woman lost her balance completely and began to fall backward, her arms flailing wildly as she tried to find something—anything—on to which she could grab hold and save herself. She was unsuccessful. Even across a distance of several feet, Nate heard the sharp crack of her head hitting a rock before the werewolf came crashing down on top of her. Her slender body disappeared under the pelt of the huge, feral animal pressing her into the forest floor.

* * *

She opened her eyes slowly. The black of the night sky was splattered with bright stars, and the full moon hung huge and low in the center of her vision. It was blurred, and she blinked in an attempt to clear it. Nothing happened, so she sighed and closed her eyes again. Her head hurt and there was a horrible smell, like rotten meat and unwashed bodies. She had no idea where she was or how she came to be here. A warm, drowsy feeling swept over her.

"Don't go to sleep." It was a man's voice. Unfamiliar and authoritative.

She frowned and opened one eye, seeking the source of those warm, well-modulated tones. A face loomed above her. The moon was behind him so she couldn't make out much of his features. She got the impression of strength and determination. As he leaned closer, she caught a whiff of his clean, masculine scent. Soap and cologne. Something woodsy, musky and warming. He wasn't the source of that gut-churning smell. Although the scent probably wasn't the most important of her problems right now.

The feeling of cold earth and damp leaves against her bare flesh brought another realization crashing over her. She struggled to move, but the pain in her head was too intense. "Why am I naked?"

"You mean you don't know?"

He asked the question in a slightly incredulous manner that could have been intended to convey almost anything. She gazed up at him in horror. She couldn't remember. Couldn't remember why she was naked, why she was in these woods, why her head hurt, who he was. Who *she* was.

"What did you do to me?" The words trembled on her lips.

"Apart from saving your life, I haven't done anything to you." The words were harsh, clearly intended to put a swift end to any possible allegations.

She shrank back farther into the dirt. "I don't believe you."

He pointed to something just to one side of her. "Believe."

With an effort, she turned her head. Inches away from her lay the body of an enormous wolf. Its jaws hung open to reveal lethal fangs, gleaming white in the moonlight. At least she had finally discovered the source of the smell.

"He was about to rip your throat out—among other things—when I shot him."

Among other things? Even through the pain and fear, she picked up on something in the man's tone. Sadness and sympathy. Regret. He referred to the wolf as "him," not "it," almost as if he was deliberately giving it an identity. That was how it felt, but maybe the shock or the bump on the head was making her overimaginative.

"I don't know why I'm here." The tears threatened to spill over, and she fought them. She might not know who she was, but she knew she didn't do crying.

"There's a big party going on at a house on the edge of the woods. Could you have come from there?" He turned slightly, presumably in the direction of the house he was talking about, and she caught a glimpse of his strong profile.

"I suppose it's possible." She risked sitting up, hugging her knees up to her chin. Her head hurt like hell, but at least she felt less exposed in this position than lying flat on her back. "It doesn't explain why I'm not wearing any clothes."

Her rescuer tugged his hooded sweatshirt over his head and handed it to her. "Put this on."

She accepted it gratefully, pulling it over her head and sliding her arms into the sleeves. The residual warmth from his body and that delicious smell were comforting. She drew the garment around herself, trying desperately to remember something—anything—about what had happened before she had opened her eyes and seen this man leaning over her. It was no use. Her memory remained stubbornly blank.

"Can you stand?" He leaned down, offering his hand.

Taking it, she allowed him to pull her to her feet. Once she was upright, the world swam out of focus and she staggered. Strong arms caught and held her, and she leaned her forehead gratefully against a chest that was hard and muscular.

"Who are you?" It seemed a little late for introductions. His hands maintained a firm grip on her hips and, even through her giddiness and discomfort, she was glad the sweatshirt was long enough to reach the top of her thighs.

"My name is Nate." He looked over her head toward where she guessed the house party must be taking place. "Maybe we should go down there and see if someone recognizes you. Even if they don't, we can call for help from there. I don't have a phone with me and I'm not from 'round here. I have no idea where the nearest hospital is, but I think you should get that head injury of yours checked out."

She lifted her chin so she could scan his face. In the circumstances, it probably wasn't the wisest move. Her head was spinning and nothing made sense. She didn't know this man, but she sensed there was a lot he wasn't telling her. Panic threatened to overwhelm her. Somehow, she had lost control of her life and now she had no idea how to get it back on track. She was so far from the track, she had lost sight of where it might be. The thought set her heart pounding and her breath coming in short pants.

As she fought to regain control, a series of questions swirled around in her head. She had no idea why she was in the woods—*let's not get into the whole naked thing right now*—but why was *he* here? How had he conveniently managed to kill that wolf just as it was about to attack her? What did he mean by "among other things"? And how was it that she could sense, beyond any shadow of a doubt, his overwhelming reluctance to go toward that house where the party was being held?

As the questions chased each other around inside her fragile head, the moonlight illuminated a glimpse of Nate's rueful grin.

"Before I do anything, I have to take care of our friend over there." He indicated the wolf's body. "This isn't going to be pleasant, and, when I'm finished, you probably won't want to come anywhere near me ever again."

With those cryptic words, he released his grip on her hips and shifted her weight so that she could lean against the trunk of a tree. Moving stealthily in the darkness, he walked a few feet away and rummaged among some items that were in a large bag on the ground. When he returned, he was carrying a curved, gleaming sword and a shovel.

The woman recoiled violently as Nate walked toward her. She eyed the sword and shovel with a look of horror. "What are you going to do with those?"

It was not an easy thing to explain. He had to decapitate this werewolf while the moon was still full, or his job was only half-done. The silver bullet had stopped his heart, but Nate had to be sure he couldn't rise again. Legend was divided on this issue. Some believed that decapitation was the only way to finally lay the tortured soul to rest. Others felt it was overkill. There were no examples that he could find for what happened if someone left the werewolf's body intact. Preferring to leave nothing to chance, Nate went for decapitation. And, since he had to be on a flight to London in a few hours, he had to do it here and now.

What sort of bad luck was this? Okay, the circumstances of their meeting weren't ideal, but for the first time in as long as he could remember, Nate felt a tug of attraction toward a woman. More than a tug, if he was honest. What he was about to do next would kill any reciprocal feelings stone dead.

The woman, who was gazing at him with huge, troubled eyes, was about to get a live demonstration of the messy side of werewolf hunting. He ran a hand through his hair, wondering if there was any way to make what he was about to do sound acceptable to her. He was never going to see her again after tonight, but the idea of figuring in her nightmares for the rest of her life didn't fit comfortably with him.

He tried for a soothing opening sentence. "This is not an ordinary wolf."

"It *is* very big." Her voice was wary. Clearly she was wondering where this was going. And whether she was humoring a madman.

"He's a werewolf." There. He'd said it. She hadn't run away screaming. But that might have more to do with her head injury than her acceptance of his sanity.

In the moonlight, he couldn't see the color of her eyes. He saw only the sweep of her long, dark lashes as they came down and rested on her pale cheeks before lifting slowly. "What do you have to do to him?"

"I have to cut off his head."

The gulping sound she made as she swallowed echoed in the silent forest. "I can't watch that."

Nate nodded grimly. "I'll tell you when I'm done."

She kept her eyes closed, leaning back against the tree. Nate worked swiftly. Although he'd lost track of how many times he'd done this over the years, he had developed a routine. It might not suit the purists who first devised these ancient rites, but it worked for him. Kneeling beside the body of the werewolf, he bent his head. Prayer wasn't appropriate. He didn't know this young man. Didn't know his background, his beliefs or his culture. It didn't matter. A werewolf was a creature of darkness. If this man had worshipped a deity before his transformation, his allegiances would have changed once he became feral. But something was needed. Some acknowledgment of who he had been, a recognition that he would die alone, that his family would never know what had become of him.

Nate owed this unknown man something. It was a duty. Just as Stella, when she laid her hands on Nate six years ago, had felt a different sort of obligation to him. Nate wasn't a necromancer. He couldn't bring this guy back to life the way Stella had with him. Even if he had that choice, he wasn't sure, knowing what he did, that he would exert it. No, his ritual was simple. He murmured a few words, lines from a poem he'd once heard, to ease the dead on their way.

The samurai sword, with its curved blade, worked best. He'd tried others, but always returned to this. Raising it high above his head, ignoring the awful silver stench, he brought it down in a single, swift stroke. The sound of the blade slicing through flesh and bone never failed to sicken him. Usually one blow was all it took. This time, clouds had obscured the moon at the crucial moment, and his aim was not true. Cursing his bad luck, he aimed the sword at the werewolf's neck a second time and finished the job.

And, just like that, the wolf was gone. In his place, the body of a slender young man lay curled on his side.

"At peace now." Nate said the words quietly. Sadly. Although whether the sadness was for the werewolf or for himself, he was never quite sure. Because Nate himself sure as hell wasn't at peace.

His voice must have attracted the woman's attention. Her gasp shattered the stillness of the forest before her hand flew to cover her mouth. Those huge eyes met Nate's across the few feet separating them.

He experienced an overwhelming impulse to go to her and draw her into his arms. After so many years of believing he wasn't capable of feeling attraction, it was as if the floodgates to his emotions had been opened in spectacular style.

He tried telling himself it was the strange circumstances that had him enthralled, but it didn't seem to be working. He was fascinated by this woman he had only just met, drawn to her in a way he didn't understand. He got a grip on the impulse to go to her, telling himself she had been through enough without the uninvited embrace of a stranger.

"It was true. He was a werewolf. When you said 'among other things,' you meant he was going to rape me before he killed me, didn't you?" There was still a trace of incredulity in her voice, but there was no longer any fear.

"The poor bastard will have had the urges of both man and wolf, with no way of controlling either." He became brisk again. "And now I have to bury him."

The ground was damp, and Nate was able to dig a grave quickly. He was worried about the woman. Although she was a complication he could have done without, she had become his responsibility as soon as he had rescued her. Leaving her standing around injured and half-naked while he completed this task didn't seem like the behavior of a hero. He almost laughed out loud at the idea of himself in that role.

Of the five band members, Nate was the one labeled by the press as "the shy one" or "the quiet one." He was the one who didn't do relationships. He was the one most likely to be tucked up in bed with a good book while the others were out raising hell. He couldn't remember the last time he'd even talked to a woman. Heroic? He wouldn't know where to start.

When he'd finished burying the body, he came back to the woman, wiping his hands on his jeans. His thoughts were focused on the problem of how to get her to safety. If that house on the edge of the forest was the scene of a werewolf get-together, the last thing he wanted to do was walk in there. But if it was where she had come from, he needed to return her to her friends. Was she a werewolf? If she had come from that party, it seemed likely she was. *None of my business.* He'd pledged to get her to safety, not judge her.

What if she's not a werewolf? What if you walk into that house with her and they have no idea who she is? A darker scenario presented itself. *What if they say they know her, but it's a lie?* He had no reason to suppose the werewolves at that party were not law-abiding citizens. Most werewolves in the mortal realm were. But this woman was alone, vulnerable and…well, she was fucking gorgeous. What if they welcomed her with open arms because they had plans for her that were similar to the feral werewolf's intentions?

No, there was no alternative. Nate Zilar, celebrity by day, werewolf hunter by night, was going to have to walk into a house full of werewolves. He had cast himself in the role of hero, and now he had to live up to it. He was going to make damn sure this woman was safe before he left her anywhere.

Chapter 3

She was conscious of so many things as they approached the house where the party was taking place. How much her head hurt. The cold flesh of her legs. How her bare feet were scratched and muddy. She wore Nate's sweat-shirt with nothing underneath it. If it wasn't for his strong arm around her waist holding her up, she'd have fallen several times.

Oh, and this man she was trusting? He'd killed a were-wolf back there in the depths of the forest. Sliced its head right off and buried the human remains like it was part of his everyday routine. And she had stood by and watched. Not the decapitation, but the aftermath. As if what he did was normal. *I might not know who I am, but part of me feels I should not be okay with this.* Yet she was wrapped in a surreal bubble where everything else was gauzy and his protective presence was all that mattered.

Although she couldn't see Nate clearly in the darkness,

she got the impression of power and energy. The moonlight gave her glimpses of strong features and dark coloring. Those things meant he was an attractive man, but they didn't explain the instantaneous connection she felt to him. *He rescued you from a wolf.* Of course that meant there was a connection. But it was more than that. It had been a bright, instant flame, sizzling the air between them. And it showed no sign of subsiding.

Overriding everything else was a hazy sense of something she could barely describe. Of not belonging. Of being in the wrong place, wrong time, wrong *everything.* Her hurt head tried to tell her what it was. Or maybe her hurt head *was* the problem.

"I can't just walk in there." She indicated the sweatshirt that barely reached the top of her thighs. "What if they don't know me?"

"Don't worry. I'm going ahead of you."

She wished she could get a proper look at him in the moonlight. Something flashed through her mind. Something about prospects. About what the word really meant. How having prospects wasn't about power and wealth, it was about how well a man would take care of you. It was a fleeting thought, gone almost as soon as it appeared.

They were in the backyard of the house now, and she could see a few people nearby standing around drinking and talking. On the immediate edge of the yard, where it joined the forest, a group of three young men appeared to be attempting to restrain someone.

"Roko, wait here. This could be a trap." The man spoke in an urgent tone.

"Too right it could." The response was panicky, almost terrified. "You know what he's capable of, Teo. He could have snatched her from under my nose."

Nate moved forward. "Wait here." He motioned her to step back into the shadows.

It was too late. The man called Roko had already caught sight of her. Breaking free of his friends, he started toward her. "Violet! What the fuck…?"

She frowned. Surely she would remember this man if she knew him. He was very handsome. As he reached her, Roko made a grab for her hands. She shrank away from him in alarm, moving instinctively toward Nate.

Nate positioned himself between them. "Who are you?"

Roko bristled. He scanned her face, his expression changing, becoming even more annoyed. "This is a joke, right? Tell this guy to butt out."

As he spoke, something was happening inside the house. There were shouts, crashes and sounds of glass breaking. Looking up, she saw what looked like a dozen people erupting from the house into the yard. They appeared to be running from something.

Roko turned to his friends. "You said we'd be safe. You promised they wouldn't find us here."

As he spoke, he gave a signal to his friends. Kicking off their sneakers and shrugging out of their outer clothing, they shifted. Just like that. No big performance, no whisper of sound, no creaking of bones or sprouting of fur.

Within seconds, the young men were gone. In their place, a pack of sleek werewolves dropped to their haunches, shaking themselves free of the final remnants of clothing that had been shredded during their transformation. Baring huge fangs, they crouched low, preparing to face the group that had emerged from the house.

Nate pulled on her arm, drawing her back into the shadows where they could see what was going on, but not be seen themselves. Her instinct was to run from this scene, but she understood what he was doing. Roko—the man who had just shifted and become a werewolf—knew her. There were clues to her identity here.

The five werewolves who approached from the house dwarfed Roko and his friends. Huge and black, with eyes that glowed gold by the light of the moon, it was clear they meant business. The crowd that had followed them from the house was a combination of humans and werewolves, and the atmosphere thrummed with a cocktail of fear and anticipation as the two opposing packs lined up.

Crouching low, the black wolves rippled with muscle and menace. Vicious snarls rent the night. The space between the warring forces crackled with rage. Roko and his pack barely had time to answer back before the black werewolves sprang at them. The fury of the attack was so intense she felt its force even from her hiding place in the darkness. Instinct made her draw closer to Nate, and he placed a steadying arm around her shoulders.

In the golden glow of the garden lamps, blood sprayed and fur flew. It was clear from the start that Roko and his pack were hopelessly outclassed, but they fought bravely. The black wolves tore into them, ripping chunks of flesh from the smaller werewolves, forcing them onto their backs and into submission. It was clear this was an organized fighting force, used to working as a team, used to getting what it wanted.

Within the watching crowd, there were screams and shouts of outrage.

"Can't we stop this?"

"Who are they?"

Even as some of the partygoing werewolves who had emerged from the house made a movement toward the fight, it was already over. The black wolves, having subdued Roko's pack, were shifting back into human form.

Five naked, muscle-bound men stood over the injured werewolves.

One of them addressed himself to the partygoers. "Apologies for any inconvenience. We won't disturb you any longer." Reaching down a giant hand, he grabbed Roko by the fur at the scruff of his neck and hauled him to his feet. "This is what we came for. He has something belonging to our master."

Dragging Roko and the other wounded werewolves with them, the five men strode through the watching crowd and out through the front of the house.

"Violet…is that your name?"

Nate still had his arm around the woman, and he could feel the tremors that ran through her slender body. He wasn't surprised. A brutal, bloody attack like the one they'd just witnessed was enough to leave anyone shaken. Following on from the earlier events of the evening, he was amazed to find she could still answer him coherently.

"It's what he called me, so I guess it must be."

"Wait here while I see if I can find out what that was all about."

She slid her hand into his, those huge, trusting eyes fixed on his face. "Don't leave me."

Something lurched in the center of his chest. In a place where he hadn't felt anything for a very long time. Six years, to be exact. He gave her a smile that he hoped was reassuring. "I'll be two minutes."

Reluctantly, she let go of his hand. An answering smile trembled on her lips. "I'm timing you."

Nate strode out of the shadows. The party atmosphere was understandably subdued following the fight, and people were standing around discussing what had happened.

He approached one group, slotting in as unobtrusively as he could.

"Who were those guys?" Nate turned to the man next to him.

"No one seems to know. Looks like they were gate-crashers who had a grudge against the other group, the ones they dragged away with them."

"So no one knows who they were, either?"

Another man joined in the conversation. "Teo is a regular at these parties, but the others hadn't been here before."

"I heard Teo call one of his friends Roko," Nate said.

"Name means nothing to me."

"Me neither." Both men shrugged.

Conscious of Violet—since that seemed to be her name—waiting anxiously for him in the shadows, Nate tried the same questions on a few other people. He got similar responses. Teo was known, Roko wasn't. No one seemed to know what the fight was about or who the black werewolves were. With no more idea about what was going on or who Violet was, he made his way back to her.

"Nothing." He ran a hand through his hair in frustration. "Let's get out of here."

"Where to?"

"Back to my hotel room. At least there we can get you cleaned up and into some warm clothes while we talk about what to do next."

Nate was getting seriously worried about Violet's ability to stick with him by the time they had trudged back through the forest to the point where he had left his werewolf-hunting kit. Although she was making valiant efforts to keep up with his pace, she was clearly struggling. From the point where he had buried the werewolf, they still had to walk to the road where he had left his rental car. Hoisting his bag onto one shoulder, Nate scooped Violet into his arms so he could carry her the rest of the way. She wrapped her arms around his neck and rested her head in the curve of his neck.

"Who are you? Really? I know your name, but that's all."

He laughed. "Just your average werewolf hunter."

How did he start with the rest? *Oh, and by the way, I'm in a band. Not just any band. We've been one of the top ten bestselling rock bands in Europe for the last two years and we're just about to embark on a world tour. Which is why I have to be back in England tomorrow.*

Somehow, nothing else mattered except how his hands felt compared with the softness of her thighs. Suddenly his fingers felt too big, too rough to be pressing into her delicate flesh. He experienced a ridiculous urge to apologize in case the abrasiveness of his touch was uncomfortable for her.

"But why are you *here* hunting werewolves. Why here, why now?" Her voice was a soft murmur in his ear, her breath warm against his cheek. Nate felt as if he was meant to carry her weight in his arms forever. *This is ridiculous*, he told himself firmly. He was getting carried away, believing himself to be taking the starring role in a child's fairy tale. Slaying werewolves was part of his routine. Rescuing maidens seemed to have gone to his head.

"I get a message when there's a problem."

She laughed. "Just like that?"

"Yeah, it's that simple." As if anything in the last six years of his life had ever been *that simple*.

They had reached the car, and he placed Violet on her feet before stowing the bag containing his kit in the trunk. The courier would collect it from the motel later and dispose of it. All part of the service. A very bizarre service.

They accomplished the journey to the motel in silence, and once inside the room, Nate locked the door and switched on the lights. For the first time, he got a proper look at the woman he had rescued…and his breath caught in his throat.

"What is it?" Violet made an attempt to pull his sweatshirt down farther, squirming slightly under the intensity of his gaze.

Nate shook himself. "Well, at least we know your name really is Violet."

She looked confused and he took her hand, drawing her over to the mirror. Turning her so that she could see her reflection, he stood behind her with his hands on her shoulders. Her eyes were enormous. Fringed by thick, spiky black lashes, they were a glorious, vivid shade of violet-blue. Her hair was a tumbling mass of midnight curls, and her skin, in contrast, was pale as milk. In the forest, he had thought she was the most beautiful girl he had ever seen. The harsh overhead glare of the neon lighting only confirmed his first impression.

Violet gave a shaky laugh. "How can I not know my own face?"

"That bump on the head must have caused you to lose your memory."

She turned to face him. "You're the only thing that seems real."

With those words, the weight of his responsibility to her hit him full force. He had rescued her from that werewolf, but it didn't end there. He couldn't abandon her now. What had he hoped to do? Take her to a doctor and sneak out the back door while she was in the consulting room? Hand her over to the police? How would that story work out? *While I was out werewolf hunting last night, I came across this naked girl…*

No, Violet was in his care. Until her memory came

back, or he found out who she was, he had a duty to look after her. A tiny voice at the back of his mind spoke up. *Are you sure that's what this is about? You haven't just been bowled over by that beautiful face and those endless legs?* Firmly, he shut it up.

"Go and take a shower or a bath while I make some calls." He hesitated. "This might sound creepy, but it's not intended to be…don't lock the door. You may have a concussion, and I need to be able to get in there if you black out."

She nodded trustingly and headed for the bathroom. Trusting. That's what she'd been almost from the start. He had to live up to that trust. Six years a loner, and now, all at once, he was having to think for someone else.

Minutes later, he heard the faucet running. Nate dug his phone out of his pocket. It occurred to him that it would be useful if he had a number for Cal. His relationship with the sorcerer didn't work that way. Cal contacted Nate when he needed to, usually turning up at some unearthly hour and surprising him when he least expected it. No, he couldn't rely on Cal being around to help him out on this occasion. Instead, he called the other person who could be guaranteed to help him out in a crisis.

Ged Taverner had managed Beast since the group formed six years ago. He was the man who knew everything about each member of the group, every secret they had, both past and present. Now, despite the time difference, Ged answered on the third ring and managed to do a good job of sounding awake. He listened in silence while Nate explained what he needed from him.

His manager's weary transatlantic groan needed no explanation. "Nate, don't do this to me. You're the sensible one, the one who never causes me any problems. I've never had to bail you out of a foreign prison. Never had to bribe a reporter to keep quiet about your antics. You're not the one who calls me up days before we start the biggest tour of our lives and gives me this sort of headache." Nate remained silent, and Ged tried for a persuasive tone. "We can find you another girl."

Nate glanced at the clock. "It's just after midnight here. I need you to sort this out today."

Ged muttered a curse. "Nate, if she has no identity documents, there's no way I can help you."

"Make it happen, Ged, because I'm not leaving here until it does."

This time the groaning and cursing held a note of defeat. "I'll call you back in a few hours."

When Nate hung up, he sank into a chair, leaning his head back and gazing at the ceiling as he listened to the sounds of splashing coming through the thin walls of the bathroom. He had made a commitment to protect Violet, and he would see it through. Even as he made the promise to himself, and to her, that little voice spoke up in his mind once more.

What if you find out that flawless face and beautiful body hide the soul of a werewolf?

Clad in a clean sweatshirt and a pair of Nate's sweatpants rolled up at the ankles and cinched in as tight as she could get them at the waist, Violet emerged from the bathroom. She had used the dryer on her hair, being careful of her head wound, and it now curled wildly around her head and shoulders. Clearly, before her memory loss, she must have had a better idea of how to style it.

"I think I left half a forest in that tub."

"How's your head?" Nate was sprawled in a chair near the window.

"Sore." She grimaced as she felt the back of her skull.

"It's not cut, but there's a lump right here that hurts like hell."

He snatched up his car keys. "Let's get you to the emergency room."

She studied him as he came toward her. He was tall and powerful, with an effortless, athletic grace to his movements. With his dark hair and eyes and masterfully carved features, her rescuer was a striking-looking man. There was something soulful in the depths of those dark eyes that tugged at her. When she looked into them, she felt like she was prying into some private grief.

But there was more to Nate than sorrow. There was an undercurrent of danger, a rawness about him that Violet thought held an untold story of hurt and anger. She guessed it provided the steel backbone necessary for killing werewolves and cutting off their heads and wondered why it didn't scare her.

"Why are you doing this?" She had to tilt her head to look up at him. At least tilting no longer caused dizziness. "I mean, I really appreciate your help. I just wondered why."

He paused, looking down at her with those eyes that had seen too much. "Because you need me."

The words caused a fluttering sensation that had nothing to do with her injury. She tried to find a suitable response. The words that came out were totally inadequate. "I have no shoes."

"We'll stop on the way."

It was intensely frustrating not to *know* things. Until Nate took her to a place called a mall, she hadn't known that it was possible to buy sneakers, jeans and a sweater at midnight. Or that a doctor was available at an accident and emergency department at any time of the day or night.

I must have known these things once. One bump on the head and they've gone? Just like that?

"My memory will come back, right?" she asked the doctor at the hospital who examined her.

"It will, but I can't offer you any guarantees about when." The woman doctor stepped back, stripping off her gloves. "It could be hours, days or even weeks. In some rare cases, it can take months for the memory to return fully after this sort of post-traumatic amnesia. Some people find things come back to them slowly. For others, their memory comes back in a sudden rush. All I can advise is that you rest, remember that you've suffered a trauma and don't overdo it."

"But there is no serious injury?" Nate asked.

"There is no external injury," the doctor said. She extended a hand, helping Violet down from the examining table. "Your skull isn't damaged. If you get any symptoms, such as headaches, dizziness or blurred vision, then seek medical help immediately. Also, I would advise a CT scan, a detailed image of the brain, just to rule out any underlying injury."

"Will she be okay to travel?" Violet looked at Nate in surprise. Where was she traveling to?

The doctor pursed her lips. "As I said, my advice would be to rest. If traveling is essential, do it in easy stages."

Violet thought she saw a flash of humor in Nate's eyes at that comment, although she didn't understand its source. Having thanked the doctor, they made their way back to the car. Violet felt exhaustion wash over her as she sank into the passenger seat. She studied Nate's profile as he drove through the deserted streets of the quiet town. *I don't even know the name of this place. This could be my hometown and I don't recognize it.* The thought caused her a moment of panic. It subsided as a flash of certainty came to her. *This is not my home. I don't belong here.*

That thought prompted a question. "Why would I need to travel?"

For a moment he didn't answer. Then he took his eyes off the road briefly so he could glance her way. "Violet, how much do you know about rock music?"

The question was so unexpected it made her laugh. "If I said nothing, it would be a massive exaggeration. Although I might have been the world expert a few hours ago."

They had reached the motel, and Nate stretched his long limbs before sliding out of his seat. Coming around to Violet's side of the car, he held open the door before helping her out. As they walked into the motel room, she glanced up at his face. He looked tired, but there was a frown between his eyes.

"Just tell me." She may not have known him for long, but she knew that frown was there because of her.

He threw himself down in the chair he had been seated in earlier, scrubbing a hand over his face as though attempting to erase the weariness. Violet sat on the edge of one of the beds. "I have to leave here today and fly to England."

"Oh." She glanced at the clock on the bedside table. Its glowing figures showed it was close to three in the morning. "Look, it's been really kind of you to take care of me. I should probably just go now…"

"Where will you go?" He sounded unexpectedly harsh.

"I don't know." Her voice refused to rise above a whisper.

"Exactly." He rose from his seat, coming to sit next to her. Clasping her hands between both of his, he ducked his head low so that he could look at her face. "I can't leave you alone here like this, Violet."

She was confused by the mixed messages he was giving. "My head hurts." All she wanted to do was lean against Nate's broad shoulder and let him take away her cares.

"I'm not surprised. Tonight has been enough to scramble anyone's brain, with or without a blow to the head." She didn't understand why, but his smile warmed her. "Let me explain. I'm in a rock band. We're just about to start a world tour, which is the reason why I have to go back to England today. If there was any way I could avoid it, I would cancel and stay here with you."

"You've done enough. I wouldn't ask you to change your plans for me." Violet felt something sharp and bright sting the back of her eyelids at the idea that he would even want to. No one had ever put her first. *How do I know that when I don't know anything else about myself?*

His grip on her hands tightened. "Violet, can you remember any details? Anything about your family, your home? Why you were at that party? That wolf called Roko? Why you were in the woods? Why you were naked? I know the doctor said don't force it, but is there anything there?"

She closed her eyes. When she tried to probe her memory, all she could feel was a gray mist of nothingness. And a sense of…not belonging. She tried to grasp it. To give it a name. *Otherness.* That was as close as she could get. Sighing, she opened her eyes and gazed into the dark, soulful depths of Nate's. He was all she had. The thought of him leaving terrified her.

"The only thing I know for sure is that I don't belong here."

"Then that settles it." He nodded decisively. "You're coming with me."

Chapter 4

Violet's memory might have deserted her, but she was fairly sure most people did not travel in their own luxury jet. As they mounted the steps of the sleek airplane, a uniformed man bowed low in greeting. That, too, seemed unlikely to be an everyday occurrence.

"Welcome aboard, Mr. Zilar. My name is Daniel, and I'm here to take care of your comfort during the flight."

"Is there any message for me from Mr. Taverner?" Nate kept his hand in the small of Violet's back, and she was grateful for that light contact. Everything felt strange and overwhelming, but his touch was comforting. Was there a possibility of it already becoming too comforting, of her starting to depend on him too much? She didn't have time to explore the thought, but like a new and exotic taste, it lingered.

"Mr. Taverner told me to tell you everything is taken care of." Daniel turned to Violet. "Your luggage has already been brought aboard, Miss Wolfe."

Miss Wolfe? She turned questioning eyes to Nate, and he grinned. Leaning closer, he pressed his lips up against her ear so he could whisper. "It was the only name I could come up with on the spur of the moment."

"My luggage?" she whispered back, as they followed Daniel inside the polished interior of the plane.

"Ged is very thorough." He seemed to feel it was an answer. Instead it raised more questions. Who was this mysterious Mr. Taverner who seemed to already have such a strong influence over her life?

The main cabin was an elegant salon with cream furnishings and walnut trim. Every feature had been designed with comfort in mind, including the finishing touches of fresh fruit, champagne and chocolates. Violet gazed around with wide eyes. Daniel held open a door, through which she could see a huge bed.

"I took the liberty of placing your suitcases in here." Daniel indicated a neat arrangement of stacked luggage just inside the bedroom door.

There were three large suitcases and two smaller ones. Although Violet might not know much about these things, she sensed that they, like her surroundings, were expensive and customized. She tried to catch Nate's eye and give him a *we have to talk about this* look, but he was turning away from her, addressing his next words to Daniel.

"There was a problem with Miss Wolfe's passport. Mr. Taverner was going to sort it out."

"It's all taken care of. The new document was delivered just before you arrived. The immigration official will come aboard before we depart to do the necessary checks."

Violet slid her hand into Nate's. *Document? Official? Checks?* None of those things sounded like things in which she wanted to participate. That sense of not belonging swept over her again. The fear of being discovered in some wrongdoing was overwhelming. Nate returned the pressure of her fingers reassuringly.

"In that case, can you leave us alone before we set off?"

Daniel bowed again and closed the bedroom door behind him as he left. When he had gone, Nate leaned against the door, watching Violet's face. "You are not okay with this."

She released a long exhale. "That's because I have no idea what *this* is." She gestured around the small but luxurious bedroom as she spoke. "Do you always travel this way?"

He laughed. "This is my manager's over-the-top way of responding to my plea for help. I told him I wasn't leaving America without you, but that you had no identification. I don't know how he has managed to get you a passport in such a short time, and I'm not going to ask. I suspect his methods weren't legal and probably cost a lot of money. All I know is I sent him your picture and he said he'd do the rest. I guess he decided there would be fewer questions asked if we flew privately."

"And the luggage?" Violet pointed to the suitcases.

"I asked him to get someone to pick you up a few things. He tends to do things on a grand scale." He smiled reassuringly. "Once we are over the passport hurdle, we can relax. I'm meeting my bandmates in London, so we have the plane to ourselves."

Daniel tapped on the door at that moment, his face apologetic. "The immigration official is here. He said it will only take a few minutes if he could just see you both with your passports."

Violet edged closer to Nate, and he took her hand again, smiling down at her. "Come on. Once this is done, we can get going."

She nodded miserably. She had no idea what her life was

usually like, but she didn't recognize this crawling feeling of fear. She sincerely hoped this constant nervousness was werewolf attack–induced and not a feature of her personality. *Or maybe it's simpler. Maybe I'm just tired.* She hadn't slept, and that big, crisp bed looked very inviting.

The immigration official was more interested in Beast, Nate's band, than in Violet. He had their latest album and was annoyed that he hadn't known he would be meeting Nate that day.

"I'd have brought it along and asked you to sign the cover."

"Write down your contact details." Nate signaled to Daniel, who produced a piece of paper and a pen. "I'll get a copy to you that's been signed by all the band members."

For a moment Violet thought the immigration official might be about to hug Nate. She knew it would not be a popular move with the intensely private man she had known for only a few hours. Instead, he recalled his position and opted for gripping Nate's hand gratefully. Turning to the passports, he checked them quickly.

"Everything is in order here. You're cleared to leave." He handed the documents back to them and left, turning back with a cheery wave when he reached the door.

"That's it?" Violet looked down at the little booklet in her hand. It had conferred a status on her she didn't have before. *Wolfe.* She wondered what her real passport said. She couldn't recall ever seeing one of these things until now. Memory was a strange thing. Somewhere, locked away in the recesses of her mind, were the clues to her identity. She just had no idea how to get to them.

"That's it," Nate confirmed. "It's a long journey. Why don't you make the most of it by getting some sleep?"

"Do you always know the right thing to say and do?"

Her words seemed to shake him, and he gazed down at her for a moment before replying. "Not always."

Do you always know the right thing to say and do? Violet's question had played on his mind throughout most of the transatlantic flight. He watched her as she slept. Lying next to her, but not touching her. Because that was what she had asked him to do.

"Will you stay with me?" She only had to raise those incredible violet-blue eyes shyly to his and he was lost.

"Anytime you need me." Would he always do what Violet asked him to? *Probably.*

His words, together with his presence, had calmed her nerves, and Violet had fallen asleep almost as soon as her head touched the pillows. Not Nate. Despite his weariness, he had remained awake, wondering about that question. Debating his motives. Could bringing her with him be considered "the right thing"?

As soon as he had taken a look at Violet in that cheap motel room, something inside him had lurched out of place. It hadn't gone back again. He studied her now. The dark fan of her lashes against her pale cheek. The midnight velvet of her hair curling soft on the pillow. The plump, inviting cushion of her lips. She was cream and rose and ebony. And, when she opened those glorious eyes, she was lavender and lilac. A fairy-tale princess. Every man's fantasy. But Nate wasn't every man. Six years ago, a werewolf had stripped away his humanity. Yes, his friends had patched him up, but they hadn't made him whole again. The part that made him human was gone forever. He didn't know what he was. A man-shaped monster. That about summed up Nate Zilar.

He had spent too much time between then and now wallowing in self-pity, and he shrugged it off, returning to the mystery of Violet. If she was a werewolf—and he felt strongly that she *was*—why wasn't he repulsed by that? He hated werewolves. But that didn't come close to describing the red-hot bitterness he felt toward them. When Nate had been at his most vulnerable, a werewolf had tried to use him as a murder weapon. That werewolf was now the Wolf Leader. The only thing that had kept Nate alive throughout the last six years was the knowledge that one day he would pay Nevan back for what he had tried to do. No matter what Cal might say, one day Nate would look that bastard in the eye before he took his revenge.

But the thought that Violet might be a werewolf didn't repulse him. On the contrary. It excited him. Aroused him. It called to something dark and primeval inside him. Something he thought had gone forever when Cal drove that knife into his heart. Something he didn't want to explore. Because, if he explored it, he would have to name it.

Violet had triggered not only his protective instincts, but so much more. A memory, a longing, stirred deep within him. A younger man's sweet dreams of romantic love coupled with a healthy dose of good old-fashioned lust. Both were things he had never thought to feel again. Yet here he was lying beside Violet with an erection so rock solid his zipper was in danger of leaving a permanent imprint on his penis as a reminder. And for a *werewolf*? He shook his head. If only he'd known. All these years and all it had needed to restore his manhood was a little wolf porn.

At that inopportune moment, Violet stirred. A soft sigh murmured against Nate's cheek, jacking his already iron-hard cock to even more uncomfortable proportions. Her eyes opened slowly. Confusion blurred their depths for a few seconds, then she smiled and Nate's heart faltered. This is what it would feel like to wake up next to Violet every day. To see her head on the pillow next to his, that smile in her eyes, to be able to kiss those sweet lips, draw her close, relieve the aching demon between his thighs…

"I'm hungry."

She means for food, he told himself sternly, forcing his mind away from his raging erection. "I'll have Daniel organize breakfast."

Daniel must have been anticipating their needs, and before long, they were seated at the table in the salon with a choice of hot and cold dishes spread before them. Nate was conscious of Violet studying his face as they ate.

"What's our story to be?" she asked eventually. "Are we pretending I'm your girlfriend?"

"I hadn't thought about it. Does it matter?"

"Surely your friends and family will wonder what's going on if you turn up with me at your side and no explanation."

Friends and family? He didn't have any. The other members of the band were about as close as he came to either, and they wouldn't interrogate him. They had never questioned each other. "Pretend girlfriend. Close friend. Whichever you choose."

A slight frown furrowed her smooth brow. "All this—" she waved a hand to indicate the plane "—I can't just accept your generosity indefinitely, Nate. You have to let me do something in return."

He quirked a brow at her. "What did you have in mind?"

A soft pink blush stained her cheeks as his meaning hit her, and she gave a little gasp before plowing on. "I don't know because I don't know what I *can* do." Her brow wrinkled. "It's hard to explain. I don't know what my qualifications are. I could be an artist or an attorney. Maybe I could clean your apartment or cook for you?" Her eyes clouded. "If I know how to cook."

Nate caught hold of her hand. "Violet—" he waved his

other hand, just as she had done "—all this means nothing. I have enough money to care for you until your memory comes back or we find your family. In the meantime,
relax and enjoy it. I'm going to. Being on the road is lonely
and boring as hell." An image of his bandmates came into
his mind. *Boring as hell?* Maybe not the first words that
sprang to mind when describing the phenomenon that was
Beast. "I'm glad to have your company."

Violet's expression remained doubtful, but she ate the
rest of her meal in silence. It was a huge meal, Nate observed, consisting mostly of meat, eggs and berries. She
shuddered at his offer of coffee, drinking water instead.
Her choice of food and the quantity she ate seemed to
support Nate's suspicion that she could be a werewolf. Or
maybe she adhered to some diet he was unaware of. Or she
had allergies. Perhaps he should stop second-guessing and
do what he had said…just enjoy her company.

As Violet met his eyes and smiled, Nate decided finding pleasure in being with her wasn't going to be a hardship. On the contrary, he had a feeling Violet's company
might prove to be addictive.

Since their arrival in London a few hours earlier, Violet felt like she had been plunged into a whirlwind of light
and sound and movement. A car and driver had met them
at the airport and driven them through busy streets to
Nate's luxurious apartment long enough for him to prepare for the tour. He had shown Violet to a guest room,
where she had showered and selected an expensive outfit
from one of her new suitcases. The unknown person who
had been sent by Nate's manager to shop for her had done
an impeccable job.

"How did they know my size?" she asked Nate as she

turned to study the fit of the tight black jeans in a full-length mirror in the hall.

"I sent Ged some details." The look in his eyes as they traveled up her legs and skimmed her ass left her feeling slightly breathless. "I guess I must be better at describing the female form than I thought."

His hair was still damp from the shower, and his chest and feet were bare. He wore hip-skimming jeans and had a towel slung around his neck. Violet was suddenly very aware of his potent masculinity. Of his upper body that was a masterpiece of well-defined, taut chest muscles and superchiseled abs that cried out to be touched. The thought made her cheeks flame, even though she couldn't drag her eyes away.

As he lifted the towel to his hair, his sharp-edged biceps and sculpted stomach tightened. His hips were so well defined that the sharp V line of his muscles drew her eye downward. Her imagination ran wild as she pictured running her hands over that broad chest, exploring those ridges of muscle, sliding lower… Raw, untamed need pulsed through her. Every cell in her body was achingly aware of him and, even though her memory was gone, Violet knew she had never felt like this before.

Aware of Nate's eyes on her face, she forced her thoughts away from such dangerous territory and back to practical matters. "What happens now?"

He grimaced. "People imagine that life on tour is glamorous. But it isn't. It's hard, boring work. In fact, it feels like Groundhog Day." He frowned. "That doctor said you needed to take things easy. Even though we'll be traveling, I intend to make sure you do that."

Violet shook her head, a slight smile trembling on her lips. "Whatever brought me to those woods on that night, it didn't just bring me an encounter with a werewolf. It also brought me a meeting with you, so I can't regret it."

His expression was slightly bemused as he smiled down at her. "What does that mean?"

"I'm not sure. I don't understand it myself. I just don't think I've ever had this feeling before, of someone looking out for me the way you do."

Nate laughed. "Having lost your memory, maybe you wouldn't know that?"

"Maybe." Violet didn't know where to begin. How could she explain that the loss of her memory appeared to have also enhanced her senses? Or was it Nate's nearness that was having that effect on her? When she was with him, her awareness was on high alert. Was he the trigger that sent her senses into overdrive? Or had this heightened perception been caused by the bump on her head? All she knew was everything felt *more*. As though adrenaline was pumping out of control through her body, causing colors to be overly bright, scents to be overly strong, sounds to be overly loud.

She didn't know if it had occurred to Nate to wonder, as she had, why she was in those woods. The most likely explanation was that she had been at that party. Certainly the man called Roko had recognized her. And he was a werewolf. All of the people at that party had been werewolves. *Does that mean I'm a werewolf?* She believed it was likely. More than likely. Why else would she have been at that party?

But what did it feel like to be a werewolf? Ever since she had stood in the shadows and witnessed the fight, Violet had tried to reach inside herself and answer that question. So far the only response she had received had been silence. If Violet did have an inner wolf, she was in hiding, cowering deep inside and refusing to show herself.

"Ready?" Nathan was pulling a white T-shirt over his head, drawing her back to the here and now.

His expression seemed to ask another question, as though he was attempting to delve into her thoughts. But how could she confide in Nate—a man who killed were-wolves in a brutal way—her fear that she might be a were-wolf? Ever since she had opened her eyes in the forest and found him leaning over her, she seemed to be living through a dream sequence. Reality had taken a back seat. Except, of course, she had no idea what her reality looked like. It was only when she looked into Nate's dark eyes that she got any sense of reassurance or well-being. He was what was keeping her going, putting one foot in front of the other, taking that next breath. Without him, she might just give up and crumple into a heap.

Placing her hand in his felt natural. "As I'll ever be."

Chapter 5

A heavy, thumping beat filled the cramped space while on the screen the camera panned around to capture the ten-thousand-strong audience. Excitement, anticipation and exultation showed on the waiting faces. The person who had made the recording they were watching had perfectly captured the energy pulsing through the crowd. Thick, theatrical smoke rolled like fog from the stage and out into the waiting audience and, within it, colored strobe lights danced in time with the music.

Through the haze, Violet caught occasional glimpses of the giant LED screens at the rear of the stage. Alternating images of fire, close-ups of snarling animals and a stylized symbol that looked like three entwined number sixes flashed up on the screens. At the side of the stage, random explosions went off, shooting orange flames into the air.

As the camera panned the crowd again, Violet noticed the three-sixes symbol on people's clothing. "What does that mean?" She managed to turn her attention briefly from the mesmerizing images on the screen to Nate.

It was Ged Taverner, lounging in a seat behind her, who answered. "666. The Sign of the Beast." Violet glanced over her shoulder to see him putting his fingers on either side of his head to make devil horns. His grin exuded confidence. "It's the band's logo."

Violet took a moment to digest that information as she cast a sidelong glance in Nate's direction. *The sign of the beast? Okay, so this band he's in is not exactly the sweet, wholesome boy band I pictured.* As if in response to her thoughts, on screen, the tension built further as the crowd sensed something was about to happen. The lighting shifted, becoming focused on a podium at the rear of the stage that supported a vast, gleaming circular wall of drums. Even above the music, the roar of the crowd filled the air as a lithe, muscled man ran on from the side of the stage and leaped into his seat behind the drums. His chest was bare and his tattooed biceps bulged as he pounded out a furious beat, his blue-black hair flopping forward to cover his face. He exuded raw, brooding vitality, and something more. Even through the screen, Violet could feel it. It was suppressed menace.

"That's Diablo," Nathan said. "The best drummer in the world. That's what he'll tell you when you meet him. If he speaks to you."

"Why wouldn't he speak to me?" Violet couldn't take her eyes from the artistic thunderstorm Diablo was unleashing before her eyes.

"It will depend on his mood."

Before she could unpick that cryptic reply, the cameras panned upward, spotlights picking up two men being lowered on twin platforms at either side of the stage. Their fingers flew in a symphony over their respective guitars as they focused intently on their playing.

"On the right, you have Torque. He's lead guitar. Dev, on the left, is rhythm guitar."

"Fire and ice." Ged spoke up again.

Violet saw immediately what he meant. Red-haired Torque was all burning drama and flickering movement. The air around him glowed with life, and he punctuated the sweeping arc of his hand on his guitar so that it was perfectly in time with the explosions at the side of the stage. In contrast, Dev held his body statue still, the movement of his flying fingers the only sign of life. His white-blond hair and pale skin added to the illusion that he was carved from ice.

She watched as Nate, taking up a position slightly to the left of center, and behind Dev, joined the group. She turned questioning eyes to him.

"Bass guitar," he said, replying to her unanswered question. "Only one person to come."

With those words, the screen erupted into life. The crowd was in a frenzy as the lead singer strutted onto the stage. *Owned* the stage. Violet saw the devil horn gesture that Ged had made repeated over and over within the audience as the man on the stage grabbed the fixed microphone stand and rubbed it suggestively against his groin. When he started to sing, his voice ranged from husky crooning to wild screaming. No matter what sound those perfect lips made, he was mesmerizing. Throwing back his red-gold mane of hair, he strutted, crouched and jumped around the stage in skin-tight black leather pants and a flowing white shirt open to the waist.

"Khan." Nate said the single word as though it explained everything.

There was no doubt about it. Beast delivered a spine-tingling performance. As the number reached its end, Diablo pounded out a crescendo and Nate slid his palm over the neck of his guitar, fingers caressing the frets, the instrument dropping down between his muscular thighs as he lunged. Torque and Dev played back-to-back in the center of the stage, and Khan howled out the final chorus while lying on his back and dry-humping the air.

As the final chords died away and the crowd went demented, Khan leaped to his feet. Tilting his head back and holding his arms wide, he half yelled, half growled, *"Guten Abend, Berlin!"*

If it was possible, the noise from the audience grew even wilder until Nate pointed the remote control at the TV set and muted it. Shifting in his seat, he viewed Violet's face. "And that's Beast."

"Wow." She was stunned by what she had just seen. By what he was a part of.

They were seated in a small room off the larger living area of the band's tour bus. In addition, Violet had seen a kitchen, shower room, two restrooms and a long narrow hall lined with bunks. Nate had explained that they used hotels when they could, but the bus was their home away from home when they were on the road. While they were waiting for the others to arrive, Ged had suggested showing her the film of the band.

"I wanted you to watch this before you met them. Beast is not like any other band," he explained now. There was a note in his voice that troubled her.

Violet turned her black leather chair to face Ged. She wasn't sure what she thought of the band's manager. Ged Taverner was a huge, dark, brooding figure with eyes that seemed to see right inside her soul. "I see what you mean."

He stared at her for a long silent moment. "I'm not sure you do…but you will."

* * *

Nate kept one eye on Violet as the men who had saved his sanity climbed—or, in the case of Khan, erupted—onto the tour bus. All at once, the vast, glossy space was filled with noise and virility. It was always like this when the five of them were together. Not so much a competition, more an unconscious demonstration of strength. The band members were such a closely knit group that they had developed their own brand of masculine pride. With five huge competing egos, it sometimes looked like machismo gone wild. Only they knew the truth. Only they knew the real story. And Ged knew it all, of course. He was the man who had brought them together. The man who had saved them.

When the backslapping and calculated insults were over, Nate spoke up, his voice cutting across the clamor. "Guys, this is Violet. She's joining us for the tour."

Four pairs of eyes turned to study Violet. Diablo's were gold with haunted shadows in their depths, Torque's gray with multicolored moonstone flecks; Dev's were like chips of ice and Khan's a brilliant, unrelenting amber. He could feel Violet's unease as she was caught in their combined beams. Nate knew what the others were thinking. Saw it in Khan's altered stance and the way he licked his lips. A flash of anger ripped through him. *No way.*

"She's with me." He kept his voice level, but his eyes challenged them. *Don't even think about it.*

Slowly, the others relaxed. The coiled tension unwound. The macho posturing gave way to casual welcome. Nate had staked a claim to Violet that the others would respect. None of them had ever brought a girl on tour before. Oh, there had been plenty of women sharing those bunks. Plenty of wild nights and crazy days. But no one had ever started out by introducing someone to the band, announcing that she would be accompanying them. It was a new dynamic. He knew Ged was watching closely, observing how it would work out.

"Welcome to the zoo, Violet." Torque's brilliant smile flashed. He brushed back his long, flame-red hair, his movements quick-fire. Torque didn't know how to be still. "Beast. Zoo. Get it?" Violet smiled, and Nate could see some of the tension draining out of her. Torque wandered away to stow his belongings under his bunk.

"Has Nate made coffee yet?" It was Dev's drawling voice.

"No." Violet looked wary. Dev's uncanny stillness and watchfulness always had that effect when people met him for the first time.

"Good. Nate's an Englishman. He can't make coffee for shit." Cool as ever, Dev strolled off in the direction of the kitchen.

Watching him, Violet was taken by surprise as Khan grasped her hand and pressed his lips to it. "Nate should have introduced you to the most important person first, beautiful Violet. I am Khan."

"I'm pleased to meet you," Violet said, casting a helpless glance up at Nate.

"Naturally. Everybody is." Khan's voice was a purr as he went to his bunk. Nate knew from experience he would curl up and be asleep in seconds, leaving his luggage strewn in everyone else's way.

Diablo was always the unpredictable one. In the end, he muttered something that could have been a welcome, but might just as easily have been a curse, as he went to join Dev in the kitchen.

Nate drew Violet down to sit on one of the large, squashy sofas that lined the living area. "These are the people you will have to live in close proximity with over the coming weeks, maybe months." He didn't mention that the tour was scheduled to last just over a year. Surely her memory would have returned by then. "What do you think?"

"I think I need another blow to the head." She gave a shaky smile. "Seriously? I think I've totally disrupted your life…and theirs. Are you certain you want me along?"

The question shook him. Gazing at her, Nate tried to analyze what he was feeling. This wasn't about his sense of responsibility toward her. It wasn't because she needed him to come to her rescue and care for her. *Are you certain you want me along?* He wanted her. It was that simple. And that complicated.

"After a few hours cooped up with us, you may wonder what the hell you've gotten yourself into. Torque's zoo comment wasn't far wide of the mark." He stretched his long legs in front of him. "The schedule is punishing. We're crossing the Channel to France tonight and starting the European leg in Paris. Things will get really frantic in a month or two when the US tour begins."

"How many of you are American?"

He should have foreseen she would want to know more about them. Questions about their backgrounds weren't easy to answer, but they had come up with a biography that suited them. Over the years, they had honed it so it satisfied even the most pressing journalist. Even so, he didn't feel comfortable telling Violet a series of half-truths. "I'm English, as you know. Diablo is Native American. Khan is from India and Dev comes from Nepal."

Violet accepted his explanation without further comment. "And Torque?"

Ah, Torque. The hardest one of all to explain. "He's well traveled."

"A child of the world, that's me." Torque returned carrying coffee. "Wherever I lay my well-worn beanie, that's my home. So it begins. Diablo has just threatened to kill Khan for stealing the best bunk." He raised his cup in a mock toast, those curious, mercurial eyes shifting color. "Welcome aboard, Violet."

As he spoke, the engines rumbled into life and the gigantic bus rolled out into the traffic.

The band was going to spend the afternoon at the stadium engaged in rehearsals. Nate explained the way it worked. Their entire stage, video and lighting rig was in duplicate, so while one stage was being erected in one city, the other one was on its way to the next venue ready to be set up there.

"It's a luxury not many bands can afford. A huge crew of professionals travels ahead of us to set everything up, so all we have to do is turn up and perform. All part of the mystery that is Ged Taverner and his billions."

Violet was bemused at the way he spoke of Ged. It was as though he was indebted to, but barely knew, the man who was responsible for the band's success. "How did you meet Ged?"

They were eating lunch on the tiny balcony of their Parisian hotel suite. It overlooked the River Seine, and the brilliant sunlight, blue skies and iconic buildings made it a picture-perfect scene.

A slight shadow crossed his features. "It was six years ago. I had been through a difficult time. I'd been ill following an attack—" his eyes were on the river, so she couldn't read his expression "—it's not something I care to remember, let alone talk about. I was a music student and I'd been in a band. Not Beast." He turned back to look at Violet, and the shadows were gone. "I'd never come across anything quite like Beast. Ged turned up at my apartment one day.

He said he'd seen me play—God alone knows how, because I hadn't done anything for a while—and he was putting together a rock band. He was looking for a bass guitarist, if I wanted to audition. At first I wasn't interested, but he left me his card. I don't know what it was, but something about the encounter, something about Ged, kept tugging at my mind. Anyway, I got in touch, did the audition and haven't looked back since."

"Is that how Ged found the others?" Violet sipped her water. The elegant menu had dismayed her, and she had ordered a rare steak with a salad instead of any of the dainty French dishes. "He scouted them?"

"I suppose so," Nate said.

Violet sensed he was being deliberately vague. Beast had been together for six years, so he had to know the details of how every one of the members joined the band. Violet thought about Ged Taverner. On the surface, he was charming, but there was something about him that troubled her. It was a watchfulness, a stillness, that was outside of her experience. He was the puppet master, the Svengali, and he reveled in the role. Maybe that was what she felt from him. That sense of needing to be in control. Whatever it was, it worked. The band clearly owed their success to him.

"Is this okay?" Nate indicated the suite behind them. They had arrived in Paris just over an hour ago and checked into this grand, old hotel that cried out "money." There were two adjoining bedrooms with a sitting room in between. "This way, the others in the band won't get any ideas that you might be available." His face darkened as he said the words.

She reached across the table and clasped his hand. "This is perfect."

Could she tell him she'd be happy to share one room—

and a bed—with him? Could she find the words to tell him that her fantasies about getting him into bed, any bed, were getting wilder by the minute? She didn't know if this longing was something she'd experienced before; all she knew was it was raging out of control. How would Nate feel about that? About her wanting him, but also about her possible inexperience? She guessed he wouldn't want to take advantage of her memory loss. *No matter how much I might want him to.*

She wondered if something of her thoughts showed in her face, because Nate's eyes flashed and his grip on her hand tightened. Just as he leaned across the table toward her, there was a wild pounding on the door.

"Nate?" It was Torque. "Get decent, man. We're leaving in five."

Nate groaned. "I have to go. You can either come and watch—but I warn you it will be boring—or you can explore the city and meet me at the stadium in a few hours."

"I choose the nonboring option." *Even though it means being apart from you.*

"Very wise." He rose to his feet, paused and then, as though unable to help himself, stooped and kissed her lightly on the lips before striding out without a backward glance.

Violet sat very still for a few seconds, then slowly raised her fingertips to touch her lips. It had been the briefest of kisses. Barely a kiss at all. So why did her lips feel like they were on fire? Why was she trembling all over? Why did she want to run after him and beg him to kiss her again? Because this attraction was growing like wildfire, consuming her to the exclusion of everything else.

The thought jerked her up from her seat like a lightning flash. No. This couldn't have happened. She was confusing gratitude with something deeper. She was still suffering the effects of that blow to her head. *I could have a husband, or a lover, waiting for me somewhere. He could be frantically searching for me even now. I may not be free to have these feelings for another man.*

She didn't think that was the case—and Nate's frequent internet searches that turned up no trace of anyone looking for her, no newspaper reports of her as a missing person, backed up her hunch—but she clung to the thought anyway. Because the alternative was that she had tumbled headlong into this intense attraction toward Nate with no real idea of who he was. Worse than that, she still had no idea of who she was. But she had a suspicion that she was a werewolf, and she knew he was a werewolf killer. It was hardly a match made in heaven.

Restlessly, she decided to push her thoughts aside, reasoning that her damaged head wasn't capable of straight thinking. After being confined on that bus with all the raw energy that was Beast for the best part of a day, she needed activity. Among her expensive new clothing, she had noticed some kick-ass running gear. Changing hurriedly into three-quarter-length leggings, a tight T-shirt and running shoes, she made her way down to the lobby and out onto the street.

The wide pavements alongside the river were busy, but there were other joggers taking advantage of the pleasant weather. Violet ran at a steady pace, enjoying the fresh air and the sunlight on her face, even though she craved more. What *more* was, she didn't know. When she tried to reach within herself to find out, it eluded her. All she got was a sense of needing bigger, freer, wilder. Frustration kicked in and she paused, leaning over a wall to view the river as she caught her breath.

That was when it hit her. A memory. The first she'd had since that blow to her head. Brief and faint, it flashed into her mind for a second or two. A man, strong, tall and powerful. He was angry. His voice was raised. She got a sense of her own anger firing back at him before the image faded. Although she tried to catch it, to hold on to it, it was gone.

Even though she had felt the confrontational mood of the flashback, she had felt something else more strongly. It was there again. That feeling of otherness. Wherever she had been when she and that man faced each other with rage quivering between them, it had been…different.

Where am I from? Where do I call home? That man cared enough to be angry at me, yet he doesn't seem to be searching for me. The mystery of her identity appeared to be tied into the mystery of where she belonged. A slight headache was forming behind her eyes, and instead of jogging back to the hotel she walked slowly, her feet dragging. Her thoughts kept returning to the only thing that mattered.

Nate. She picked up the pace. *I need to be with Nate.*

Chapter 6

Nate tried to drag his focus back onto the forthcoming gig. Around him, everything was the usual organized chaos, but he hardly noticed. His mind was on Violet. *Face it*, he told himself. His mind had been on Violet since the moment he met her. But she'd been unnaturally quiet ever since she'd turned up at the rehearsal. In the whirlwind of preparation, he'd barely had time to speak to her.

Typically, before a performance, the big personalities in the band would take up most of his time. Nate was the peacekeeper. He wasn't the showman. He was a classically trained musician and, just as his guitar playing brought the music together, it was his temperament that held the team in place. He was the one who didn't need his own ego massaged. There was a definite pecking order, starting with Khan. The closer they got to the start time of the gig, the more outrageous the lead singer's behavior became. Khan was so high maintenance, he was off the scale. By the time they went onstage, he was often lucky to still be alive.

Diablo would generally become even more moody, often disappearing off on his own. There would sometimes be a preshow panic as a search party was raised to find him. Torque became more talkative, his jokes and gibes stoking everyone else's nerves. Dev, meanwhile, was so laid-back he was almost horizontal and getting him to do anything became a Herculean effort. Tempers frayed as they clashed among themselves. Because Ged would be busy organizing and liaising, it usually fell to Nate to keep the band members calm and make sure they all got to where they should be on time and in one piece.

On this particular night, he left them to it. Armageddon would probably break out backstage, but to hell with them. He needed to see Violet. Getting her here had been a logistical nightmare. Their first concert on the European leg of the tour was a sellout. Paris had welcomed them with something approaching a frenzy. It was the same story for the rest of the sold-out tour. The world was going wild for Beast.

Outside the stadium, chaos had reigned for hours. Lines of people queued behind metal barriers from one end of the street to the other, waiting to get inside the stadium. The surrounding area was cordoned off and police patrolled the roads around the venue. The press was out in force, their trucks lining one side of the street. A group of screaming fans had congregated at the rear of the stadium, convinced that they had seen Khan sneaking in that way. Security faced them in a black-clad, mirror-shade-wearing wall.

Nate had arranged for Violet to be brought by cab from the hotel and escorted through the crowd by security. She was waiting for him in one of the executive boxes that perched high above the stadium floor, its height affording her a bird's-eye view of the stage. From her stunned expression, he guessed that she was only now getting a sense of just how big the band was. Below them, roadies bustled about like worker ants. Wearing wired headsets to communicate, they moved equipment, did final lighting and sound checks and ensured that the band's instructions were followed to the letter.

"My God, Nate. I thought those people outside were going to attack the cab in case you were in it."

He drew her into his arms, the gesture as natural as breathing, and dropped a kiss onto her hair. "You seem quiet today."

"While I was out running I remembered something." Her face was troubled as she raised it to his. "Almost remembered something. It was too fleeting to call it a real memory." Violet frowned as though straining to recapture the image. "It was a man and he was angry."

"Husband? Boyfriend?" Nate's chest tightened painfully as he questioned her.

She wrinkled her nose. "I don't think so. But I felt he was someone close to me. Maybe my father? Possibly my boss. There just wasn't enough for me to make any sort of connection. I'm sorry."

Sorry? How could he explain that he didn't want her memory to come back because that would mean she would leave him? How selfish did that make him? "Will you be okay up here?"

"Okay?" She tilted her head back, her eyes sparkling. "I can't wait to see this concert."

"It should be a good one. Khan is on fine form. When he's in this skyrocketing mood anything could happen."

"I won't be watching Khan. I'll be looking at you." There was a husky note in Violet's voice.

And, because he couldn't help himself, Nate bent his head and kissed her. Fire spread through him as soon as his lips connected with hers, so hot he thought he might burn up with it. Her lips were soft and sweet beneath his. When his tongue stroked the seam of her lips, they parted readily for him and he probed the honeyed warmth of her mouth. Violet's hands bunched in the material of his T-shirt as though she was using him to stay upright. He groaned, kissing her harder, and she trembled, returning the caresses of his tongue eagerly. She tasted sweeter than ice cream or strawberries. She tasted like everything he had ever wanted and never knew he needed until now.

On the floor of the stadium, the doors were opening, the crowds, carefully controlled by security, beginning to fill the vast space. Nate raised his head, gazing into Violet's glowing eyes. God, he could lose himself forever in their depths.

"I have to get back down there." He kept his arms around her.

"In that case, maybe you should let me go?" There was a hint of shy mischief in her smile. The smile that shook him right to his soul.

"I said I have to. I didn't say I want to."

She laughed. "Go. I don't want to be the reason all those people riot."

He moved reluctantly away. As he reached the door, he turned back. Closing the space between them again, he pulled her quickly back into his arms and kissed her once more. Long and lingering.

"What was that for?" Violet asked, when she was able to speak again.

"Because that's what I want you to think about while you watch me onstage."

She blushed. "I'll let you in on a secret. That's what I would have been thinking about anyway."

Violet knew she was witnessing something truly amazing. The band had grown so much since the film she had seen on the tour bus had been made. Beast's music was incredible. The way the band played together was creative and intuitive. Each member was individually talented, but as a whole they came together and made so much more. From Khan's raw yipping, screeching tones, through Diablo's wild drumming to Nate's haunting basslines, their unique sound pulsed with primal energy.

They were also visually stunning. She wondered if that was mere serendipity, or if Ged had deliberately recruited them for the way their looks complemented each other. She decided he could have searched forever and not found five men who were such perfect specimens of masculinity. Perfect, yet such a contrast to each other. It occurred to her only now, as she watched them own the stage, just how different they were. There was Khan, with his strutting, purring egomania. Diablo, so solitary, stealthy and quick tempered. Torque with his quick-fire restlessness and Dev, in contrast, so cool and aloof. And Nate. Her eyes were drawn constantly to him, just as she had promised him they would be. Even on that stage, with the explosion of life and sound going on around him, he seemed slightly apart. Detached. Yet, even across the distance that separated them, she could feel his coiled strength, sense the latent power in that lean, muscular body. As a cast of characters, the band came together with a presence that couldn't be manufactured. They were one of a kind. They were Beast.

Behind them, the LED screens were like a giant art installation showing their signature three-sixes logo, roaring flames and the snarling jaws of various wild beasts. The frenzied crowd was dutifully demonstrating the horned sign of the beast by pointing their fingers at the sides of their heads.

But even the performance below her couldn't keep Violet's mind away from that devastating kiss for long. Her lips still tingled with the memory, and her fingers strayed to touch them. Her whole world, already off balance, felt as if it was spinning wildly. The only thing she knew for sure was she wanted more of those kisses. It sounded like madness, but if someone offered her a trade, right here right now, her memory or Nate, she would take Nate. *What does that mean?* She bit back the panicky laugh that rose in her throat. *I think it means you are in trouble.*

Trouble because she didn't know what her future held. Didn't even know what her past contained. *How can I be considering my feelings for another person when I don't know how I feel about myself?* It didn't matter what she told herself, how much she tried to rein in her out-of-control reactions. She wanted Nate with a fierceness that common sense couldn't overcome. It was about raw, primeval longing. She couldn't halt it any more than she could stop herself from taking her next breath.

The concert ended on a wild finale with Khan climbing the lighting rig at the side of the stage, hanging precariously in an upside-down position as he howled out the final number. Violet waited patiently until a member of security came to collect her. Nate had explained that the after-party was a necessary part of the tour.

"It can get a little wild," he had warned her. "But don't worry. I'll be there."

She hadn't thought much of it at the time, but now she was starting to wonder exactly what he meant. Just how wild could Beast get? Having seen them onstage and spent time up close with them, it didn't take much imagination to figure out the answer to that question. Beast could get feral.

The security guy who came to escort her backstage was the same one who had brought her to the stadium from the hotel. His name was Rick and he was shaped like a barrel, a huge, no-nonsense man with a surprisingly soft-spoken manner. He held the door open for Violet to precede him.

"Looks like Khan is keen to get the party started. The green room is already full."

"What does that mean?" Violet asked as she accompanied him along a series of corridors.

Rick shook his head. "I guess you'll see for yourself when you get there. Just keep an open mind, okay?"

Rick led her to a large room. A bar occupied most of one wall, and there were low-level sofas, beanbags and coffee tables clustered together in groups to create distinct seating areas. The lighting was subdued, and a bank of screens on the wall opposite the bar showed a series of images of the band. Beast's music played in the background. This, Violet decided, must be the infamous green room. There were a number of people gathered there already, most of them women, many of them scantily clad. Frosty glances were sent her way as Rick escorted Violet to the bar. She felt decidedly overdressed in her jeans, heels and off-the-shoulder white lace gypsy blouse.

"Where's Nate?" She cast a nervous glance around the room.

"Ged needed to talk to him. He'll be here soon." Rick beckoned the bartender over. "What do you want?"

"Just soda, please."

The bartender looked at her as if she was from another planet. *Perhaps I am. That would explain the otherworldly feelings I get. Maybe I was dropped naked from a space-ship just before that werewolf attacked me.* Hysteria was setting in, she decided. It must be a side effect of the amnesia. After all, she was hardly following doctor's orders and taking things easy.

Accepting her drink from the bartender, she turned to

view the room. Khan was already lounging on a beanbag in one corner with three barely dressed girls at his feet. One of them had her hand on his thigh, and Violet looked away as her fingertips inched higher, brushing the enormous bulge in his groin.

"Who are all these women?" She turned to Rick, who had remained at her side, no doubt on Nate's orders.

"Groupies." In response to her raised brows, he looked slightly bemused, as though she couldn't possibly have never heard the term. "Girls who follow celebrities around hoping to have sex with them."

"You mean all these women are here because they want to have sex with one of the band members?"

"One, two…all." He cast her a sidelong glance, checking her reaction to the shocking information.

Violet choked slightly on her drink. "At once?"

"That would be the ultimate dream. It's well-known on the groupie network that the guys in Beast like to share."

Violet digested that information. There was no doubt was Rick was serious. Was that what Nate did? Shared girls with his bandmates? A hollow feeling hit her low in the stomach. Was that part of his plan for her? Was the sweet-as-honey kiss they had shared earlier intended to warm her up prior to the main act?

As if on cue, a hand slid around her waist and Torque pressed his warm lips to her bare shoulder.

"Angel, you look good enough to eat."

As she skittered out of his hold, Violet realized that the three women at Khan's feet were now naked. He was lying back on his beanbag with his hands behind his head, while one of them bent her head over his groin. Although Violet's view was impaired, it was clear what was going on. When she twisted her head in the opposite direction, she saw Dev in an embrace with another groupie, his hands roaming under her clothing.

"I have to get out of here."

Ignoring Rick's look of surprise, she slammed her drink down on the bar and ran out of the room. Once she was in the corridor, she couldn't remember the way, but she decided she would have to stumble on an exit sooner or later. Anything was better than staying in the scene of debauchery she had just left. Bitter disappointment welled up inside her. Nate was her knight in shining armor, but she had just discovered he might have plans to share his damsel in distress with four other guys.

Gradually it dawned on her that she was becoming lost in a maze of narrow corridors. She seemed to have found her way below the giant stadium and was in some sort of maintenance area. The walls were bare brick, the floor concrete, and the overhead lighting created a gloomy atmosphere. Violet was about to turn back when she became aware of movement on a ledge just above her. As she turned to look, a large black-and-white cat arched its back and hissed at her.

The animal, with nowhere to go, was clearly afraid of something. Violet, very aware of sharp claws in line with her face, took a step back just as a man in a janitor's uniform emerged from a nearby room.

"Ah, *mademoiselle*. Do not be afraid of *le gros chat*. What do you say? The cat who is fat?" His English, although heavily accented, was very good. "She is too lazy to hurt anyone."

Violet eyed the cat warily. It didn't look lazy. It looked terrified. As the man approached and reached for the animal, it lashed out at him, scratching his arm. He muttered under his breath, and the cat jumped to the floor. Backing against the wall as though trying to blend into the bricks, it hissed at Violet again.

"How strange." The man regarded the cat's behavior in surprise. "She is an old lady. Once she caught mice. Now all she does is sleep and eat the food I bring her." He turned to Violet. "Why are you here, *mademoiselle*?"

"I got lost. Can you show me the way to the exit?" She would worry about what she did next once she got outside.

"But of course." He beckoned for her to follow him.

As he passed the cat, it remained in place. As Violet made a move toward it, the animal let out an agonized yowl and ran in the opposite direction. *It's me.* The realization hit Violet as she watched the creature's retreating form. The cat was afraid of *her*. The thought jolted her. *I scared that placid, old cat just with my presence.* It seemed to be confirmation of her suspicion that she was a werewolf.

As they made their way to the next level and rounded a corner, Nate was coming toward them. His face was drawn with worry and, when he saw her, he hurried to Violet's side. The janitor, obviously feeling his services were no longer required, walked back the way they had come.

Nate reached out as though to grip her upper arms, but Violet took a step back. "Where did you go? I've been out of my mind with worry." His voice certainly sounded concerned.

The temptation to melt into his arms was overwhelming, but she needed to know what came next if she did. "I saw what was going on in the green room with Khan and his groupies. Rick said you all share your girls."

A range of emotions crossed Nate's face. Starting with incredulity, it passed through confusion and settled on rage.

"Rick said that, did he?" His lips tightened. "Come with me." He made no further attempt to touch her, merely turning on his heel and marching in what she now recognized as the direction of the green room.

"I'm not going back in there."

"I'm not asking you to." His features softened slightly. "Although things have calmed down and I'm sorry you saw what you did. Khan was out of order. Apparently Ged walked in minutes after you left and restored order." He drew a deep breath. "Wait here. Please?"

Violet found something out in that moment. She found out how hard it was for her to say no to him. She drew the line at being passed around among his friends, but there was very little else she could refuse him. When she nodded, some of the tension left his frame, and Nate went into the green room. When he emerged a minute or two later, he was accompanied by Rick.

"Tell her." Nate's voice was close to a growl.

Rick looked shame-faced. "When I said the guys in the band share their girls, I should have made it clear that Nate doesn't do that."

"And the rest." Nate kept his eyes on Violet's face as he spoke.

The big security guy looked like a little boy caught in an act of misbehavior. "He never has done that. And he doesn't go with groupies." Rick swallowed hard. "You can ask anyone connected to the band. They'll all tell you the same thing."

Violet felt like a huge weight had been lifted from her shoulders. Rick could have been saying those things out of loyalty to Nate, or to keep his job, of course. Something in Nate's expression told her that wasn't the case. He looked like he desperately needed her to believe this. She could sense the emotion coming off him in waves. It was incredible how in tune she had become with his moods in the short time she had known him.

"I believe you." As she said the words, a relieved Rick took the opportunity to try to sidle away.

"Wait right there." Nate barked out the words. "It's your job to get us past the press in a few minutes." His voice was softer when he spoke to Violet. "So we're okay?"

She smiled. "If it wasn't the truth, why would you go take the time to convince the troublesome girl you found in a forest? For a lot less bother, you could just go in there and have your pick of those groupies."

His expression was unreadable as he gazed down at her. "Why indeed?"

Chapter 7

Getting past the waiting fans and press proved to be a nightmare. Rick had a car waiting in the underground parking space below the stadium, but, when Nate and Violet arrived, the security guard was regarding the vehicle with displeasure.

"This is not what I asked for." He pointed to the windows. "They're not blacked out. Ged won't be happy if the paparazzi get shots of you with Violet."

Nate shrugged. "We're not waiting around while you get another car."

"We could put my jacket over Violet's head," Rick said with a hopeful light in his eyes.

Nate glared at him. "Just drive."

"Won't Ged be angry with you for leaving the party early?" Violet asked as they got into the back of the car.

"Right now, he's too pissed off with Khan for starting the tour off on the wrong foot to even notice what I'm doing." He took her hand. "When I said those parties get wild, you have to believe that was *not* what I meant. Even Khan has never gone that far before."

"Is he determined to be the wildest man in rock?"

"Despite all the posturing, there's a lot more to Khan than that." Nate couldn't hide the sadness in his voice. Of all of them, Khan was probably the most damaged. When he considered what they'd been through—Nate included—that was saying something. Before dark thoughts of the past could overwhelm him, they were exiting an underground tunnel and all hell broke loose around them.

Camera flashes went off like explosions, and Nate instinctively reached for Violet, turning her face into his shoulder. He could hear the fans chanting his name as they clustered around the car, banging on the windows and pressing their faces to the glass. The sign of the beast was all around him, and while he should have been flattered, the car was beginning to rock alarmingly. Rick was unable to move the vehicle forward even an inch through the throng.

"Get on your phone to the police. They'll have to escort us out of this," Nate said.

Rick followed his instructions, speaking in a combination of English and French that seemed to get his message across. A few minutes later, sirens were heard, and before long, the crowd parted, as police motorcycles cleared a path, allowing Rick to drive through. The officers stayed with them until they were clear of the waiting fans. It was only when Rick took the route back to the hotel that Nate breathed a sigh of relief. The fans were the reason for their success, and he appreciated them, but moments like that were scary.

When they reached their suite, Nate didn't bother with the lights. There was enough illumination from the streetlamps outside for them to see, and all he wanted to see was Violet. Back at the stadium, when he believed he had lost her… He ran a hand through his hair. *She isn't mine to lose.* The thought was killing him.

"I would never hurt you." She had seen him decapitate a werewolf, but he wouldn't harm a hair on her head. He would lay down his life to protect her. "You have to believe that."

Her smile tugged at that point in his chest. The place that had been cold and shriveled for so long. Until she had come along and breathed new life into him. "Don't you understand? It wasn't just about being afraid." She stepped closer to him, enveloping him in her delicate scent. "I was jealous."

She couldn't have delivered a more erotically charged force if she'd touched him intimately. He was instantly hard, achingly aroused, needing to hold her. But this was dangerous territory. Nate knew it even if Violet didn't. She had no idea who she was. What her past might be, what her relationships were. She had placed herself in his hands and in his power. Her trust in him was absolute. What sort of lowlife would take advantage of that? The invitation in her shining eyes was unmistakable, and, if it was repeated when her memory returned…well, that would be the most wonderful moment of Nate's life. But right now she was at her most vulnerable. When he had kissed her back at the stadium, he had acted on impulse. The most wonderful, never-to-be-repeated impulse of his life. He had to resist the overwhelming temptation to do it—and more—again.

Ignoring his supercharged senses with an effort, Nate moved to the minibar fridge, gesturing to Violet to see if she wanted anything. Even in the half-light, he could see the hurt and confusion in her eyes at his apparent rejection of her shy advance as she shook her head. Steeling himself to ignore her pain, he took out a bottle of water and drained half of it in one gulp.

"Beast is back on the road tomorrow. We should get some sleep."

Violet nodded, moving slowly toward her room. When she reached the door, she turned back. She was framed with the darkness behind her. God, she looked so beautiful in that white lace blouse, the creamy flesh of her shoulders exposed and her black hair tumbling around them.

"Can I ask you something?" Her voice was husky.

"Always."

"Why don't you join in with the others?" It was hard to see in the gloomy light, but he sensed she was blushing. "With the groupies and the sharing? If it's what your friends do, why do you keep yourself apart from it?"

He felt his throat tighten. How could he begin to tell that story? A story that started six years ago and not only destroyed a young man's dreams but also his ability to have any sort of normal relationship. How could he tell another person that, when he was attacked, he was a virgin? That, since the attack, every time he thought about sex, he couldn't get hard unless his fantasies included a woman who was half wolf? That the only time he'd tried to have sex with a woman—one of those eager, grasping groupies—he hadn't been able to get it up and she'd laughed at him? That he was terrified this soul-destroying attraction to Violet might be because deep down he suspected she was a werewolf?

He bowed his head in an attempt to hide his eyes and with them his shameful, tangled thoughts. "I just never have."

She remained in the doorway for a moment or two, then he heard her exhale. It was a soft sigh. A sound of regret and missed opportunity that almost brought him to his knees. "Good night, Nate. Sleep well."

She closed the door behind her.

Sleep? She had to be fucking joking.

Violet woke with a start, sitting up abruptly, her heart pounding wildly. What was that awful noise? It came again, and she identified its source. It was coming from Nate's room. The sound of a creature in torment, it was a piercing, guttural cry. Not quite the howl of an animal, but not exactly human. In between the cries, she could hear a man's voice. Although the words he was saying were indistinct, it sounded like he was exhorting someone or something to leave him alone.

She hurried out of bed and across the sitting room that separated her room from Nate's. When she entered his room, he was lying curled in the middle of the bed in a fetal position with his arms protectively raised over his head. He had left the drapes open, and she could see he was naked. The bedding lay in a heap on the floor as though he had kicked it aside. As Violet approached him, Nate let out another agonized wail.

"Get out of my head, you werewolf bastard." The pain in his voice brought tears to her eyes.

"Nate?" Tentatively, she reached out a hand to touch his shoulder.

She had a scant second to register that his flesh felt like it was on fire, even though his body was bathed in sweat, before Nate flung away from her. Hurling himself from the bed, he threw himself into the corner of the room, bringing his knees up under his chin. Cowering there, he gazed around with wide, unseeing eyes. His breath was coming in uneven gasps, and his lips were drawn back in a snarl. Violet was fairly sure he hadn't regained consciousness.

She knelt in front of him. "Nate, it's me. It's Violet."

He gave a shuddering sigh and his eyelids fluttered. "Violet?"

"You were dreaming." She gave a shaky laugh. "Well, a nightmare to be exact. A bad one."

Nate scrubbed a hand over his face. "Night terrors. I didn't know I still had them. I'm sorry I woke you." He became aware of his nakedness and brought his knees up a little closer to his body. "Could you pass me something to cover myself?"

Violet untangled one of the sheets from the pile on the floor and handed it to him. "Can I get you something?"

"Some water would be good." His voice still sounded shaky.

She went through to the minibar to get a bottle of water. When she returned to Nate's room, he was sitting on the edge of the bed with the sheet wrapped around his waist and his head in his hands. Violet sat next to him, placing the water on the floor.

"What causes these night terrors?"

He straightened, and she saw the lines of tension in his face. "I told you I was attacked."

"Yes, but you didn't tell me the details." She wanted to reach out to him, to wrap her arms around him and hold him, but his earlier rejection of her was still fresh in her mind. She didn't know how welcome her touch would be.

When he turned his head, his eyes were hollow pools of pain. "I was attacked by a werewolf."

Violet did close the space between them then, wrapping her arms around him and holding him close. She felt his whole body tense and then relax in her embrace. "I don't understand. You are not a werewolf now."

"It's a long story."

"I'm not going anywhere. You helped me when I had

no one else." She tilted her chin so she could look at his face. "That works both ways."

He nodded. "I've never told anyone. Not all of it. Six years ago, I was attacked by a feral werewolf. I was just like that poor bastard who came after you, driven mad by an urge inside me I couldn't understand. I could live a normal life until the full moon came around, and then I believed I was going mad as I shifted and became a werewolf against my will."

"But those werewolves we saw at the party in the woods didn't need the full moon to shift."

"Werewolves have evolved over time. The original werewolves *did* need the full moon to shift. Feral werewolves, like the one who attacked you and the one I became, still need the full moon. That's because we are the remnants of an intended kill. We were not meant to survive the attack. In my case, I only lived because the werewolf who was attacking me chose to do it in a town. He was interrupted by a group of passersby."

Violet shuddered and tightened her arms around him. "I'm glad."

Nate placed his hands over hers and gripped them. "I wasn't. Not for a long time. Not until recently." Before she could ask what he meant by that, he continued, "I tried to resist the werewolf cravings, but they were too strong. Then I started to hear a voice in my head. It was driving me to find a young woman called Stella and kill her. This is going to sound crazy, but Stella is a powerful sorceress. At that time, she was in hiding because she was being sought by the leaders of a place called Otherworld."

Violet shivered. *Otherworld?* Had she heard that name before? She wasn't sure if it was that word that had such a strong effect on her, or if it was Nate's story. A story involving werewolves was far-fetched enough—but having seen them for herself, her imagination could stretch that far—now she had to open her mind even further and include a sorceress.

"Are you cold?" Nate looked down at her in concern. She was wearing only thin cotton pajamas.

"A little. Can we go into my room, where the bedding is intact so I can get into bed? You could even join me."

He hesitated. "I'm not sure—"

"We shared a bed on the plane and you emerged unscathed." Violet rose. "I only want to listen to your story without getting any colder." That might not be strictly true, but Nate didn't need to know that she had other plans for him. Not yet.

"I'll come through when I've put some clothes on."

A few minutes later, Nate, clad in a pair of sweatpants, followed Violet into her room and slid into the bed next to her, perching on the extreme edge as far away from her as he could get. Violet had switched on the bedside lamp, and she could see the strain on his face.

"Tell me about Stella," she said.

A slight smile flickered across his features, then it was gone as though a painful memory wiped out a pleasant one. "I tried to resist the voice in my head. It was a man's voice, but I knew he was a werewolf…a very powerful one. Over and over, he was telling me to kill her. I knew it wouldn't go away until I did. Next time the moon was full, I tracked Stella down to her hiding place. But she was too strong for me." He shook his head as though in surprise. "I can hardly remember the details now, but, even though I was in wolf form, she overpowered me. And she wasn't alone. Stella had a protector." He laughed. "This is where the story gets *really* incredible."

"Because it's not incredible enough already?"

"Believe me, there's more to come. The man who was

protecting Stella, the man who is now her husband, is the most powerful sorcerer the world has ever known. His name is Merlin Caledonius. He was known throughout the centuries as Merlin. These days he prefers to be called Cal."

There it was again. The faintest flicker of recognition this time. Not at Merlin Caledonius or Merlin. But Cal? That name sparked a tiny response deep inside the recesses of her memory. *Otherworld and Cal.* They meant something to Violet. She just had no idea what.

"So there I was, writhing on the ground, an injured feral werewolf, and standing over me were the two most powerful sorcerers on the planet. That was when Stella took pity on me and came up with a plan."

"It sounds like it would have to be something out of the ordinary," Violet said.

Nate's laughter was soft and not altogether pleasant. "Oh, it was. Cal stabbed me through the heart with a silver dagger and killed me."

Violet gave a start of horror, slewing her whole body around to face him. "What?"

"It's the only way to kill a werewolf." He spread his arms wide, pointing to his chest. She could see the ragged white outline of scar over his heart. "And look at me. You said it yourself. I'm not a werewolf."

"But you are alive...aren't you?"

"Yes, I'm alive. In every sense that counts, and none that matters." She didn't like the bitter, self-mocking note in his voice as he said the words. "In the instant after Cal stabbed me through the heart, Stella used her powers of necromancy to bring me back to life. While he drove out the wolf, she restored the human."

Violet gazed at him in confusion. "Surely that's a good thing? Yet the way you say it makes it sound like it's bad."

"That's because I've never known which it is." His voice was so tortured that her heart ached.

Violet wasn't looking at him in disgust. She was looking at him with huge, dark blue eyes in which sympathetic tears swam. The delectable cushion of her lower lip trembled, and it was taking every ounce of Nate's self-control not to close the distance between them and take her in his arms.

"When they did this, your friends couldn't have known the impact it would have on you."

"Oh no. They did it with the best of intentions. As far as I know, I'm a one-off." He gave a bitter little laugh and saw her flinch slightly at the sound. "An experiment that went wrong."

"Don't say that. Don't speak about yourself that way." Her voice throbbed with an emotion that sent a thrill through his body. "Although I don't understand why you kill werewolves when you used to be one."

"I only kill feral werewolves, and I do that out of sympathy for their suffering. I understand the nightmare they are going through. I also know what they are capable of doing to the humans they attack. It's my way of helping them, and of giving something back to Cal for the way he helped me. His job of policing the border between both worlds is hard enough."

"It sounds like you went through a living hell." Violet placed her hand on his arm.

Nate glanced down at her slender fingers, so pale and delicate against the tanned flesh of his forearm. Even that light touch was doing something primeval to his nerve endings, something that would frighten her if she ever became aware of its intensity.

"Since that day, I've existed rather than lived. Stella

restored the living, breathing me, but I lost something vital that day. I lost the part of me that feels. She made me human again, but she couldn't give me back my humanity." He smiled at the bemused expression on her face. "I'm not making sense, am I?"

He couldn't put into words the other things that had happened to him as a result of that day. The fears that he lived with daily. That maybe Cal had killed the werewolf that lived within him, but not the wolf instincts. That his wolf had died while his human lived, but his humanity had perished while his—he searched for a word: *wolf-ness? lupinity?*—survived. Nate didn't know if that was true or even possible; he only knew how he felt. Driven to rid the world of the curse of feral werewolves, sworn to kill Nevan, he told himself he hated all werewolves. When he was being honest with himself, Nate knew it wasn't true. Werewolves held a dark attraction for him, one that might just call to something deep within himself.

And could he honestly say he had lost the part of him that knew how to feel? He had truly believed it…until that night in a Vermont forest when he had met Violet.

She moved closer now, seriously endangering his equilibrium, and placed her head on his shoulder. "Is that why you don't behave the way the others do? Why you don't go with groupies and share girls?" He couldn't see her face, but her voice was shy. "Why you don't want me?"

Nate groaned. Turning his body so he could slide a finger under her chin and tilt her head up to look at him, he gazed at her face. "You don't understand."

"I want to. Explain it to me." Her voice was husky. Nothing in his life had ever tempted him as much as her parted lips.

"That night changed my life. I was twenty-two. Before that, I'd been a normal guy, doing what students do.

Going out, drinking, dating—" he shook his head "—but I'd never had sex with anyone."

Her eyes widened. "Never?"

He shook his head. "I've always believed there should be an emotional connection as well as a physical one. I'm not pretending I never had any encounters, but at the time of the werewolf attack, I'd never had a serious girlfriend and I hadn't lost my virginity."

"So you still haven't...?" Violet's eyes were growing rounder.

His smile was self-mocking. "No, I never have."

"I see." She drew in a deep breath. "No wonder you didn't want to do the groupie thing."

"If that's what the others want, then that's their choice and I'm not criticizing them for it. It's just not my choice."

"And I understand now why you don't want to get involved with me." Her voice was quiet.

"No, you don't." He dragged a hand through his hair in frustration. "You don't understand that at all."

Her small white teeth tugged at her lower lip. "Explain it to me, Nate."

He gripped her shoulders. "Violet, I want you so much it's killing me. I never knew it was possible to feel like this, but can't you see how wrong it would be?"

She shook her head slowly. "No. How can it be wrong when I want you every bit as much?"

Her words, her nearness, her scent...none of it was helping. "Because we don't know who you are." He ground the words out. "You have no memory. You could be married, engaged, in a long-term relationship. You could have kids, for God's sake. You are vulnerable, and I would have to be the world's biggest louse to take advantage of that."

Her eyes flashed. "I'm not vulnerable if this is what *I* want."

"Yes, you are." He had to make her see before he forgot everything but the intoxicating longing in her eyes as she gazed at him. Before he drowned in wanting her. "You are saying this with no knowledge of what the real you wants."

She moved closer. Close enough so that even through the thin cotton of her pajamas her hardened nipples brushed his chest. Her breath was a whisper across his cheek. "This is the real me, Nate. Don't ask me how I know that. I just do. In the same way I know that if we don't follow our instincts, we will regret it forever."

"This is wrong." Even as he said the words, his gaze was fixed on her lips. How could anything so perfect be wrong? "You don't know what you're doing."

She gave a soft laugh. "You are a virgin. I may be the one who *does* know what she's doing. I may even do this for a living."

With a shuddering sigh of surrender, Nate brought his hands up to grasp her waist. "Is that what you think? That you are an experienced seductress?"

She shook her head, her dark hair tumbling about her shoulders. "I may have no memory, but I know I have never felt like this before. This is the first time for both of us, Nate." She reached up a hand to stroke his cheek, her breath quickening. "How exciting."

Chapter 8

Violet wrapped her arms around Nate's neck, twisting her fingers in the hair that grew long over his nape to draw him closer. His tongue licked hungrily over the seam of her lips, and her mouth parted eagerly for him. He slanted his lips over hers, holding the back of her head and tilting her into a kiss that became hard and deep. Need surged through her, wild and wanton. She might never have felt it before, but she welcomed it, her need for him escalating, spiraling out of control until she was shaking with the intensity of it.

Nate jerked his head back and stared at her. "Are you sure about this?" His eyes gleamed with a hunger that scared and delighted her.

"More than I have ever been about anything in my life."

"You can't know that."

"Believe me... I can. I do."

She drew his head back down to hers, brushing her lips

against his, triggering a return to the hungry kisses of moments earlier. She couldn't get enough of him. Couldn't get close enough to him. She needed his tongue in her mouth, the hard muscle of his chest against the softness of her too-sensitive breasts, his hands exploring her body. She needed everything he could give her. Measured and gentle wouldn't do. Self-control wasn't good enough. What Violet wanted was raw and out of control. Something in her was wild, ready and aching for him.

Nate eased her down so that they were lying side by side. Violet pressed her hips tight to his, feeling the heavy ridge of his erection pressing firmly against the intimate mound between her thighs. Her hands slid to his chest, her fingers trembling as they slid through the crisp hair. Hunger raged out of control throughout her body. She was intoxicated by the sensual storm gripping her.

Nate tugged her pajama top up, and she raised her arms so he could pull it over her head and cast it aside. His lips were an impatient heat against her nipple as he drew first one delicate tip then the other into his mouth. Violet arched her back and cried out, as a whole new spectrum of sensation swept over her. She was sinking, falling, spinning out of control, giving herself up to the rapture provoked by Nate's lips as they sucked and licked her hardened nipples.

"I thought you said you didn't know what to do?" She managed to gasp out the words as she clung to his shoulders as though her life depended on it.

"I'm working on instinct here." His eyes glittered in the half-light as he raised his head. "I know I want to taste you. I don't need a manual to tell me how."

Oh. Maybe she should do that. Follow her own instincts. Tentatively, she ran her hand down the front of his body, smoothing over the hard muscles of his chest and down over the ridges of his abdomen. Nate sucked in a breath as her fingertips lightly brushed his straining erection.

"Can I touch you here?"

He gave a shaky laugh, taking hold of her hand and guiding it so she could wrap her fingers around his shaft. He was raw, pulsing heat beneath her touch. "You can— and it feels like heaven—but it may test my self-control to the limit."

As she caressed his warm flesh, Nate's hand moved inside the elastic of her pajama pants, one finger parting her swollen folds. Violet gave a gasp and he paused. "Is this okay?"

She nodded vigorously. "It's wonderful."

"Then let's get rid of these." She raised her hips so that he could pull her pajama pants down over her hips and legs. Nate pressed a kiss onto her lips. "I have to go and get a condom from my bedroom."

"A virgin with condoms?" She quirked a brow at him as he slid from beneath the bedclothes.

His expression was somewhere between a grin and a grimace. "It's a Ged thing. He insists on keeping us supplied. He calls it our 'emergency kit.' Can you imagine what would happen if I said I didn't need them? The virgin rock star? Ged would have me in therapy or find me a hooker faster than I could blink."

Violet was still giggling when Nate returned. She let her eyes wander down his body. He was so big and hard, his erection heavy and straining toward her. His silken flesh was made to be stroked. She knelt on the bed, moving toward him on her knees.

If this was about acting on instinct...

"I want to taste you."

She wrapped her fingers around the base of his cock and lowered her head, swiping her tongue over the engorged tip. Nate's whole body jerked, and he hissed in a breath. Violet gave a little hum of pleasure. He liked that. She had taken the initiative and pleased him. Repeating the action, she flicked her tongue back and forth over the throbbing crest. His flesh tasted clean and salty, yet darkly erotic. As she became more adventurous and closed her mouth over his head, Nate moaned, thrusting in small movements against her lips. It seemed natural to suck, and he fisted a hand in her hair in response. Violet looked up at his face, watching his response. His eyes were half closed, the cords of muscle in his neck standing out.

"So good," he crooned. "Too good." Gently he eased away from her. "I don't want to come before we've even started."

Placing his knee on the bed, he tipped her onto her back. Pressing her onto the bed, he lowered his head between her thighs, and her senses went wild. His tongue rasped over her most tender flesh with the lightest, softest strokes, licking at her, and she writhed in ecstasy, burning to lift herself closer.

"Nate…" She needed more. But she didn't know what "more" there could be or how to ask him for it.

Luckily, Nate seemed to know what her wail of need meant. His tongue found the tiny bundle of sensitized nerve endings and flickered over it, sending fire pulsing through her. Violet dug her hands into his hair in an attempt to draw him even closer. His hands hooked under her knees, pushing them back and wider apart as his tongue stroked her entrance. She felt a pressure, then he was probing just inside her. Color flamed in her cheeks. It was so sweetly, deliciously erotic.

An aching need was building inside her, hunger driving her toward an unknown, longed-for release. His lips covered her, his tongue returning to torment that tiny nub, and Violet's whole body exploded. It propelled her into a cataclysmic ecstasy, tightening her muscles and sending shooting stars of rapture through to every cell in her body. Nate held her down as she writhed and convulsed, calling out his name deliriously.

She became vaguely aware of Nate tearing open the condom wrapper before moving in place between her thighs. His lips were gentle on hers as she felt the heavy pressure of him pushing against her still-throbbing entrance.

"We'll go slow." His voice was thick with desire.

"I don't want slow." She lifted her hips to accommodate him, gasping as her muscles began to stretch, easing the way for his steel-hard erection. "I want you...all of you."

A powerful thrust of his hips pushed him deeper into her, the tight friction causing Violet to arch up to him. She twisted mindlessly beneath him, demanding more, and Nate pulled back before driving into her again, seating himself fully inside her this time. A brief flare of pain—sharp and pinching—gone as quickly as it appeared, flashed through her, to be replaced by a feeling of elation. She felt as full as she could be. Full of Nate. It was glorious. Now she needed him to move. To pound in and out of her. Until she screamed.

"Are you okay?" His eyes scanned her face.

Violet nodded. He didn't know what she was feeling. He thought she was some fragile little thing to be treated with care. She was going to have to tell him. "Please. Do it now. Hard and fast."

"This is your first time..."

She wrapped her legs around his hips, urging him on, and heard his groan of surrender. He drew back, then filled her again, impaling her on his thick length. Mindless pleasure washed over her. *I would know if this had happened to me before.* It was her last coherent thought. She gave herself up to sensation. Reality was lost as Nate drove into her hard and fast, exactly as she had begged.

His erection was a hot length of iron powering into her, rubbing over tender tissue, building the friction, stoking the pleasure, until Violet thought she might go crazy. Her breath was suspended, meaning she couldn't even scream as he increased the tempo, his rapid-fire thrusts driving her ever closer to the edge.

This time, when her release slammed into her, her muscles gripped Nate's cock, heightening the intensity of each spasm. It felt like liquid velvet had been poured into her veins. Her body was languid, yet every sense was heightened as she pulsed and contracted, each perfect wave ebbing and flowing rapturously over and around her.

She felt Nate's hard flesh stiffen further, his body jerking to a standstill as the white-hot force of his own release claimed him. Violet wrapped her arms around him, wanting to hold him to her, to capture the moment for all eternity.

Eventually, she collapsed beneath him, shuddering in the aftershocks of unimaginable pleasure.

"That was..." When her breath returned, she floundered, searching for the right words.

"Amazing? Incredible? Perfect?" Nate drew her into his arms, punctuating each word with kisses. "Worth waiting for? I know I'm glad I waited. I hope you are."

"How would we know if it was perfect?" Violet looped her arms around his neck, pressing closer against him. "We've only just started."

"What do you mean?"

"Well, we're hardly likely to have got it right on the first attempt, are we?" She kissed her way along his collarbone. "And you know what they say about perfection."

Nate lay back as her lips moved lower. "Remind me."

"You have to keep practicing to get there."

It was the same story whenever they toured. The bus was ready to go, but there was always at least one band member missing. Khan had the worst track record, but he was by no means the only offender. The next morning, it was Dev who couldn't be found. Ged had sent the roadies out to look for him and was on his cell phone in the hotel lobby, pacing back and forth as he left increasingly heated messages for Dev to call him.

When he saw Nate, Ged beckoned him over. "Any sign of him?"

Nate shook his head. "He went to a club with Torque and Khan after the party last night and left with a girl. No one has seen him since."

"We won't have to worry about him going off with any more girls after I've finished with him." Ged's expression hardened. "Because I'm going to remove his balls without anesthetic."

"This is not like Dev," Nate said. "And, to be fair, we all know you tell us to be on the bus at least an hour before we need to set off."

Ged laughed. "It's the only way to get everyone organized." He cast a sidelong glance in Nate's direction. "Where's Violet?"

"Already on the bus. She found a tourist guide to French cities so she's reading about where we're going next." He sensed Ged wanted to say something more.

"Who is she, Nate?"

How was he supposed to answer that question? *I don't know?* That would be the truth. *She's everything I ever wanted.* Also true. Sex with Violet had been the most incredible experience of his life. His body was still on a high, reveling in the memory. His emotions were equally rapturous. He desired her the way an addict craved a fix, not just thinking about the next time he could take her to bed—although that had started to occupy a lot of his thinking—but he needed to be near her, to be able to touch her, to know she was close, to look at her whenever he wanted to. Which was just about all the time. She had enchanted him, and that enchantment instilled a mix of fear and wonder in him because he knew it couldn't last.

"Why?"

He knew from Ged's face he wasn't just asking. This was more. Ged could sense something about Violet. And if Ged's supercharged senses were involved, that could mean only one thing…

Ged shook his head. "None of my business."

"No, but it's mine." Nate felt his jaw clench with tension. "Tell me."

"Not here." Ged cast a look around the hotel lobby at the people milling past. "Come outside."

There was a small courtyard with a central fountain and rustic benches just off the main reception area. Its sole purpose seemed to be decorative. They made their way out into this haven of cool and quiet. Nate could feel tension curling through him, like a residue of the werewolf memory he tried so hard to forget. He wanted to protect himself from it by crouching low, slinking away, dealing with it on a purely sensory level.

Because he knew what Ged was going to say. Hadn't he known all along what Violet was? He wanted to cover his ears, to tell Ged it didn't matter, to follow those hidden werewolf instincts and walk away. To tell Ged to shut the fuck up even before the other man had opened his mouth.

He did none of those things. He had promised Violet he

would help her find her lost memory and restore her to her family. Nate was a man of his word. "Well?"

Ged looked uncomfortable, a fact that probably had a lot to do with Nate's tone. "You know what I do."

"You've never come right out and said it." Nate crossed his arms over his chest. Ged had been good to him, but he was in no mood to make this easy. On the contrary, he was determined to make the other man work for it.

Ged scrubbed a hand over his face. "Hell, Nate. Okay, if that's the way you want it. You must know I rescue endangered shape-shifters. You've seen the evidence, been a part of it for long enough."

He stared Nate in the eye as though daring him to challenge what he had just said. Nate couldn't. Just because it had never been said out loud didn't mean he hadn't known. He almost laughed aloud at the thought. Weren't they—Beast—the living, breathing proof of what Ged did? A perfect example of a successful rescue effort?

In spite of his annoyance, Nate's lip quirked in a half smile. "I sort of got that."

Ged laughed. "The clues were all there, right?" His face became serious. "I know shifters, man."

"And your point is…?" *Make him sweat.*

"Violet is a shifter." *Blunt and to the point. Thank you, Ged. I can always rely on you.* "She's a werewolf…" Ged hesitated, his expression bewildered as though he was struggling to explain his thoughts. "But—and this is the hard part, the thing I've never come across before—she may not know it."

"You can read her that closely?" Nate was interested enough to overcome his antagonism for a moment.

Ged ran a hand through his hair. "You have no idea. Talk about blessings and curses. But, yeah, I can get that much information from her. And I'm not saying this because I think her being a werewolf is a bad thing. I'm just telling you because you need to know. If you didn't already." He cast Nate a sidelong glance. "For what it's worth, I think she's good for you, werewolf or not. You've been—" he searched around for the right word "—restored."

Restored. It was true. That was what Violet had done. She had breathed new life into him. From the moment they had met in that dark, loamy forest, she had gradually been making him whole again, rebuilding him. Into what? His worst fear had always been that there were traces of werewolf left over from that attack. What if she was slowly but surely finding them and using them in this reconstruction job? Not deliberately. If Violet didn't know she was a werewolf, she was hardly likely to be consciously building herself a new mate. But Nate was so smitten by her, so utterly captivated, that wasn't it possible his *wolfness* was responding by becoming more dominant? Another question, one he had never thought to ask himself, surfaced as he thought this through. *Do I care?*

He had to care. When Violet was gone, he had to cling to his principles. They would be all he had. Them and his memories of a sweet interlude with the girl who had taken his breath away. And his principles told him that the Wolf Leader was evil and manipulative. A cold, vicious bully who would use a confused and frightened young man as a weapon to further his own political ambitions. His principles still told him Nevan had to die.

As for Ged and his strange talent... Beast was the result of his obsession with rescuing damaged shifters. Their audiences knew they were witnessing something unique when they attended one of the band's gigs, but no one could ever guess just how unusual the group was.

"Don't mention this to Violet." Nate drew his mind back into his conversation with Ged with an effort.

Ged held up his hands. "Of course not. I wanted to make sure you were okay. That's all."

"I'm okay." Nate smiled. "I'm better than okay."

It was the truth. For the first time in six years, here now, in this moment with Violet, he was happy. Anxious to get back to her, he moved toward the door that led back to the hotel reception area.

Turning his head to look at Ged, he asked the question that had always puzzled him. The question he was able to ask now the other man had been open with him. "If we are a band of shifters, where do I fit in?"

Ged's expression was confused. "What do you mean?"

Nate explained patiently. "The other four guys are shifters, but I'm not. I'm the odd one out. Why did you recruit me?"

Ged stared at him for a moment, a strange, sorrowful look dawning in his eyes. "You may not be a shifter anymore, but you still needed rescuing."

A commotion in the lobby distracted them, and Nate didn't get to question him further about that statement. They hurried forward to greet Dev, who, looking disheveled and with cuts and bruises to his face, stumbled to his knees.

Chapter 9

"Leave Dev alone." Violet adopted a protective manner as Khan attempted to ruffle his friend's hair.

Dev opened one bloodshot eye. "You heard Violet. I need peace and quiet. You don't do either of those."

Khan snorted with laughter. "Tell me again what happened, just so I can fix it in my mind."

"Fuck off." Some of Dev's cool had deserted him since Nate and Ged had picked him up off the floor of the hotel lobby and carried him onto the tour bus.

Ignoring him, Khan sat on the sofa at a right angle to the one on which Dev was stretched out at full length. "No, seriously. How did it happen? You go home with some girl, right? Then, when you wake up the next morning and try to leave, she asks you for money and that's when you find your wallet has gone. Am I getting this straight so far? When you begin to search for it, that's when her three brothers burst in and start kicking the shit out of you."

"Make him go away." Dev turned pleading eyes to Violet, who was kneeling on the floor next to him, holding a cold compress to his head.

Khan snorted and looked over his shoulder. "Nate, are you sure this story isn't some fairy tale just to get Violet here away from you?"

Nate looked up from the book he was reading. "Isn't it time for you to find Diablo and piss him off?"

Khan unwound himself gracefully from his seat. "Thanks for reminding me." He ruffled Dev's hair again before sauntering away. A few minutes later they heard the sounds of an altercation coming from the kitchen.

Nate rolled his eyes at Violet. "I feel bad about setting him on Diablo, but I know he'll stand up to him and I thought Dev had been through enough."

"You should get some sleep," Violet told Dev. His face wasn't too badly bruised. She suspected his ego had taken more of a beating than his body.

He stretched his long body, before rising tentatively. "Good idea. Thank you, angel." He blew her a kiss from the tips of his fingers before making his way through to the sleeping area.

"Is it always like this?" Violet rose from her kneeling position and curled up next to Nate. She had been feeling curiously fatigued ever since she woke up that morning. Maybe it had something to do with not much sleep and lots of amazing sex?

Nate ran a hand down the length of her hair. "No. Sometimes it can get quite dramatic."

She turned her face into his neck. "I want to be alone with you again."

"We are alone." He gestured to the empty living space.

Violet felt a blush heat her face. "No, I want to be alone with you in bed."

Nate sighed regretfully. "One night and you're already sunk beneath the depths of depravity."

"I know. It's wonderful, isn't it?"

He kissed her. "Beyond wonderful. But you will have to control your wanton lusts until we get to Toulouse."

"That's another seven hours," Violet grumbled.

"I'm worth waiting for," Nate said.

"One night and you're already convinced you're a sex god."

"Who's a sex god?" Torque strolled through from the kitchen. "Has Khan been boasting again?"

"There is no privacy on this bus," Nate complained.

"There is no privacy anywhere, my friend." Torque tossed his cell phone to Nate, who caught it with one hand. "Check out the top story on the celebrity pages. Ged is not a happy man."

Violet leaned closer so she could read along with Nate as he scrolled down the screen on Torque's phone. The simple headline Who Is Nate's Mystery Lady? was followed by a picture of Nate and Violet in the car as they left the stadium the night before. Nate's face was clear, but Violet had her head buried in his shoulder. All that could be seen of her was her dark hair and one slender, naked shoulder emerging from the white lace of her blouse. The text was more speculation than the story.

Nate Zilar, gorgeous, enigmatic bass guitarist of rock supergroup Beast, didn't hang around to celebrate at the after-party following last night's sold-out gig in Paris. Sources say Nate couldn't wait to get back to his luxury hotel room to be alone with the new lady in his life...

The article concluded with a plea. *Are you Nate Zilar's new love? Do you know who she is? Contact us with details.*

"Enigmatic? That's just another word for *odd*," Nate said with a touch of outrage.

"I'd take enigmatic." Torque sounded envious. "I always get *fiery* or *hotheaded*." He lowered his voice. "Leader alert."

Violet wondered how Ged managed to convey annoyance without speaking. It wasn't as if his facial expression was particularly disapproving. He just gave off an aura of condemnation. Now that she thought about it, Ged always managed to communicate his emotions without any effort. *Or is that just me?* She glanced at Nate and Torque but couldn't tell if they were picking up on Ged's mood in the same way. Anyway, Torque had already warned them that Ged wasn't happy, so maybe she was just projecting that information onto him.

Nate held up Torque's phone. "We've seen it."

"Fucking marvelous. What a great start to a tour. We have tiger-boy Khan doing his best to get arrested for violating French public decency laws. Now we have an online campaign to find out who you're dating. No offense, Violet, but that means even more press wherever we go."

"There's no such thing as bad publicity," Torque said helpfully.

"You would say that." Ged flicked a glance in his direction. "How many times have I had to make a statement to haul you out of some shit-hole or another that you've dug yourself into?"

Torque gave a cheerful grin. "Happens all the time," he told Violet. "Last month, I had a bit of an incident that brought me to the attention of the London police. Ged had to come and bail me out."

"Again," Ged said, with a long-suffering sigh. "I had to come and bail you out *again*. And this 'bit of an incident' Torque dismisses so lightly was actually him breaking into the house of a girl he liked the look of."

"She liked me, too," Torque protested. "It was her father who objected. He thought all rock musicians were the devil incarnate. Anyway, it wasn't my fault he came home early and found me in her room. I had to jump out of her bedroom window, stark naked. But there was no need for the shotgun…"

"You set fire to his barn," Ged said in an outraged voice.

"That was an accident. I don't know how it happened."

Getting a grip on his emotions with an obvious effort, Ged turned back to Nate. "I suppose that's a timely reminder that you being photographed with Violet isn't so bad, after all. Just be careful in the future."

After Ged and Torque had gone, Violet bit her lip. "I'm sorry to have caused any trouble."

"You haven't. No one saw you, and there is no harm done. Although in a way it would have been useful if we *could* have published your face in the press. That way your family might see it and come forward." Nate shuddered. "But Ged is right. In the middle of a tour, it doesn't bear thinking about. We'll have to keep checking online to see if anyone is looking for you and hope that your memory comes back."

Violet nodded, resting her head on his shoulder. *Or I can keep hoping it doesn't.*

They arrived in Toulouse in the late afternoon and had the luxury of free time the next day. Ged had secured invitations to the luxury home of a millionaire friend, but Nate suspected that Violet was less than enamored about the idea of a day spent lazing beside the pool. He knew from past experience that pools, alcohol and his bandmates tended to result in days that were anything but lazy, but he kept that information to himself.

"What do you want to do?" he asked as they lay in bed that morning. "We don't have to follow like sheep."

A wistful look came into her eyes. She seemed subdued, but it was hard to pinpoint what that meant exactly. "I know it sounds foolish, but we drove past a beautiful forest on the road from Paris. I would love to go there."

Nate felt that slightly panicky sensation tug at him. The one that always surfaced whenever he got an inkling that she might be a werewolf. But hadn't the signs become stronger than inklings? Ged had come right and out said it. *She's a werewolf, but she may not know it.* And Ged had been very clear. He should know because shifters were his business. His very lucrative business.

Nate gazed at the beautiful face on the pillow next to his. Should he tell her what he suspected, and what Ged seemed so sure of? He was afraid that, if he did, it might do more damage to her memory. He had tried researching this dilemma online, but there didn't seem to be any consensus. He wanted to know for sure what would happen if one told someone suffering from memory loss a shocking fact about themselves. If, for example, they believed they were human and he told them they were a werewolf. Would it help their memory to return, or could it drive it away forever? Could it send them into a state of emotional shock so deep that they might never recover? Nate couldn't find the answer to those questions and, until he did, he wasn't prepared to risk it.

He wondered if Violet had noticed the clues about herself. There was that incredible appetite of hers. Violet was always hungry. And usually for meat. The guys on the tour bus had started to joke that Nate hadn't wooed her with chocolates and flowers. They said he must have turned up at her door with a pound of rare hamburger. Then there was her energy. She needed to run. Not jog. She had to run flat out for miles each day, but the exercise never tired her. Now she wanted to go to the forest.

Wolf signs. Can't you see them, Violet?

He was aware of Violet scanning his face as if she was trying to read his thoughts. "We can go to the forest."

"We met in a forest." Her expression was guarded. "Do you ever wonder why I was there? Why I was naked?"

"Of course." Maybe she had been able to read his thoughts. Perhaps his expression had given them away. That certainly seemed to be where this was heading. "It was hardly an everyday situation."

"Do you think I could be a werewolf, Nate?"

And here it was. The question was out in the open at last. The truth. That was all he could offer her. "It has crossed my mind."

"You hate werewolves." Her voice was very small.

"I don't hate you. I couldn't if I tried." The words were such an inadequate expression of everything he felt for her. He wanted to draw her into his arms, but he sensed she wasn't ready for that right now. "Do you think you're a werewolf?"

"I think I might be, but, if I am, I've lost it." She flapped a hand in a helpless gesture as she tried to explain what she meant. "It's gone, along with my memory. If I'm a werewolf, I've forgotten how to *wolf*." Tears sparkled on the ends of her long lashes. "But, deep inside me, I feel things that make me think I'm missing a part of myself." She moved nearer, resting her head on his shoulder. "If I'm a werewolf, I'm a broken one."

Nate held her close. "Then we're two of a kind. I'm a broken human. The difference is, you can be put back together again. I might be past repair."

"Might be?" He was caught in the intense violet-blue beam of her gaze. "That means there's a chance you can be fixed."

As she reached up and drew his lips down to hers, Nate

realized she was right. He had admitted there was a chance. For the first time ever, he had seen a glimmer of hope in his future. The problem was, that glimmer depended on one thing. It relied on a future that contained Violet. And that was by no means guaranteed.

They walked for miles through the Forêt de Bouconne, leaving the paths and making their way through the denser trees. Violet was drawn to a meandering river and led Nate along its banks, pulling off her shoes and rolling up her jeans so she could paddle in its crystal waters. Later, they followed a steep incline and sat on a rocky ridge, enjoying the views across the surrounding valley.

There was something missing. This forest wasn't right, but she couldn't say why. Oh, it had all the right ingredients to make it a forest. Ancient skyscraper trees reached high into the cloudless sky. It was wild, yet peaceful. Its shades were leafy green, bark brown and silver birch. Its carpet was pine needle and primrose. Its scent was resin, fir and wild garlic mingling with the clear tang of fresh summer air. Its sound was silence, punctuated occasionally by a bird call or the subtle rustle of forest creatures lurking in the bushes.

It was a forest in every sense of the word, but it wasn't the forest her body craved. Deep within her, there was a longing for a darker, denser place. A woodland where she could lose herself. Her imagination knew it well, conjured it until she could almost believe it was real. *Otherworld.* Did it exist beyond her imagination?

"If you believe you might be a werewolf, why not try to shift?" Nate's question interrupted her daydream.

Was she brave enough to do this? She was half seated, half lying, propped between his legs, with her back against his chest and her arms resting on his raised knees. She turned her head now to look up at his face. "Because I'm scared."

"What of?"

She hesitated. If she gave him an honest answer, she gave him everything. She gave him her heart. Was she ready to do that? In the end, she decided he probably already knew how she felt. "I'm scared of what it will do to us."

She held her breath, waiting for his response. This was his chance to say *"There is no us"* or *"You're right, I can't be with a werewolf."* Nate did neither of those things. He kept his gaze fixed on hers. "From the first moment I saw you, I thought you might be a werewolf. That didn't stop me falling in love with you."

Her lips formed into a soundless *O* of surprise. "You love me?"

"You must know I do." His lips were feather-light on her temple.

Her throat tautened with tears. "I guess I hoped you did, but I couldn't understand how you would."

He tightened his arms around her. "I don't think we get to understand love."

"I know I love you and nothing will change that." She rubbed her cheek along his jaw, and then stopped.

Wolf gesture. I do wolf gestures.

"We don't know what the return of your memory will bring." She hated that note of sadness in Nate's voice. "As much as you love me, there may be someone you love more."

Not someone, somewhere.

The thought was crisp and clear, jolting her out of the sweet, warm bubble of his love. There wasn't someone she *loved* more than Nate. But maybe there was somewhere she *needed* more than here. No. She pushed the intrusive idea aside. She could overcome these longings for a place she didn't know. A place that might not exist. This was where she belonged now. With Nate. At his side. What had happened before didn't matter. They could make new memories together. Even as the thoughts came tumbling along, a strange fatigue followed in their wake, as though challenging her to try to feel normality in a place she didn't belong. It was as if the Fates were laughing behind their hands at her attempt to fit in here in his world, prodding her with these feelings of tiredness and insecurity whenever she began to feel comfortable.

A contrasting surge of restless energy drove her to her feet. "Let's go."

Nate gave a mock groan. "You're too fast for me."

Laughing, Violet caught hold of his hands, pulling him to his feet and propelling him along with her as she broke into a run. Slowing her pace so Nate could keep up with her, she ran back down the ridge and into the shade of the forest. High above them, green garlands of leaf and branch formed a protective canopy, almost shutting out the freckled blue of the sky. Leaving the moss-veined trail, she plunged deep into the trees, brushing past clinging vines and berry-encrusted bushes. Nate crashed behind her, panting now as she picked up the pace, spurred on by the scents of mulch and resin. Finally, she halted in the darkest place she could find.

Could she shift? Where should she start? Closing her eyes, she tried to find that place deep inside herself, the place where she felt something was missing. That was where her wolf self must be. She could feel Nate's presence close by, could sense the watchful guardianship of the forest. The woodland itself was like an elixir to her, spurring her on. She had no idea how to do this, but something within her triggered a series of prompts.

I am human and wolf. Both are equal. I do not have a hand. I have a paw. I do not have a nose. I have a snout. I do not have skin. I have fur. The chant became woven into her psyche, no longer separate words. Simply part of her thoughts. She felt something inside her give way...*shift.*

After a few minutes, she opened her eyes, expecting something to have happened, some change to have occurred. There was nothing. She looked exactly the same. *But I felt it. I felt a change.*

The only difference she could feel was taking place inside her body. Every nerve ending was buzzing, alive with an urgency that had only one focus. It was dark here, and seductively enchanting. She turned to face Nate, her back pressed against the crinkly bark of a tree, her eyes shining.

"It's like our own secret place." Slowly she began to unbutton her blouse.

"Here?" He was still breathing hard.

The blouse slipped from her shoulders. "Remember the night you found me naked in the woods?"

Before she could say any more, Nate had closed the distance between them and was pushing her hard up against the trunk of the tree. Although his breathing was still labored, Violet had a feeling it was now for a different reason. His hands pushed the blouse the rest of the way down her arms until it fell to her feet. As his lips found hers, he lifted her so she could wrap her legs around his waist.

Violet clung to him, something about this place calling her, driving her. "I couldn't shift. I may not know if I'm a werewolf, Nate, but maybe now is the time to find out?" She nipped a line along his collarbone with her teeth. "Don't be gentle with me. I want this to be wild..."

"You want wild?" She barely recognized his voice as he

fisted her hair into a ponytail and yanked her head back. "I can give you wild, Violet. Just be sure you know what you're asking for."

Chapter 10

Nate couldn't describe the blaze of emotion storming through him as he gazed down into Violet's eyes. A lone shaft of sunlight had stolen through the branches to illuminate the scene, highlighting the excitement on her face. It matched his own. *God help me, this is the wildness I have tried so hard to hide.* Something within Violet had found these animal urges deep inside him and released them. A chord inside her perfectly matched one inside him. Their souls were in tune. And this place, these sights and scents and sounds, had fanned the flames of desire that already existed between them until they blazed out of control.

Violet's fingers gripped his biceps as her head tilted farther back, exposing the vulnerable curve of her neck. She shuddered, then cried out when Nate lowered his head and scraped his teeth over the tender flesh.

His lips covered hers. His tongue sweeping into her mouth and meeting hers, caressing it, luxuriating in the sweet, wild taste of her. She tasted like summer meadows and freshly ripened berries. Violet murmured against his lips, and a growl emanated from his chest—a sound he barely recognized—as he released her hair and moved to caress the soft swell of her breast above the lacy cup of her bra. She whimpered, pressing into his hand.

His lips left her mouth, moving along her jaw to her collarbone, sucking and licking until he reached her breast. Her nipples were rock hard, jutting against the soft lace. She trembled in his hold, her body arching toward him as a desperate moan left her lips. Her nails dug circles of fire into his arms.

He tugged her bra cup down, and the first touch of his lips on her nipple had her writhing in desperation. Nate's thigh slid smoothly between her legs, and she tightened her muscles around him instantly.

"Nate." It was a cry of need as he sucked her sensitized flesh into his mouth. His tongue rasped over the hardened tip. He nibbled at her as she clenched on his thigh, silently begging for release.

"Please, Nate." Her eyes were dazed in the half-light.

This pulsing, throbbing need was intensifying, consuming them both. "My God, Violet. What is this? What are these feelings?"

"I don't know." Her voice was a soft moan. "I only know I never want this to stop."

She moaned again as his thumb raked her nipple before he covered it with his mouth once more. Her hands went to his hair, holding him close, as this time his tongue stroked her gently. She squirmed, pressing her lower body tight against the hard bulge that threatened to burst the zipper of his jeans. The scent of her arousal was overpowering him. So hot and sweet. His need for her was like spiraling flame consuming him.

Violet was shaking wildly. "Take me now, Nate. I can't wait any longer."

Nate lowered her to the mossy leaf-strewn carpet. The moment her back touched the ground, he moved over her, his lips taking hers. Violet's tongue responded eagerly to his, and his lust spiked again, reaching a new high. He was like a drug addict and Violet was his fix. He couldn't get enough of her. But it was working both ways. Violet's hands gripped his hair painfully, keeping him tight to her as his mouth devoured hers. As their tongues mated, Nate tugged aside the rest of her clothing, scouring her delicate flesh with his blunt nails, delighting in the shudders that raked her slender body.

She twisted beneath him, panting like a wild animal. Her fingers clawed at his clothes, and Nate assisted her by pulling them off and throwing them aside. His thighs parted hers, and he moved a hand to cup her breast, still kissing her. He licked and nibbled at her lips, drawing her tongue into his mouth and sucking on it. Violet arched closer, the naked softness of her mound pressing against the throbbing length of his erection. A low rumble of pleasure started somewhere deep inside Nate's chest.

He bent his head to lick her breasts, and she cried out. Moving his hand between her parted thighs, he pressed two fingers into her hot, narrow entrance. Violet tensed around him, her eyes closing and her head falling back.

"Open your eyes." His voice was raw with the intensity of his emotions.

Indigo heat glittered between her half-open eyelids as she watched him raise his glistening fingers to his lips. With a growl of pleasure, he licked her juices from his fingers. "You taste so sweet. Nothing ever tasted as good."

"Nate." Her head thrashed from side to side. "Stop torturing me."

He smiled, feeling his jaw muscles tight with savage lust. "Prepare for a little more torture, because I'm going to devour you, Violet."

He edged down her body, pausing over her sex, and her hips jerked toward him. He used his fingers to spread her wide, gazing down at her heat-glazed flesh.

He rasped his tongue along the length of her slit in a slow, erotic motion, delighting in the way she melted into him. His hands gripped her thighs, holding them apart to stop her locking them around his head.

Nate hummed a low moan of pleasure, feeling Violet buck in response as he closed his lips over her clit. He licked her there once before dipping his tongue into the tight entrance of her vagina, swirling inside, gathering more of her delicious taste as his heated growl of pleasure vibrated against her.

He could feel the sensations building in her. She was shaking all over, the tension in her muscles increasing as he returned to lick her clitoris again, sucking the tiny bud into his mouth.

"Oh yes, Nate. Just like that." Violet was gasping out words of need as she writhed against him.

Her body tightened, every muscle straining toward his mouth. As she tensed, Nate slid one finger past the delicate folds of her skin. His mouth continued to suckle her, and he drove his finger into her, hard and fast.

Violet screamed as pleasure overcame her. Her hips bucked uncontrollably as her climax tore through her, flinging and shaking her body around like a rag doll. She held tight to Nate's hair as she shuddered through the ferocity of it. He kept his lips on her, feeling the hot relief spasming through her muscles, causing them to clench and unclench around his finger.

As the shudders subsided, he reached into his discarded

jeans, grabbing a condom and slipping it on. He moved over her, his hands lifting her as the thick head of his cock rested against the entrance to her vagina. One quick, hard thrust buried his steel-hard erection in her to the hilt. Nate closed his eyes, savoring the moment, his body tense and tight with pleasure.

She was so hot around him, her muscles gripping him like a glove. This raging beast within him was insisting that he take her hard, fast and fierce. Violet was demanding the same. She was thrashing beneath him, grinding her pelvis against him, driving him as deep into her as he could get.

He eased back, groaning at the unbelievable rush of pleasure from the friction of her flesh resisting him. He thought nothing could feel better. He was wrong. When he thrust back inside her tight depths and her heated muscles clasped him, he thought he might go insane with the sensations flooding through his body.

Nate gritted his teeth as he braced his body over Violet's. Her hands went to his shoulders, her nails clawing at his skin. The added sensation of the sharp pain shocked him. His cock swelled further in response. A growl left his lips, and he bent his head to nip her collarbone, hard enough to sting. Violet gave a gasp, and he saw her eyes darken.

"Yes."

The knowledge that she wanted that pain-pleasure feeling, too, sharpened his own enjoyment. Nate drove into her faster and harder, one hand moving under her shoulders, lifting her breasts to his hungry mouth. Her nipples were rock hard as he feasted on them, catching at them with sharp teeth while her nails raked his flesh in time with each nip.

He was getting close. He could feel tingling, fiery fingers tracking down his spine, tensing his buttocks and tightening his balls. It was too much, and it tipped him over the edge. He slammed inside her. The pleasure was unlike anything he had ever known. Violet's body arched, her eyes widened, and she stared at him in confusion before her second orgasm hit. She clenched around him, drawing him into her and holding him there. Nate was tipped off balance as his body followed hers. With a harsh growl, he was ripped apart by a climax so extreme there was nothing he could do except surrender and cling to Violet.

When their bodies had finally stopped trembling, he withdrew from her and pulled her into his arms. It occurred to him that it didn't seem strange to be lying naked in a forest in the middle of the day, but he decided he was delirious. The sex had been so good it had messed with his mind. He ran his hand down Violet's cheek and realized it was wet with tears.

"Did I hurt you?" He sat up, studying her face in concern.

She shook her head, attempting a smile through her tears. "It was amazing." She seemed to be struggling to find the right words. "It's just…here, in the forest…this was the right place. This made it even better. Does that make sense?"

He lay back down again. Yes, it made sense. Perfect sense. For so long, he had kept this side of himself hidden. It was as he had always feared. He was an animal, out of control and subject to primitive lusts. Yet he still didn't know what he truly was. He was caught between two worlds. A human who wasn't fully human. A werewolf who could no longer shift. He was whole only when he was wrapped in Violet's arms.

Violet stretched her body against Nate's. Half an hour had passed and they had remained in the forest, wrapped in each other's arms. Although they hadn't spoken, she knew what was troubling him, and maybe it should have bothered her, as well. The dominance he had shown, the roughness of the sex they had shared, the loss of control they had displayed together had triggered a lust so powerful it had shaken them both to the core. Yes, it was further evidence of who they really were. But Violet was willing to embrace that. To welcome it. There was just one thing that would make it perfect...

She ran her hand down Nathan's chest. "I want you again. I need it to be—" She bit her lip, knowing what she wanted, but unsure of how to ask. The bond between them was unbreakable, but would he understand?

Something flared in the depths of Nate's eyes. She saw understanding in his expression. Without speaking, he shifted their positions, raising her so she was on her hands and knees. Rearing over her with his chest pressed to her back and the front of his thighs tight against hers, his lips were warm on the shell of her ear. "This?"

She nodded vigorously as she heard him reaching for a condom. "Yes. God, yes."

Nate gripped her hips, tucking her buttocks tight against his pelvis, allowing her to feel how hard he was once again. Violet gave a gasp as the thick length of his cock entered her, stretching her, sliding in deep once more. She tightened around him, shivering as his teeth nipped the back of her neck. His hips began to thrust, driving him deeper inside her, the pleasure so intense she wanted to throw back her head and howl to the treetops.

Primitive and throaty, his growls demanded her submission as he powered inside her. Violet's body tightened, spiraling desperately. She arched her back, feeling Nate's chest hair harsh and abrasive against the sensitive flesh of her back, the powerful muscles of his thighs tensing and relaxing in time with his thrusts. Violet saw stars as her climax ripped through her. She convulsed against him as Nate bit the soft skin between her neck and shoulder. Just painful enough to drive her wild. Nate plunged deep and hard, a deeper growl rumbling from his chest as she felt the heat of his release inside her, the tension of his muscles, the sharp edge of his teeth.

Violet felt her body shaking, her muscles refusing to hold her up, and Nate lowered her gently to her stomach, easing slowly out of her. Turning her, he held her close to him, wrapping his limbs protectively around her. They lay still, hearts beating in time, both breathing hard and fast.

After a long time, Violet turned her head to look up at Nate. "I tried to shift and nothing happened. But it triggered something inside me. It triggered this."

"You think us having sex in the forest is about your wolf self?"

"I know it is. I can feel it." She tried to find the words to explain it rationally. It was difficult, because the whole situation caused her distress. Not the amazing sex with Nate and the lying here in his arms. That part was wonderful. But the fact that she knew—just *knew*—there was a hidden facet to her being, a side to her she ached to find and couldn't. That was hurting her, causing a restless, burning longing she needed to assuage. "I couldn't shift, but something happened inside me, something that made me want it to be different between us. Wanted it here, in the forest, in the open, wilder, rougher, like animals—" she buried her head against his shoulder "—it was amazing, wasn't it?"

He nodded, but didn't speak. Violet tried to interpret what his silence meant. Was he disgusted at what she was suggesting? Was the idea that he had succumbed to her fantasy and had sex with her while she was in the grip of a wolflike frenzy repugnant to him? She knew, more from what he didn't say than what he did, just how much he had been damaged by his time as a werewolf. She knew, without knowing quite *how* she knew, that a feral werewolf was different from others. A feral werewolf was the ultimate outcast, a being whose very soul was so damaged there could be no redemption. Hated and feared by humans and werewolves alike. That knowledge gave her an understanding of Nate's feelings surrounding what happened to him six years ago.

But there had been redemption for Nate. The man called Cal—the man whose name sparked a tiny flare of recognition deep within her—and the woman called Stella had used their remarkable powers to destroy the feral werewolf inside him and restore him to humanity.

"Maybe they didn't destroy all the wolf." She spoke her thoughts aloud.

"Pardon?" Nate's shocked expression scared her. It was as if she had also spoken his thoughts out loud and he was scared of what he was thinking and hearing.

Violet swallowed hard. This was Nate. How could she possibly be afraid of saying anything to him? "I wonder if, when Cal stabbed you through the heart, what he destroyed was the feral part, but something of the wolf—the untainted part—remained in your body." There. She had said it. She held her breath, waiting for his reaction.

He exhaled a long sigh. "That there was wolf left behind in my DNA, you mean? I've wondered about that so many times. It would explain a lot about the feelings I get, but I don't get the urge to shift." The pain in his voice tugged so hard at the midpoint of Violet's chest that she wanted to cry out at the unfairness of it all. One night, one random attack. If he had been a minute earlier or a minute later. If Nate had chosen a different route that night. If the feral werewolf had picked a different victim. *If.* Such a little word with such a huge impact on the lives it shattered.

Violet wrapped her arms around him. "I don't know how it works, but perhaps that urge went away with the savageness?"

He kissed the top of her head. "I think there was some savageness left about the way we had sex. Your wolf definitely appealed to me."

Violet breathed a sigh of relief. There was no disgust in his voice. Quite the opposite. There was a definite note of husky appreciation. "So neither of us knows how to shift?" She ran her hand down his chest. "Maybe we need to keep having sex until we find a way?"

Nate laughed. "Or until we die of exhaustion? Or end up behind bars for public indecency?" He caught hold of her hand as it began to descend lower. "As much as I would like to explore this theory, it's getting late and I have to be onstage in a few hours." Violet made a grumbling noise as he pulled her to her feet. "There will be other forests."

He didn't say what they were both thinking. *Unless your memory returns.*

The concert in Toulouse had been just as successful and exciting as the one in Paris. From there, the tour bus took them to the Mediterranean port of Marseilles. Violet, studying her maps and tour guides, was bemused by the apparent lack of planning.

"Why are we going to Spain next and then doubling back to get to Italy?"

Ged, flopping into the seat next to her in the dressing room, looked tired. His big, muscular frame drooped with tiredness that seemed to match her own. The difference was, Ged could trace the reason for his weariness. He never stopped working. Violet didn't understand this sudden fatigue that had descended on her and that was getting worse by the day. By the hour, if she was honest.

"It's all about timing as well as routes," Ged explained. "When this tour was planned, Beast weren't as well-known as they are now. The fame wagon was beginning to roll, but it hadn't reached the crazy levels we're seeing now—" His cell phone buzzed, and he made an apologetic face in Violet's direction. As he listened to whoever was talking, his expression became increasingly thunderous. "Is this some kind of fucking joke?"

When he ended the call, Ged stared at his phone for several seconds before throwing the offending object against the wall. He glared around the room. Everyone was gathered there in preparation for the afternoon's rehearsal. All except for one person.

"Where the hell is Khan?"

Rick had been lounging near the door, but he sprang to attention at the quick-fire words. "He got here early to try out the microphones. Said something about an echo in Toulouse."

"Tell Tiger Boy to get his ass back here in the next two minutes. If he argues, I'll wring his goddamn neck."

For a big man, Rick could move fast when he needed to. He returned just within the allotted timescale with Khan in his wake.

"This had better be good…" The words died on Khan's lips as soon as he caught a glimpse of Ged's face.

"Sit down, shut up and for once in your life cut the wise-cracks and listen." Ged drew a breath. "All of you listen, because this doesn't just affect Tiger Boy here. Someone had a hidden camera at the after-party in Paris." He jabbed a finger at Khan. "There is a graphic video of you and those three groupies that is being auctioned to the highest bidder. I've been offered the chance to enter the bidding, but the guy who just called me said the editor of a UK newspaper is prepared to offer stupid amounts of money to get his hands on it. I may not be able to get you off the hook this time."

There was a horrified silence. "How much?" Nate was the first one to speak.

"Millions. I can't match that. Everything I have has gone into this tour."

"And how detailed are the images?" Nate was the only one who seemed able to say anything. Everyone else was standing around looking stunned.

"Oh, they're good. Almost professional quality. Whoever did this knew exactly what they were doing. According to the guy who called me, they are clear enough to be featured on a porn site. He even asked me to congratulate you on the impressive size of your dick and commented on your interesting piercing."

Khan started to smirk, but Torque clenched a hand on his shoulder and gave a warning shake of his head. "This is not the time, man."

"It gets worse," Ged said, massaging the bridge of his nose. He looked at Nate. "Remember those pictures of you and Violet leaving the Paris Stadium?"

"What about them?" Nate's tone was wary as he placed a protective arm around Violet's shoulders.

"We thought there was no harm done, right? Violet's face couldn't be seen, so she couldn't be identified. All the press had to go on was her dark hair and her white lace blouse. There was a flurry of interest. A few 'do you know who Nate Zilar's new lady is?' articles, that sort of thing." Ged turned to glare at Khan. "Thanks to our horny friend here and his inability to keep it in his pants, the press now have pictures of Violet's face, as well."

"How is that my fault?" Khan snarled.

"Because she was in the background while you were putting on your little performance, and she can be recognized because of her hair and the distinctive blouse she was wearing."

"They don't have Violet's name," Nate said.

"No, but I'm warning you now, it will renew their interest. Violet's picture will be everywhere if it isn't already. I give it twenty-four hours before her name gets out there." Ged shrugged at Violet. "Sorry, sweetheart, it's time to kiss your anonymity goodbye."

Chapter 11

Violet took up her favorite position at the side of the stage. She had learned that she preferred to be alongside where the action was, rather than watching a concert from a distance. This was where it felt real. She could hear the roar of the crowd, experience the anticipation and energy, feel the thumping beat of the music inside her body. This was where she got the full impact of Khan's gravelly growl, Diablo's soaring energy, and Torque and Dev's amazing partnership. Most of all, this was where she could see and feel up close how amazing and intuitive Nate could be when he got that guitar in his hands.

Ged had been unable to prevent the sale of Khan's sex video from the Paris after-party, and the news had been plastered over the world's press ever since they left Toulouse. Alongside the story of Khan's indiscretion, the minor story about Violet had achieved a notoriety all its own. Even though her face had hit the headlines, no one had yet come up with a name for Nate Zilar's beautiful new girlfriend. The mystery had acquired epic proportions. She had become the girl no one knew.

Where did I come from? Violet had been over and over that question in her mind. *I didn't drop from the sky into that forest seconds before Nate rescued me. So how did I get there?* That man at the party, the one called Roko, had known her name. *He didn't just know my name; he knew me.* The werewolves who launched that vicious attack had taken him away. What could have happened to Roko since then? How could he not have seen these images of Violet's face in the press and on the internet? As they hauled him away, they said he had something belonging to their master. She swallowed hard. Was Roko dead? Had those werewolves killed him that night? Even if that was the case, surely he wasn't the only person who knew who she was? Her memory continued to elude her, and so did the answers to her questions.

The crowd had reached a point that was close to delirium as the band prepared to go onstage. Nate kissed Violet's cheek before he dashed into place with his guitar in hand. Khan, always the last to appear before the crowd, observed this and grinned at her. "You won't have eyes for Nate when I get out there, baby girl. I can just stand still while this place rocks itself to my presence."

Violet had Khan's measure by now. She gave him a friendly shove in the direction of the stage. "Save your voice for the fans and stop wasting it on me."

He kissed the tips of his fingers at her. "Get ready for the vocal orgy of your dreams. I'll be sending some hardcore eargasms your way tonight."

He burst onto the stage to a cacophony of screaming. Grabbing the mic stand, he held it like it was an extension of his penis. Violet, who had a good view of the crowd from where she was standing, saw various female undergarments land at his feet. Right at the front a group of three women lifted their T-shirts to show the slogan written in black pen across their breasts: Khan's Next Foursome. Khan kissed his fingers at them as he screeched out the first lines of the opening number.

"Totally unrepentant." Ged came to stand next to Violet, his expression a mix of admiration and annoyance.

"He wouldn't be Khan if he worried about what people thought of him," Violet said. She knew the band members well enough by now to understand their individual personalities.

They watched in silence for a while. As usual, Beast owned the colossal stadium. Powerful, theatrical and energetic, they also managed to include the massive crowd in every number. Each person at the back of the stadium felt as important as the one on the shoulders of their friend at the front.

Violet looked past Khan, the performer, at the other members of the band. Diablo created a furnace of energy around him as sweat dripped down his face, while his huge, muscled arms and deft hands wielded the drumsticks with lethal magic. Dev stood statue-still, eyes half-closed, in his own world as he played along to the music in his head. In contrast, Torque was all burning energy. He played like a man possessed, throwing himself around the stage with scissor kicks and gymnastic moves. When he lifted a hand from his guitar and pointed at the side of the stage, mini-explosions went off in perfect timing, making the depths of his curious eyes glow orange with reflected light.

And then there was Nate, with his perfect, elegant bass lines. Not as still as Dev, nowhere near as wild as Torque. Maybe Violet was biased, but to her, it was Nate's assured technique that anchored the music in the chaos around him. Her eyes were drawn away from Torque's pyrotechnics and Khan's theatricals to Nate, the musician. He held her attention above all the others.

"Nate's technique is astonishing." Ged followed her gaze. "He has incredible musicality, with a style that can be subtle, delicate and sweet or wild, energetic and slamming. He is able to find the right coloring or expressive nuance for every piece we play." Ged watched Nate for a moment or two. "Most of our biggest hits were written by Nate."

"He never told me that." Violet was surprised.

"That's Nate for you. Mr. Modesty. People think the band revolves around Khan because of his showmanship, but each one of them brings an equal measure of talent into the mix."

"How did you find them? I mean, Nate said they come from all over the globe." Violet turned her head to look up at Ged. "You must have searched forever to find a group of people who would fit together so well."

Ged's face was in shadow, so she couldn't read his expression. "You could say that."

The show was nearing its climax when Rick approached Ged, his expression serious. "We've got a problem." He gestured to the crowd.

Before Rick could elaborate further, Violet watched in horror as five figures who had been plowing their way through to the front of the crowd leaped onto the stage. She gave a horrified gasp of recognition as the men simultaneously shifted into werewolf form. There was no way of knowing for sure if these were the same huge black werewolves that she and Nate had seen at the house in Vermont, but they certainly looked like them. Crouching low at the far edge of the stage, they bared their teeth at the band members.

Believing this to be part of the show, the crowd went

wild. Violet could see the sign of the beast being made throughout the stadium as howls of appreciation rent the air. Rick was yelling instructions into his two-way radio, and Ged moved closer to the stage.

Onstage, everything went from stillness to action in the blink of an eye. Unable to believe what she was seeing, Violet did a double check. No, it was real. Instead of being afraid of the werewolves who had invaded their stage, Beast turned as a group to face them. Was it her imagination, or did they actually seem *pleased* at the prospect of the coming confrontation? Khan, leading the advance, had a bring-it-on snarl on his face as he moved with muscle-bound stealth toward the werewolves.

In the blink of an eye the stage erupted. The werewolves sprang from their crouching position, and Violet cringed in expectation that the members of Beast would be torn apart before her. Instead, a series of incredible transformations took place. Khan's clothing burst apart. Beneath it rippled brilliant orange fur slashed across with diagonal stripes, each as thick, black and straight as a hand-drawn charcoal line. In Khan's place a giant tiger covered the distance across the stage in one bound, his lips drawn back in a snarl that revealed huge white fangs.

Tiger Boy. That was what Ged called Khan. The thought hit Violet at the same time that the tiger plowed into the wolves. She had always assumed the half-sarcastic, half-affectionate name was a reference to Khan's larger-than-life persona. Now she knew the truth.

She barely had time to process that idea before she realized that there were two other big cats on the stage. Diablo had disappeared and, in his place, a muscular black panther was prowling the space before joining the tiger as an unlikely ally. Finally, Dev cast aside his guitar, shifting stealthily as a ghost into a huge snow leopard, sharp and white in contrast to the blur of color around him, before throwing himself into the fray. Landing on the back of one of the startled wolves, the mighty creature lowered his head and used its lethal fangs to tear a chunk of flesh from its victim's neck.

The crowd, still convinced they were watching a series of awesome special effects, continued to cheer and howl. Rick and Ged were screaming at the security team to get everyone out of the stadium and bring down the emergency screens. Meanwhile, Violet's eyes were drawn to the startling new phenomenon that was unfolding before her eyes.

Striding across the stage, Torque was raising his hands and unleashing a series of explosions in his path. As he walked, he grew in stature until he towered over everything around him. Even from a distance of several feet, Violet could see his eyes were bright red, the color filling the entire surface. The pupils had become vertical black slits. As he blinked, both top and bottom lids moved in time to meet each other.

As Torque broke into a run, his clothes tore from his body. His arm and leg muscles thickened, and he dropped onto all fours, giant claws the size of a mechanical digger churning up the surface of the stage. His skin was replaced by shimmering scales that reflected back the neon colors of the strobe lighting. Giant wings unfurled, and a spiked tail flicked out before he opened his mouth to shoot a stream of blue-white flame in the direction of the wolves. Transfixed, Violet watched as her friend Torque became a fearsome, beautiful dragon. He rose and hovered, his wingspan covering the entire stage.

Next minute, she was almost knocked off her feet as Nate cannoned into her, catching her around the waist and propelling her along with him. "Time to go. This is about to get messy."

* * *

Nate lifted Violet onto the tour bus, diving up the steps behind her and clambering into the driver's seat. Ged had handed him the keys as they met in the middle of the stage, and Nate shouted the words, "This is about Violet" at him, seconds before Torque shifted. The good thing about Ged was he didn't ask questions. There were never any recriminations, unless a sex scandal was involved. He just acted.

Starting the engine and locking the door, Nate spun the wheel, tucking his arm around Violet as he pulled her into the seat next to him and swung the huge vehicle out of the underground parking lot.

"Where are we going?" Violet's voice quavered slightly, but he was pleased to hear she sounded quite lucid. Not many people would cope so well with seeing a group with whom she had spent the last week living in close proximity suddenly shift before her eyes.

"I'll drive around the nearby streets until Ged sends me a message to come back and pick him and the guys up." He fumbled his cell phone out of his pocket and handed it to her. "Let me know when he does."

"So we're the getaway vehicle?" She gave a nervous giggle. "You've done this before, haven't you?"

"Once or twice." He kept his eyes on the road.

"It was all real." Violet's throat gave an audible click. "What I saw back there…"

"It was real." He allowed his eyes to briefly flick from the darkened streets to her face. "How much does that bother you?"

"Probably not as much as it should," she confessed. "It was a shock, and Beast was magnificent, but I don't understand how it could have happened in front of all those people. How did your bandmates shift and become—" she ticked off the different creatures on her fingers "—a tiger, a black panther, a snow leopard and a dragon and that didn't cause a riot? Instead, the audience seemed to enjoy it."

"Because this has happened before, Ged has a contingency plan. He projects an image of the band onto the stage, so it looks like we are still playing even though the real band has shifted and might be creating havoc behind the scenes. The crowd might get a glimpse of something surreal, but it looks like a special effect."

"Ged really does think of everything. What bothers me more is those werewolves." Violet drew a shaky breath. "It wasn't a coincidence. They were the same werewolves who attacked Roko and his friends in Vermont. They were there for me, weren't they?"

Nate nodded, his expression grim. "It looks that way. It looks like someone did recognize you from those pictures of the Paris after-party. They just decided to introduce themselves in an unconventional way."

"But why? Why not approach me in a normal way? Why this? Whoever those werewolves are, or whoever they represent, why couldn't they come to me and say, 'Hey, Violet, we know you. We're your brothers, or cousins, or whatever.' Why the violence?"

"I don't know. But until they offer us some explanations, I don't think you should go anywhere with them."

Nate examined his motives. Were they pure? He wasn't just saying that because he couldn't bear the thought of parting with her? Yes, he could place his hand on his heart and say he was unselfishly looking out for Violet's interests. No one in their right mind would hand a vulnerable young woman over to a pack of snarling werewolves. The fact that he loved her? That meant he would go to the ends of the earth to keep her away from those evil bastards. He would use everything at his disposal. And that included a formidable group of shape-shifting friends.

As if in response to his thoughts, his cell phone buzzed. Violet checked the display. "Ged says to collect them from the rear exit."

When he turned the bus around and retraced their route, the streets around the front of the stadium had become busier with departing fans and other vehicles. Everything was calm and there didn't seem to be any panic. Just as Ged had planned, the crowd was still laboring under the mass delusion that they had just witnessed one of the greatest displays of special effects ever.

He shook his head. It was hard to believe the way Ged pulled this trickery off. Thousands of people must have taken camera phone footage of that scene. It would be scrutinized and analyzed in minute detail. The world's finest special effects geeks would pore over it forever. He couldn't wait to hear the theories about how it had been done and see the attempts to replicate it. You want to transform your lead guitarist into a flying dragon? Stage a fight between wolves and big cats? No problem. Just press this button…

Violet clutched his arm as they neared the rear of the stadium. "Over there." She pointed to a shadowy side street.

Nate didn't dare risk taking his eyes from the road for too long, but he caught a glimpse of what she was looking at. Five men were walking briskly away from the stadium. Something about their build and stance was familiar. Could he swear they were the same five men who had dragged Roko away from that party in Vermont? Maybe not in a court of law. Did he believe in his heart it was them? *Hell, yeah.*

He has something belonging to our master. That was what they had said as they hauled Roko and his friends away. Nate's heart gave an abrupt lurch. It was starting to look like that "something" might be Violet. So who was their master? That was the all-important question.

Rick was keeping a lookout for the tour bus at the rear entrance to the venue. As Nate pulled up, the big security guard gestured to someone just inside the building, and the four band members burst out of the door and bounded onto the vehicle. They were followed at a more leisurely pace by Ged.

Nate knew from experience that they would be on a post-shift high for some time, but this took those energy levels to an all-time record. They were almost ricocheting off the sides of the bus with elation as they relived every second of the action back at the stadium.

Rick took the wheel so that Nate and Violet could join the band members in the seating area. The bus was soon thundering along the coast road, keeping just under the speed limit. Ged gave a terse order to keep the noise down while he took calls and fielded questions, doing his best to convince a constant stream of reporters that the whole thing had all been a trial run of Beast's latest special effects software.

Nate kept his arms around Violet as she huddled into a corner of the sofa, listening to the conversation with wide eyes. He could sense the emotion running through her. Beast were shifters. She was one of them, yet she couldn't find her inner wolf. He could see the changing play of emotions on her face. He saw admiration, envy and sadness in differing degrees.

"Five puny werewolves?" Khan's voice was disdainful. "Didn't they know who they were dealing with? No offense, guys, but that party was over before any of you had shifted."

"Why were they there?" Torque's eyes always remained disquietingly red for some time after he had shifted. They narrowed now as he looked at Khan. "Don't tell me. Have you been getting some wolf action?"

"Fuck off." Khan turned to Dev with a taunting grin. "Was your little friend in Paris a werewolf, is that it?"

"It's me." Violet's voice shook slightly as she cut across their banter. "They were looking for me."

"You don't have to do this." Nate could tell by her face how much she was hurting. She didn't know how the band was going to react to this confession. Would they be sympathetic because she was a fellow shifter? Or furious because she was responsible for bringing about the chaos that had brought their concert to an abrupt and premature end?

"Yes, I do. I can't keep pretending." Her hand shook as she raised it to brush a strand of hair out of her eyes. "I'm a werewolf, but I've lost my memory, so I don't know how to shift. I don't know who those werewolves were, but they had come to take me away from Nate." A single tear tracked down her cheek as she looked around the group. "And I don't want to go."

"Then you don't have to." The voice was gruff with emotion. Ged, leaning against the door frame, met her eyes with a reassuring look in his own. Ged, who had been through his own hell, would never allow another shifter to experience pain if he could prevent it.

"Fuck, no. You are one of us." It was one of the longest speeches Nate had ever heard Diablo make.

"And we know how to look after our own." Torque's still-red eyes blazed inner fire.

"What if they come after me again?" Violet's voice sounded very small.

"Then we'll be ready for them again," Dev growled.

"Yeah." Khan's lips drew back in a snarl. "I doubt those pathetic mongrels will try it again, but, if they do, they'll get another taste of Bengal."

"We are all agreed on that." Ged came to sit on one of the sofas, stretching his long limbs wearily. He gave Violet a look that said there would be no more discussion on that matter.

"We have to consider the practicalities not only of keeping Violet safe, but also of making sure those bastards don't disrupt the tour any further," Nate said.

"We'll kill them all." Khan was so wired, Nate thought he might just try to jump off the tour bus in the middle of the freeway and go in search of the werewolves.

"No one is killing anyone." Nate's voice was firm.

"Nate is right." Ged nodded agreement. "The only reason we will get away with convincing the press that tonight was a supercharged visual effect is that no one died. If there had been werewolf body parts on that stage, we'd have all been screwed. Beast would have been over. None of us want that." He cast a glance around the room. "Right?"

That had the desired effect. Nate knew what Beast meant to each of them. The band was all they had. It was their oxygen, their lifeblood. It kept their hearts beating and gave them a reason to live. The broken, beaten beings Ged had brought together had nothing without this. They didn't do this for the money or the fame. They were part of this band because they had to be. Because without it they were nobody. It had been the same with him. Once. It used to be how he felt about the band. Now it was how he felt about Violet.

Because Nate had hustled Violet out of the stadium while the chaos was still going on, he hadn't seen the ending of the onstage fight. He had assumed the worst. Knowing how vicious his friends could be, both individually and as a group, he believed he had left a massacre behind him.

"How did you make sure it didn't end in a bloodbath?" Nate asked Ged.

Ged's tiredness vanished as a mischievous grin lit his features. "I shifted, as well. Haven't done that in as long as I can remember. Man, it felt good."

"Spoiled all our fun," Khan said, with a suspicion of a pout. "Those wolves ran like frightened puppies when a giant werebear joined us on the stage."

Chapter 12

Violet was tired. So tired she could barely hold her head up. She didn't want to worry Nate, so she forced herself to pretend everything was fine, but this awful fatigue had been getting worse for days. Even her appetite had deserted her.

She knew what it was now, and wished she could find a way to make it go away. *I need to be able to find my inner wolf. She is inside me somewhere, but until I can set her free, I am only half-alive.*

I don't belong here. The thought became more terrifying with each passing minute. How could that be true? How could she love Nate so much but be destined not to share his world? Surely fate couldn't be so unkind. Yet, as her strength continued to fade, it seemed fate might have the cruelest trick of all up her sleeve. *I don't know where I belong, but I can't stay here. This world is draining the very life from me. Nate's world is slowly killing me.*

She could temporarily reenergize herself in the fresh

air. A walk, or better still a run, in a forest, would give her a renewed surge of energy that lasted for several days. A secretive little smile touched her lips. Sex with Nate in the outdoors—preferably in a woodland—now *that* was the best medicine of all.

After leaving Marseilles, they had traveled across the border into Spain and their next venue. Violet had been right when she questioned Ged about their convoluted route. They had traveled into the heart of the country, staying in a hotel in the center of the capital city of Madrid. There, Nate had been so worried about Violet's safety that he had extracted a promise from her that she would not go out alone. Since then, she had been a virtual prisoner, able to snatch only brief spells of fresh air when Nate was with her. And that was part of the problem. Cooped up indoors, unable to release the excess energy trapped inside her, burning with a half-understood restlessness, searching for a lost memory, she saw her health had taken a nosedive.

Everyone connected to Beast had been on high alert since Marseilles, but the werewolves had not made another appearance. The band had played in Madrid, then traveled south to Valencia before moving along the coast to perform in Barcelona without interruption. The only problem at each venue had been the disappointment of the crowd. Word had traveled fast about the incredible special effects and stunts in Marseilles, and the Spanish audiences wanted a similar show of their own. Alongside the familiar sign of the beast, there were calls for *el dragón* and *los felinos grandes* to make another appearance. Beast audiences never went away disappointed, but there was a definite sense of anticipation. When would the dragon and the big cats appear again? Which concert would be the next to get the full impact of Beast's genius special effects?

Now the band was spending the night in a beautiful,

exclusive hotel just outside Barcelona. Set in elegant parkland, it was a two-floor traditional Spanish-style building
of terra-cotta brick with wrought iron balconies and in-
tricate plaster work. The hotel was arranged in a U shape
around a central courtyard onto which the balcony of each
room opened. The mingled scents of citrus, geraniums and
red carnations filled the air.

Violet sat with Nate on the tiny balcony to their room,
listening to the flamenco music that filled the air and
thinking how happy she should be. This was surely the
most idyllic setting in the world, and she was here with a
man she loved so much it hurt.

She was conscious of Nate's eyes scanning her face.
She knew he was desperately worried about her. "You've
hardly eaten anything."

"I'm not very hungry."

He reached across the table and took her hand. "Try,
Violet. Please." She could hear the fear in his voice, and it
made her heart ache. What was she doing to him…to them?
But she couldn't stop this, whatever it was. She wasn't
choosing it, would give anything to make it go away. But
it was as if her body had set itself on a downward path and
there was no way she could pull it back up.

To please Nate, she cut a few more pieces of rare steak
and forced herself to swallow them. Her stomach rebelled
as she ate, and the feeling frightened her more. She remembered Paris and Nate's wide-eyed reaction to the amount
of food she could consume. *That* was the real Violet, not
this delicate creature. The woman whose designer clothes,
purchased only a few weeks ago, hung loosely from her
because they were several sizes too large. *I want that Violet back. I have to find her.*

"Tell me what to do." Nate's dark eyes were deep wells

of pain as they scanned her face. "We have to be able to beat this."

"It's my wolf. She needs to get out." She smiled sadly at him. "I think she's dying, Nate."

"Don't say that." His voice hitched. "Oh, God, Violet, we can't let that happen."

She moved around the table, coming to sit on his lap, curling into the warmth of his body and resting her head in the curve of his neck. He held her close to him for a long time. It felt to Violet like he was trying to imprint her onto his skin, to inhale her, to hold her in his arms forever.

A shout from the courtyard below broke the spell.

"We've got company." It was Diablo's voice.

Reluctantly, Nate placed Violet on her feet and moved to lean over the balcony rail. "What's going on?"

Diablo was standing in the center of the courtyard. He tilted his head back to look up at Nate. "Our werewolf friends are on their way."

"Get the others together. I'm on my way down." Nate turned back to Violet. "Promise me you'll stay here?"

"But it's me they've come for. How can I ask you and your friends to place yourselves in danger and not even show myself to them?" Her heart was pounding with fear. Fear for herself, but even more fear for Nate and the confrontation he was about to walk into.

"Unless they are prepared to say why they want you, we have to assume you are in danger from them." Nate drew her close for a second, pressing his lips to hers. "Until then, you stay out of sight. No arguments."

She nodded. "I'll listen from up here."

The truth was, she felt too weak for any coming showdown. She felt too weak to find that next breath.

He smiled down at her. "That's my girl."

"I'll always be your girl." Why did saying those words make her want to cry? "I love you."

Beast was already lined up on one side of the courtyard when the werewolves arrived. The five huge black animals bounded into the courtyard and halted when they saw the five men standing there.

The werewolves hesitated, then, as if acting in response to a silent signal, they shifted back. Five naked men faced the members of Beast across a distance of several feet. One of them, the one Nate recognized as the man who had apologized for interrupting the party in Vermont, took a single step forward.

"I am Dario. Give us what we want and there will be no trouble."

Nate matched the forward step. "That depends on what you want."

"We have come for the girl."

"Why?" Nate wanted answers. If he knew what this was about, maybe they could find out who Violet was. Perhaps she would be able to finally find her inner wolf and put an end to this mystery illness of hers. *Dear God, let that happen...before it's too late.*

The other man's lip curled. "That need not concern you."

Behind Nate, Khan made a low rumbling sound deep in his chest. Nate held up a hand to warn him to back off. "Unless you tell me what your interest in the girl is, you and I can have nothing more to say to each other."

"I am authorized to get the girl and take her back to my master. Entering into negotiations is not part of my remit." The werewolf's voice was haughty.

"Who is your master?"

Dario remained silent.

"Where will you take her?"

Nothing.

"Fuck this." Torque was getting restless. "Let me torch these bastards and then we can go and drink the bar dry in celebration."

"Sounds like a plan." Khan bared his teeth in an expression that might have been a grin, but was probably a snarl.

"This one is mine." Even as he said the words, Nate wondered what the hell he was doing.

His friends clearly thought he had lost his mind. Dev caught hold of his arm, drawing him back slightly. "Have you forgotten one very important detail? Like the fact that you can't shift?"

"He's mine," Nate insisted stubbornly. "You take care of the others. Leave the leader to me."

"What do you want us to tell Violet when we take her the pieces of your body?" Torque asked.

"Let Nate do this." Ged stepped out of the shadows, his eyes lit by a curious golden glow. He handed Nate a knife with a long, thin blade. It wasn't silver, but it was better than nothing. "This moment has been a long time coming."

In the instant it took Nate to turn away from Ged's mesmerizing gaze, the werewolves had shifted. Dario crouched low and fixed Nate with a hungry stare. Nate examined the tiny feeling of elation he felt—*this is for Violet*—as he decided the only way to do this was to seize the initiative.

Something deep inside him, something he had ruthlessly suppressed for a long time, gave a silent, triumphant howl as he crouched and launched himself at Dario. Leaping high into the air, he closed the distance between them, landing on the back of the huge animal. Nate might not be able to shift, but from somewhere within him, he found the fighting instincts of a wolf. His free hand formed into claws, digging deep, bringing the werewolf down as they rolled on the ground, face-to-face, teeth bared. Dario was strong, but Nate had the advantage of surprise on his side. And he was fighting for Violet's life as well as his own. Nothing was ever going to be a stronger incentive for Nate than that.

Even so, it took every ounce of Nate's strength and new-found fighting ability to prevent his opponent from sinking those huge canines into his throat for the death blow, or slicing his abdomen open with claws like razors. He twisted and turned, bit and clawed as he rolled around the terrace with Dario alternately above and then below him. He was only half-conscious of the mayhem around him. The other members of Beast had shifted, and the snarls and growls of the big cats mingled with the flapping of wings, the roar of dragon flames and the bear roars that filled the night air. Luckily, they were the only guests at the hotel that night.

The werewolf was slipping from Nate's grasp, his sinewy body twisting and turning in an effort to break free. The whole time those huge canines were snapping close to Nate's wrists, threatening to snap them in two. With a final lunge, Dario sprang free of Nate's grip and ran across the terrace.

Nate moved with lightning speed, covering the ground between them and throwing himself on the huge werewolf as it was about to dash into the darkness of the hotel gardens. His fingers dug like claws deep into his opponent's hind leg, bringing Dario crashing to the ground. With a surge, he managed to bring the knife up and plunge it into the muscle of the werewolf's leg. Wolf howls rent the night.

Tightening his grip on the werewolf against the odds, he managed to straddle the creature and get his hands around its throat. Dario writhed furiously, his lethal claws slashing into Nate's side. Stinging pain followed by the warm sensation of blood soaking through his shirt indicated that the blow had done Nate some damage.

No one knew better than Nate that he couldn't kill this werewolf. Even if he had the strength in his bare hands to break its neck, he would only slow it down. *What kind of werewolf hunter am I that I don't have my kit with me when I need it? Silver bullets and a samurai sword: that's what this occasion calls for.*

Keeping his hands around Dario's throat, he leaned close so that the creature could hear every word as he spoke. There was fury and pain in the werewolf's eyes, but there was also understanding.

"Take this message back to your master. The girl is not a possession to which he can stake a claim. I'm willing to talk to him…if he comes here alone and behaves like a reasonable man."

Dario shifted back. Nate's hands were no longer sinking into thick fur. They were pressing deep into human flesh. He loosened his hold slightly. The man beneath him winced in agony as he spoke. "You have no idea what you are up against."

Nate let him go and got to his feet. "Nor has he."

The werewolves had gone, Dario limping and trailing blood in his wake. Ged had persuaded the hotel manager that the whole incident was typical rock-star horseplay. The addition of a hefty wad of money to the conversation had helped to ease the man's concerns on the subject. The other members of Beast had retired to the hotel bar to re-live the fight in detail.

Breathing a sigh of relief, still astonished that he had managed to fight and defeat a werewolf, Nate made his way back up to his room. He knew Violet would be worried about what had happened, and he wanted to reassure her. He just wanted to be with her. The knot of worry in his chest whenever he thought about her was tightening.

She was fading fast, and the decline had happened so suddenly. There had to be a way around this. Somewhere, somehow, in time and space, there had to be an answer to this problem that would allow them to be together. They had to be together. He couldn't imagine a life without her. There wouldn't be a life for Nate without her.

He opened the door to their hotel room, his eyes going to the open balcony doors where he expected her to be waiting. She wasn't there. His gaze swept the room, and he let out an exclamation of horror when he saw her lying on the floor near the bed. Nate dashed to her side, dropping on one knee as he felt for her pulse. It was barely there. Her breathing was shallow, and she was so cold her skin chilled his fingertips when he touched her.

"Don't you leave me." He muttered the words through clenched teeth. His throat was tight and painful, and sharp moisture burned the backs of his eyelids. "Don't you dare."

Snatching up the quilt from the bed, he wrapped it around her. Scooping her up in his arms, he carried her down the single flight of stairs, across the terrace and out into the darkened gardens. He kept on going until he reached a wooded area of the parkland. Finding a dense clump of trees, Nate lay down on the leafy ground, cradling Violet against his chest.

I don't know how to do this. For six long, lonely years his life had been an empty void. The only feelings he'd known were bitterness and hatred. Inside his chest, in place of what should have been his heart, there had been a fossilized relic. When he looked back on that time it had a color. It was stained a bleak, dark gray, like residual clouds after a fierce storm.

Then Violet had come into his life with her brightness and beauty. She had shown him other feelings. From the moment he first saw her—really saw her in that hotel room—he had felt life begin to flow back into his heart. He had started to believe in himself again as a person, not simply as a killing machine. Violet loved him. That meant he was worth loving. And Violet? She was everything. Those gray storm clouds had lifted and his life had the same color palette as everyone else's. Except he had Violet, so his colors were more vibrant and spectacular than other people's. He had been offered a future…and now he was watching it fade away.

It shook him to the core of his soul that, after being ruled by hatred for so long, this brief chance at love could be snatched away from him so fast. *And then what? My next big emotion will be grief? How will I ever deal with that? How will I ever get over losing her?*

Nate buried his head in the scented mass of Violet's hair. *I can't. I can't let her go. There has to be a way.*

He had never felt so helpless. *Stay with me, my beautiful wolf, my beloved Violet.* It was the ultimate irony, the cruelest twist of fate that he seemed to be finding his wolf, just as she was losing hers.

He could feel a vague ache from where the werewolf had cut into him with its razor-sharp claws. That was nothing. The pain he felt when he thought about losing Violet was like losing a part of his body. It was as if a giant crescent-shaped wedge had been sliced from his shoulder, down the middle of his chest and out through his ribs, piercing his heart and damaging his lungs in the process. The pain was brutal, choking in its intensity.

The utter helplessness got to him as much as the pain. If there were only some clues. If he only had some idea about what he could do to make this right. But all he could do was hold her in his arms and rock her frail body gently while the tears poured down his face.

He made a vow that the pain and tears wouldn't be wasted. *Let her live and I'll be able to walk away from her with no regrets.* That he would remember this moment and be happy to let her go. He would do the noble thing and be content just knowing there was a part of the world that contained Violet, even if they could never be together. *I can do that.* He forced himself to believe it.

Gradually, during the night, the natural environment of the forest worked its magic and went some way to restoring her. The problem was, it was taking longer each time to do it, and it wasn't restoring her to full health. The decline was too steep to be reversed.

The dawn light was filtering through the trees when Nate finally carried Violet back to the hotel. She was sleeping peacefully now. Her breathing was even and regular, some of the warmth restored to her limbs. As he placed her in their bed, she lifted a hand to stroke his cheek and murmured his name. He caught her fingers and pressed them to his lips. Something, there must be something.

Leaving her to sleep, he wandered through to the sitting room of their suite and headed for the minibar. Spanish brandy sounded like a good idea. Taking out a miniature bottle, he found a glass and sloshed the amber liquid into it. As he was about to raise the glass to his lips, he was interrupted by a familiar voice.

"You look like you could use a double."

Cal was lounging in a chair, his long legs stretched before him. Nate raised his glass. "This will do to begin with." He took a hefty slug of the brandy, feeling the instant warming effect as it hit his gullet. "Care to join me?"

Cal shook his head. "I'm like the police. I don't drink when I'm on an interwordly peacekeeping mission."

"Is that a grand way of saying you have another feral werewolf for me to kill?" In the past, Nate never would have believed the day would come when he would turn Cal down, but this was it. Watching the woman he loved nearly die had sharpened his priorities. "Only, I have rather a lot on right now." He cast a glance toward the closed bedroom door. He didn't want this conversation, didn't have time for explanations. All he really wanted to do was get back to Violet.

"Funnily enough, that's not why I'm here." Cal's curious silver eyes probed Nate's face. "You look like shit."

I feel it. "Thanks. You always did have a way with words."

The sorcerer's eyes dropped lower, taking in Nate's torn and bloodstained T-shirt. "I'm here because I've been hearing stories about a group of werewolves terrorizing one of your concerts. Oh, yes. Gossip manages to travel even as far as Otherworld. The werewolf population here in the mortal realm tends not to draw attention to itself in such a spectacular way. As the person responsible for overall control of the borders between the two worlds, I need to be sure this isn't the start of something bigger. Since I know you, I thought I'd come straight here and find out what's going on."

Nate sighed, flopping into the chair opposite Cal's. "I don't know much about them. There was an altercation with my bandmates, and the werewolves ran off." He lifted his T-shirt, indicating the scratches to his side. "They turned up again tonight, and I fought their leader."

Cal raised a brow. "Man against wolf?"

Nate grinned. "Turns out you might not have destroyed all of my werewolf six years ago. I can't shift, but there is still a lot of the wolf left inside me."

Cal shook his head in a gesture of frustration. "I don't

know who these guys are. The werewolves in Otherworld are in chaos right now. I'm not Nevan's biggest fan, but I thought he might provide strong leadership. Things have been going badly, though, since he captured and imprisoned one of the young rebel leaders with no obvious reason. Roko escaped and since then—"

"Whoa." Nate's heart gave a violent thud. "Back up a bit. What did you just say?"

"Roko, one of the rebel leaders. He didn't have much of a following until Nevan imprisoned him without reason. Now he's free and is drumming up considerable support. Werewolves don't like injustice." Cal paused, watching Nate's face. "What is it?"

"I know that name. Roko." Even to his own ears, Nate's voice sounded hollow. He had a horrible feeling about where this might be going. "Never mind. Continue with your story."

"And Nevan is still going crazy over his family problems. His critics think his judgment has been affected because, even after all this time, no one has come up with any information on the whereabouts of his missing daughter." Cal shook his head. "Just my luck. I get the faerie political scene to calm down and the wolf dynasty decides to erupt."

With a hand that wasn't quite steady, Nate lifted the glass to his lips and drained it. "What's her name?"

"Who?"

"Nevan's daughter." He didn't know why he was asking when he already knew the answer. Cal was looking from Nate to the brandy glass with a bemused expression. Impatience flared in Nate as he repeated the words. "What is her name?"

"Violet. Is her name important?"

"Very." Nate rose to his feet and began to move toward the bedroom door. "There's someone I need you to meet."

Chapter 13

Violet came awake slowly, as if she had crawled down a long, dark tunnel to get here. It felt like her brain and her body were fighting each other. Her brain was forcing her to do this thing, to open her eyes, to look around her. Her body was telling her it wasn't worth the effort, to curl up, stop fighting…just fade away.

No! She forced her eyelids apart, even though the effort made her want to sob. When she did, the room swam dizzyingly in and out of focus, but she caught a glimpse of Nate's long, denim-clad legs and fixed her gaze on them. *Focus on him. Fight for him…for us.* She forced every cell in her body to obey her. Something was different, and she frowned. Two pairs of denim-clad legs? Was she seeing double, or was there someone else in the room?

Nate knelt beside the bed and brushed her hair back from her face. His expression was tender, and she wished he wouldn't smile at her that way. *That is how he'll smile at my memory when I'm gone.*

"There's someone I want you to meet."

Another man crouched down next to him. "We've met before."

Violet frowned in an effort to remember. She should remember this man. He was strikingly handsome, with strong features and unusual silver eyes. "I've lost my memory." She tried to explain, but her voice was so feeble she wasn't sure if any sound came out. He must have heard her, because he replied.

"That's why I'm going to take you home. My name is Cal." That name. She had heard it before. He was Nate's friend, the one who had saved him when he was a feral werewolf. But there was something else about it, something she should know. "I'm going to take you back to Otherworld."

Otherworld. So it wasn't just part of her imagination. It existed. It was her home. Tears stung her eyelids. *I'm going home.* She closed her eyes. A dozen feelings swirled around inside her, trying to claim her attention. There was joy that she might get well again. Relief that she hadn't been going mad when she had believed there was another world. Shock that she would be leaving this world and everything in it that she had grown to know here. But there was one feeling that rose above and overwhelmed all the others. It was determination. Because there was one person she would never leave.

She opened her eyes again and stared directly at Cal. "Not without Nate." This time she made sure her voice was strong enough to be heard.

"Mortals cannot enter Otherworld." His tone was regretful.

"Then I will stay here."

Nate took her hand. "Violet, you know you can't remain here. Your wolf self is dying. Now we know why. You were right when you said you didn't belong here. For some reason, you are unable to survive in the mortal realm. You have to go home to Otherworld."

"I belong with you." With a huge effort, she managed to raise their joined hands to her cheek.

Nate turned his head to look at Cal, a desperate appeal in his eyes. "Violet will die if she stays here. You are Merlin, the greatest sorcerer the world has ever known. If anyone can make this happen, you can."

Violet watched as Cal's eyes traveled from her face to Nate's and back again. There was something about those silver eyes, something that made her feel he could read the secrets of her very soul. "Very well. But there is no time to lose. We must leave at once."

"The band...?" Violet was so tired she could barely speak.

"Leave the details to me." Nate kissed her cheek. "Rest. We have another journey ahead of us."

She nodded, allowing her eyes to drift closed. The two men rose and moved away from the bed. Although Violet dozed, snippets of their conversation penetrated her consciousness.

"I wondered if seeing you again might bring her memory back," Nate said. She heard sounds of him moving around the room and decided he must be packing their belongings for the trip to Otherworld. The thought had a surreal quality to it. She would soon be traveling to another world. One that was her home.

"I think that was too much to hope for." Cal kept his voice low in an attempt not to disturb her. "We are acquaintances rather than friends."

"Once we reach Otherworld, her memory may return immediately." Violet could tell Nate was looking at her by the way his voice softened.

"And if it doesn't?"

Nate sighed. "Then I'll tell her. All of it. But only when she is strong enough to hear it."

"You can stay at the palace." Cal became brisk and businesslike. "It's not my palace, of course. It belongs to the Faerie King and Queen, but they happen to be good friends of mine. Stella and I have our own wing, as our home and for the Alliance headquarters."

"What is the Alliance?"

"The Alliance was formed several years ago to keep the peace in Otherworld when the previous Faerie King, Moncoya, was threatening to take the territories of the other dynasties by force. All the rulers of the dynasties are members of the Alliance, and we hold regular meetings to iron out any issues. I am the leader of the Alliance," Cal explained.

"It all sounds very official."

"It's a fucking nightmare." Cal might be the leader of this Alliance, but his language tended not to be diplomatic. He gave a frustrated groan. "When I took the job, it was meant to be temporary. Don't get me wrong, it's a hell of a lot easier now that Moncoya is dead, but there are always issues, like this one with the werewolves, to contend with. Are you ready?" He lowered his voice, but Violet could still catch what he was saying. "I think we need to leave straight away."

"I have to explain to Ged, the manager of the band, why I'm leaving in the middle of a tour." Violet heard Nate's footsteps heading toward the door.

"Will he be okay with that?"

"No, but I'm hoping he'll understand."

"I don't understand." Ged looked at Nate with an expression of blank astonishment. "You can't seriously be intending to leave us in midtour."

"You know I wouldn't do this unless I had to." Nate was pleading with his friend for acceptance. "Violet will die if I don't take her home."

Ged ran a hand through his hair. "I had no idea things were so bad."

"Her condition has deteriorated fast." Nate felt the tears burning his eyelids and forced them away. This man had picked him up when his life was meaningless. Letting him and Beast down didn't feel good and it didn't come easy, but he had to make Ged see how important this was. And he had to do it fast. Time was running out for Violet. "You have spent your whole life saving shifters who are hurting, or in danger. Now it's my turn to save just one." His lips wobbled into a smile. "My motives aren't as pure as yours. I'm being selfish and doing this because I love her. But the principle is the same."

He didn't tell Ged the devastating news that Violet was the daughter of Nevan, the Wolf Leader. Nate had never told Ged about that whole side of his life, and now, when he could actually have used a friend with whom to unburden, he didn't have the time to tell the story.

The truth was that, on top of the pressure of dealing with Violet's illness, discovering her true identity had sent him into a state of emotional shock. His thoughts were alternating between stalling and racing into a confused jumble.

He had spent the last six years of his life clinging to one certainty. It wasn't pleasant, and he sure as hell didn't like the statement it made about him, but the only truth Nate had known about himself was that he hated Nevan, and that he intended to kill him.

Then Violet had entered his world, and a whole new vista had been opened up to him. She had brought love into his life and lifted the dark clouds. Through her eyes, he had begun to see himself differently. Vengeance had been relegated to second place. Even, if he was honest with himself, half-forgotten.

To discover that the two driving forces in his life were linked. That the man he hated and the woman he loved were father and daughter? His brain, already overwrought by Violet's illness, was having a hard time dealing with that.

All he knew for certain about this devastating piece of information was that it didn't change how he felt about Violet. Nothing could. That was the simple, unalterable truth. As long as he lived, no matter what life threw at him, he would love her.

Did it alter how he felt about Nevan? He couldn't answer that. His shellshocked brain refused to let him think beyond the fact that his whole world had just been turned upside-down.

And, before he could deal with anything else, he had to make sure Violet was safe and well.

Ged must have sensed something of his inner turmoil, because he rose to his feet, placing a large hand on his shoulder. "If you have to do this, then go."

"What will you do about the band?"

"Finglas will step in." Finglas was a young Irish werewolf. Ged had rescued him from a horrible situation a few years ago when he had been captured and faced certain death. He played guitar in an Irish folk band and was a diehard Beast fan. "He's not you and he can be even wilder than Khan, but he'll do."

Nate nodded. "Finglas is okay. He has real talent."

Ged held out his hand, shaking his head in disbelief. "I can't believe this is goodbye."

"It's not forever. I'll be back once I know Violet is safe." Nate took the huge, paw-like hand.

"No." Ged continued to shake his head. "You won't be back."

Nate didn't have time to argue. As he took Ged's hand, the other man drew him forward, enveloping him in a genuine bear hug. When Nate left the room, he took the stairs running, two at a time.

Cal had moved their bags to the door. "Ready?"

"Ready." Nate lifted Violet into his arms. Alarm ran through him again at how frail she was. She felt as light as a child, and he could feel the protruding bones of her ribs under his fingers. Her head slumped against his shoulder, but he felt a tingle of relief as she placed her arms around his neck.

When they reached the courtyard, his bandmates were waiting for him. It was clear from their faces that Ged had told them what was happening. He registered their shocked expressions when they saw how ill Violet was. Nate had never pictured a scene in which he said goodbye to Beast. These were his fellow broken souls. Ged had rescued each of them from a place that was darker than death. With sudden clarity, he knew Ged had seen the shifter inside him, even when Nate couldn't see it himself. This was his brotherhood, and he had thought he would be part of it forever. He gazed down at the pale face in his arms and knew he had found the only thing strong enough to break his bonds to this group.

Torque stepped forward first, his unusual, mystical eyes filling with tears. He pressed his hand to Nate's shoulder and lightly touched his lips to Violet's marble cheek. "Make her well again, man."

"That's the plan." Nate's throat was in danger of closing up as each of his friends copied Torque's gesture and stepped close to wish them well. "We have to go."

Ged raised a hand. The gesture had a curious finality to it. "We'll take good care of your gear."

Nate smiled as he walked away. His gear. Once he would have been ready to kill at the thought of someone else touching his precious guitars. Now? He shrugged. Finglas was welcome to them.

Having loaded their bags into the trunk, Cal was waiting behind the wheel of a hired car. It seemed strange that a sorcerer should need to travel by mortal means, but Nate wasn't going to argue with the ways of magic. He eased Violet carefully into the backseat and slid in beside her, supporting her against him.

"How fast does this thing go?"

Cal laughed as he started the engine. "You sound like Stella. She always wants her transport to be supercharged. Don't worry, we don't have far to go."

"How does this work? How do we travel from here to Otherworld?" Nate asked. "Do we have to travel into space or journey to the center of the earth?"

"Nothing quite so dramatic." Cal swung the car out of the hotel grounds and onto the road that led into the city. "To understand Otherworld, you have to stop thinking logically. All ancient mythologies—Roman, Greek, Norse, Indian—believed in the existence of an Otherworld in some form, but didn't agree about its location. It variously existed in planetary space or in subterranean caverns. My own ancestors, the Celts, thought it was a series of islands set far out in the Atlantic. Even now, there are stories that it will appear magically now and then to sailors, only to disappear when they get closer. The truth is simpler and yet more complex. Otherworld exists everywhere. It is right here, alongside our mortal realm, out of sight but easily within reach. All we need is a belief in its existence and the desire to go there."

"So I close my eyes and click my heels three times?"

Cal laughed. "Not quite. There are portals all over the world. You just need to know where to look for them. Some, like Stonehenge, made a grand statement. Most are quieter. Some portals, like those used in the past by Moncoya for his darkest schemes, are known as dark houses. Others, like the stone circles of the Druids, have existed for thousands of years. Getting in? Easy. All you have to do is believe Otherworld exists."

They drove across the bustling city, following a route that led them to the hilly outskirts. When Cal halted the car, they were on a quiet, tree-lined street in an exclusive area. Elegant mansions overlooked the road, and Cal indicated the one opposite. Although very little of the house could be seen in the darkness, Nate gained an impression of a unique property with quirky architectural features, including asymmetrical turrets and balconies of twisted wrought iron. Tucked away behind high, ornate gates, the house clung to the hillside in what must surely have been the most prestigious location in Barcelona.

"La Casa Oscura." Cal's voice held a world of memories, some affectionate and some distasteful. "Once the most notorious dark house of them all. Until recently, this was Moncoya's headquarters. Until his death, this was the portal used by Moncoya to traffic beings between worlds. Dark houses hide Otherworld's sleazy secrets. Older than time, dark houses are the gateway to an underbelly darker than the pit of hell itself." He shrugged off his introspective mood. "Now the *casa* is just another portal. Follow me."

Cal got their bags from the trunk while Nate carefully lifted Violet from the car. The barbed wire that was wrapped around his heart tightened painfully as he held her poor fragile body. She was so still that he had to check she was breathing. The tiniest sigh touched his cheek as he bent his face close to hers. This time, she didn't lift her arms to his neck. Panic, a foul, choking sensation, rose in his throat.

"We have to hurry."

Cal led him through the gates and across a darkened courtyard. Skirting the house itself, they made their way around to the terrace at the rear of the house. From this point, the views across Barcelona were second to none. Below them, the whole city was spread out like a jeweled carpet, its lights flickering in the darkness.

"The best time to do this is at dawn or dusk, but, because you are with me and my power is so strong, now should work just as well." There was no arrogance in Cal's tone, only certainty.

"What do I have to do?" Nate was impatient to get started.

"Take my hand." Cal's grip was firm. With his other hand, he clasped Violet's limp fingers. "Close your eyes and believe."

Nate obediently closed his eyes. He wanted this so much, how could he *not* believe? This was Violet's last chance. Her weight in his arms felt like no weight at all. Like she was leaving him already. Otherworld was her only hope. He forced his mind, his heart, every fiber of his being to believe in this. His sweet, beautiful love needed this from him as much as she had needed that silver bullet in a werewolf's heart on the first night they met.

"Open your eyes."

Slowly, Nate followed Cal's instruction. As he did, the sensation of being in a dream made him feel light-headed. He was standing on a different terrace, high on a rocky cliff. Far below him the twinkling lights of Barcelona had disappeared. Moonlight illuminated a chain of tiny islands clinging to a turquoise-and-gold coastline. He turned his head, gazing upward in disbelief. La Casa Oscura was gone, too. In its place was a soaring, white marble fairy-tale palace of endless turrets and towers.

"Welcome to Otherworld." Cal's smile was one of pride.

Nate wasn't sure what he had expected to see. The name *Otherworld* had conjured up images of darkness and danger in his mind. This place was so beautiful it took his breath away.

He followed Cal from the terrace onto soft, springy pasture. Nate bent his head to whisper in Violet's ear. "We're here. You are home."

Something was wrong. It hit him like a thunderbolt of pain, as if someone had punched him in the gut. Even that tiny breath he had felt earlier was gone.

"It's too late." His voice broke as he called out to Cal. "She's dead."

Cal dropped the bags onto the ground and broke into a run. "Wait here."

Gently, Nate placed Violet's body on the grass of her homeland and knelt beside her. This wasn't how he expected to feel when he lost her. He expected to feel a giant hand punch a hole in his chest and rip out his heart. But there wasn't a heart to rip out. There was nothing. No pain. No ache. No tears. Just nothing. The world just got a whole lot smaller and a whole lot darker. And Nate felt numb.

She looked so beautiful lying there in the moonlight. Like a beloved memory. He wanted to feel something. He *owed* her some feelings. But nothing came. He wanted to tell her what the last few weeks had meant to him. How much she had changed his life, but his voice didn't want to work. It was lodged somewhere in his throat. Everything inside him had stopped working. And he dreaded the moment it all started up again because he knew, when it did, the pain would be unbearable.

He was barely aware of running footsteps crossing the grass toward him. A small whirlwind of a woman dropped to her knees beside him, and Nate had time to register her short, spiky hair and elfin features. As she placed her hands on Violet's shoulders, his mind transported him back in time six years to a similar scene. It was Stella, the necromancer star. The woman who had brought him back to life after Cal had stabbed him through the heart with a silver dagger.

"There is a trace of life left inside her." Stella's words rocked Nate back on his heels. Violet was still alive? But she was as marble, still as a statue. There was no rise and fall to her chest, no trace of any sign that she was breathing, and her skin was cold as ice. "It's the tiniest flicker, but she is fighting desperately to hang on to it." Stella turned her head to look at Nate. "There must be a very powerful reason why she won't let go."

"Can you help her?" His voice was thick with the tears that suddenly forced their way to the surface.

"I can try." Stella placed her hand on Violet's forehead. *"Awacnian."*

The word stirred something deep inside Nate. He hadn't been conscious when Stella had laid her hands on him in the same way—*face it, I was dead*—but somehow he knew that ancient English was the language of the necromancers. He knew Stella was telling Violet to awaken. He also knew Stella was the most powerful necromancer in the world. There was a hierarchy of the rare sorcerers who were able to commune with the dead, and Stella was at its peak.

If anyone could help Violet, it was this fearless, feisty woman. This was the woman who had taken on and defeated the evil Moncoya. The woman who had breathed life into a stranger—a feral werewolf who had tried to kill her—because she could, and because she pitied him.

For the longest minute of Nate's life nothing happened. Then, to his utter amazement and joy, Violet's chest hitched as she drew in a deep, gasping breath.

Without thinking, Nate clutched Stella's hand. "Is that it? Is she okay?"

At the sound of his voice, Violet's eyelids fluttered and she murmured quietly. It was impossible to know what she was saying, but Nate liked to think his name was in there somewhere.

"She has a long way to go before we can say she's okay, but she's alive. That's a start." The moonlight shone briefly on Stella's face, highlighting the faerie green of her eyes.

Kneeling on the damp grass, Nate leaned over and hugged Stella. It was the awkward hug between a man who tried to rip out a woman's throat and the woman who restored a feral werewolf to life. They had met only twice, but both times, Stella had performed a miracle for him. He owed her a hell of a lot of gratitude.

"Let's get Violet into the palace." Stella rose to her feet.

The little procession, with Stella in the lead, Nate carrying Violet and Cal bringing up the rear with the bags, made its way across rolling pastures and landscaped gardens until reaching the entrance to the palace. Even though his concentration was on the precious package in his arms, Nate spared a moment to notice his surroundings as they passed through an imposing portal and into a majestic hall.

They traversed several corridors before mounting a winding, red-carpeted staircase. Stella threw open a set of gilded double doors and ushered Nate into a vast suite of rooms. "I hope you'll be comfortable here."

Nate placed Violet on the huge bed that occupied most of one side of the room, exulting in the soft sigh that escaped her lips as she sank into the luxurious mattress. He had never thought to hear that sound from her again. "I think we'll manage."

Chapter 14

Violet opened her eyes slowly. The last time she had attempted to lift her eyelids, every part of her body had ached and the effort had been too great. Now, although she was still desperately tired, she no longer felt as though her very bones were infused with weariness. A slight frown tugged at her brow. This palatial room wasn't familiar. It certainly wasn't the Spanish hotel where she had fallen asleep. All of which made her wonder just how long she had slept.

And those dreams. A man with silver eyes who spoke to her about going home. A feeling that she was leaving, despite fighting with every ounce of her waning strength to stay. There were so many reasons why she couldn't go. All of them to do with Nate. So many things she needed to say to him. So many things they had to do together. So many reasons why it was unfair to end their story this way. Then there had been a warm, capable hand on her brow and a woman's voice telling her to awaken.

A new contentment had replaced the fragility and fear. She lay still for a moment, examining it. She remembered why she had become so weak. Her inner wolf had been unable to survive in the mortal realm, and because she was dying, Violet's human was declining with her. She didn't understand why that should be when she had seen other werewolves living and thriving there. Possibly it was because of her lost memory. With it she had lost her ability to shift. Had her wolf been trapped inside her, stifled and distressed? All she knew for sure was that she had been growing weaker. Then she had lost consciousness completely. Now? For some reason she was—if not whole again—sensing that the deterioration had been reversed. Could she say she was on the road to recovery? That might be stretching things a little too far.

She turned her head, pleased that the action didn't cause her any pain or dizziness. Nate was sitting in a chair beside the bed, watching her. The light in his eyes was so warm and loving that it caught in the back of her throat.

When she smiled at him, he leaned forward, resting his elbows on the edge of the bed so that their faces were inches apart. "Hey, you."

"Why am I in a room that looks like it could be part of a castle?"

He gave a soft laugh. "I have friends in high places." He took her hand and kissed it. "We are in Otherworld."

Violet's brow furrowed. The man with silver eyes had talked about bringing her home to Otherworld. "So that wasn't a dream?"

"No. Cal came to see me just at the right time. We brought you home."

There was a question in there somewhere, but it eluded her. Instead, she asked the most important question of all. "Will you kiss me?"

The smile in his eyes deepened. "I may have the most horrible morning breath in the history of the world."

"I'll risk it."

His lips brushed hers tenderly, and Violet melted into him, transported by the feel and taste of him. It was more than a kiss. It was a restoration of all they thought they'd lost. Nate kissed her like he wanted to imprint himself on her, breathe fire into her, burn the love and passion he felt for her into every part of her body. When they drew apart, Violet's cheeks were wet, but she couldn't tell whether it was with her tears or his.

She sat back against the most comfortable pillows imaginable with a sigh. Nate held a glass of water to her lips, and she sipped it gratefully.

"You've been through quite an ordeal. You should get some more rest."

"Can't." She tried for a sorrowful expression.

His eyes were troubled as they scanned her face. "Why not?"

Violet grinned at him. "Because I'm hungry."

His laughter was one of the most beautiful sounds she had ever heard. "Let me guess. Meat?"

Violet nodded appreciatively. "The rarer, the better."

"I'll see what I can do."

When Nate had gone, Violet lay back on her pillows and studied the view from the window. She couldn't see much because the room was several floors up, but she caught a glimpse of soaring cliffs, clear blue skies and whirling seabirds. It wasn't so much what she could see that told her this place was different from the mortal realm but what she could sense. It was something indefinable. It was the feel of home.

And that was the question that had been niggling at the back of her mind ever since Nate had said those words.

We brought you home. It had been the right thing to do. Clearly, this was where she belonged. *But how did you know this was my home, Nate?*

Who would have believed he could derive so much pleasure from watching Violet as she ate a nearly raw steak? Perhaps the happiness was intensified because he had believed he would never again see those little, familiar things about her. Having already believed he had lost her, he witnessed the realization that she would live send a hit of pure joy fizzing through his veins.

Having discovered Stella in the palace corridors and been directed to the kitchens, he had soon discovered that nothing was too much trouble for the staff here. They were used to catering for the leaders of the Otherworld dynasties. Vampires, faeries, werewolves, elves, dryads and countless others passed through these rooms on a regular basis. Rustling up a rare steak was nothing compared with some of the demands they faced.

Having opted for a more conventional breakfast of toast and coffee, Nate was beginning to feel the events of the last few days catching up on him. He was tired and dirty, and his side ached from where the werewolf had clawed him. None of those things mattered. Violet would live. Everything else faded into insignificance.

"There are some things I don't understand." Violet pushed her plate aside. He was pleased to see she had eaten most of the steak.

Nate had been prepared for questions. Maybe not quite yet, but Violet seemed to be on a fast track to recovery. Stella had done a remarkable job. "Go ahead."

"How did you know to bring me here?" She was watching his face closely.

Nate had thought long and hard about how much to tell

her. Maybe it was wrong to keep the whole story from her, but he wanted to wait until he was sure she was strong enough to hear it. He knew how hard it would be for her to know who her father was. To know he was the man who had caused Nate so much pain six years ago. That he was Nevan, the man Nate had sworn to destroy. He knew the truth would tear her in two, the same way it had done to him.

For Nate, the shock of learning who she was had been muted by everything else that was going on. Even so, he was forcing himself to come to terms with it. Violet was everything he had ever wanted, but her father had poisoned his life. When he finally told her the truth about her identity, it was going to have an impact on their relationship, no matter how much they tried to avoid it.

Of course, there was always a chance that, now she was in Otherworld, her memory would return before Nate could tell her anything. Either way, Violet discovering the truth in her own time, or him telling her when she was strong enough, would be better than risking a setback to her health by telling her now and trying to force the memories. Worse, by forcing her to confront the competing worlds in which her father and the man she loved existed.

"Because you had talked about your feelings of not belonging and of an Otherworld. When Cal turned up in Barcelona and I told him about you, we decided your only chance was to bring you here." It wasn't exactly a lie.

Her eyes were like indigo headlights probing his face. Because she had lost so much weight, they appeared even bigger. "But I still don't feel I can shift, so how come I am feeling so much better?"

"You weren't, not at first." He took her hand, his heart aching anew at its slenderness. She was like a bird in her fragility. "When we first arrived here, it looked like you weren't going to make it. Then Stella worked her magic on you."

She was silent for a few moments. "Stella is the one who brought you back to life, isn't she?" He nodded, and she swallowed hard. "Did I die?"

"Not quite."

Her breath hitched on a sigh, and a single tear rolled down her cheek. "I couldn't bear the thought of leaving you."

"Stella said you were holding on for a very important reason."

She clutched the front of his T-shirt. "It was you, Nate. You were my important reason." He drew her close, holding her to him, dreading the next question. Knowing it would come. "How can you be in Otherworld? I heard the man with the silver eyes—the man called Cal—say mortals are not allowed here."

"I was able to enter because Cal is working his magic."

"Tell me you can stay." It was a whispered plea. He could see the way her mind was working. If he couldn't stay in Otherworld, and she couldn't risk returning to the mortal realm, what did the future hold for them? There was only one answer, and it didn't contain a happy ending.

"We don't have to talk about this now." It was a blatant avoidance tactic. He knew it. Violet knew it. He saw it in the flash of pain in the purple-blue depths of her eyes. There was agony and something more. It was gone almost as soon as it appeared, and he wasn't sure what it was. Anger? Determination? Refusal to accept the inevitable? In its place he saw exhaustion. It was as if, whatever that flash of fire had been, it had drained every other feeling from her. "You need to rest."

"Can I take a bath first?" Violet fingered her hair with an expression of distaste. "I need to wash my hair."

The bathroom was a masterpiece of Victorian-style elegance. Larger than most apartments Nate had lived in, the bathroom's crowning glory was the central, roll-top tub. Set on a platform, this larger-than-life feature had claw feet and gold fittings. The rest of the bathroom, with blue-and-white flowered wallpaper and patterned rugs on the floor, added to the old-fashioned feel.

Nate ran a warm, scented bath. Having removed Violet's clothes—and heroically ignored his raging arousal—he carried her through to the bathroom and lowered her into the water. She gave a sigh of satisfaction and, closing her eyes, let her head rest against the back of the bath.

When she opened her eyes, she tilted her head to look at Nate. "Why don't you join me?"

"You're ill." His voice was husky with tiredness. And something more.

"I'm asking you to bathe with me, Nate. That's all." There was a hint of her old mischief in Violet's smile. "For now."

The warm water did look mighty tempting. So did Violet, but that was a whole other story. He could control his desire for her until she was stronger. He was sure he could. Stripping off his clothes, Nate slid into the bath. He hadn't realized how tense he was until his muscles relaxed with relief. Positioning himself so that Violet could lie between his knees with her back against his chest, Nate gave a groan of pure contentment.

"I need to meet your friend Stella and thank her." Violet rested her head on his shoulder. "Being brought back from the dead is proving to be quite enjoyable."

"You will meet her soon enough, but your main focus needs to be on getting well."

"I'll do that." Violet traced a finger through the hair on his chest. "As long as you promise to help me."

The message was clear. *Don't leave me.* And, since Nate had no intention of going anywhere until she was well enough to cope without him—and who knows when that might be, an insistent little voice whispered at the back of his mind—he had no problem agreeing to her terms.

While Violet leaned back, Nate poured water over her hair before shampooing the long, thick length. She murmured contentedly as his fingers massaged the lather into her scalp. When he had finished washing her hair, he took the soap and smoothed it over her body.

"You are good at this," Violet murmured dreamily as his hands slicked up her rib cage and over her breasts.

No matter how hard he tried to fight it, telling himself she wasn't ready for this, his errant body decided otherwise, and Nate's erection lodged firmly against her lower spine. Violet didn't seem to mind. In fact, she shifted position, pressing her buttocks tight up against him. His instincts told him that unique connection between them, the one that heated up their bodies into a fiery frenzy as soon as they touched, meant his caress would help to heal her.

He slid his soapy palms over her torso, inching them down over her sex and finally gliding his fingers between her feminine folds. With a sigh of satisfaction, Violet lifted her hips to greet him. Nate lifted her knee and draped her leg over his while pressing one finger deep inside her. Any fears that she might not be ready for this disappeared as soon as Violet's head fell back against his chest and she gave a soft, appreciative groan.

Her hips rose again, and Nate added a second finger, stretching and filling her. Using the index finger on his other hand to gently rub her sensitized clitoris, he pumped his fingers in and out of her. Before long, Violet was arching her back and crying out his name.

"Oh, God." She turned slightly so she could press her lips to his throat. "That was exactly what I needed."

"But possibly not what a doctor would prescribe."

"Doctors are overrated." Her eyes were closing as she rested her head on his chest. "Unlike the orgasms you deliver."

Easing her carefully out of his arms, Nate stepped out of the tub. Lifting Violet gently, he set her on her feet briefly while he wrapped her in a huge fluffy towel. He dried the excess moisture from her hair and body with another towel before carrying her through to the bedroom. She was asleep before he placed her on the bed.

Returning to the bathroom, he quickly finished bathing. When he slid into bed next to Violet and fitted his body to hers, he was so tired he felt sleep begin to overwhelm him almost immediately. There was only one thought on his mind as he drifted on to the realms of slumber. She was healing fast. He should probably prepare himself to say goodbye sooner than he had expected. The thought triggered a sharp pain in the center of his chest.

Oh, hey. I know what that is. Guess what? Heartbreak really does hurt like hell.

He guessed that hurt was going to get a whole lot worse before it got any better. If it got better. He couldn't imagine life without Violet would offer him anything that would heal the agony. For now, he was going to hold her close and imagine he never had to let her go.

The next few days slipped into a pattern. Violet spent most of her time resting. Her appetite was slowly returning and, with it, her strength. On the third day after their arrival in Otherworld, she was able to walk from the bed to a chair by the window and sit for a while, gazing out at the stunning view of the bay.

She held Nate's hand, a tiny frown creasing the smooth-ness of her brow. "I feel something for this place, but it doesn't bring back any memories."

"Give it time. You've been through quite an ordeal."

There was a knock on the door and Nate went to an-swer it. He returned with a petite, dark-haired woman. "Violet, this is Stella."

"Nate has been keeping me updated on your progress, but I thought it was time I came to see how you were doing for myself." Stella's vivid green eyes seemed to see beyond Violet's face and into her thoughts. Maybe that was part of being a necromancer. Although Stella didn't conform to the stereotype of the secretive, cloaked figure of leg-end. She was fresh-faced, smiling and very down-to-earth.

"I'm glad you came," Violet said. "I've been wanting to thank you for what you did for me."

"Being a necromancer can be a burden, but it some-times has its high points. Being able to help in a case a like yours is one of them." Stella turned to smile at Nate. "Cal is looking forward to showing you his maps and charts of Otherworld." She pulled a face at Violet. "He misses the times when he was Merlin, the greatest sorcerer the world had ever known. Now he's Cal, leader of the Otherworld Alliance. People come to him for diplomacy and advice instead of magic, enchantment and dark arts. It does him good to be with a friend from the mortal realm, someone who'll let him be Merlin for a change."

There was genuine affection in her voice as she spoke about her husband, and Violet felt a tug of envy. A spark of "if only." Stella was the key that tied her and Nate to-gether. She had brought them both back from the dead. The thought sent a shiver down her spine. *But we can't be together. He is forbidden to remain in my world, and I can't survive in his. I'll never talk about him in the fu-*

*ture with that easy, long-term familiarity with which Stella
speaks of Cal.*

Those green eyes probed her face again. "Why don't
you go and see Cal in his study while Violet and I have a
chat?" Stella asked Nate. "I promise not to tire her out."
Her smile became mischievous. "I'll save that for when I
introduce you to my children."

Nate raised questioning brows, and Violet nodded. "I'd
like that."

When Nate had gone, Stella pulled up a chair so they
were sitting close together. "How is he? I've thought about
him often over the years, and wondered if what we did
was the right thing."

Violet gave her answer some thought. Telling Stella
the truth—that for most of the last six years Nate wished
she had left him to die—was not going to be helpful. She
tried to come up with something diplomatic. "I think for
a long time he struggled to come to terms with what happened to him."

Stella nodded. "Cal has seen him in the intervening
years. He was worried about how the need for vengeance
seemed to have taken such a strong hold in Nate's mind."

"Vengeance?"

"On the werewolf who sent him to hunt me down. Even
at the time, I know how hard it was for Nate to deal with
that lisping voice in his head urging him to kill me. It's
no wonder Nate swore to one day take revenge." Stella
scanned Violet's face thoughtfully. "Now what have I said
to make you look so worried?"

The truth was Stella had said a number of things that
troubled Violet, but one stood out above the others. "You
said there was a lisping voice in his head?"

Stella's animated face froze. It was the expression of

someone who knew she had said too much. *They are keeping something from me.*

"I talk such nonsense at times." Stella gave a forced laugh. "When you are well, you will have to come to dinner and meet the children. We have a daughter, Thalia, who is named after my mother, and twin boys. Their names are Arthur and Jethro. That's quite a complex story because they are named after the same person. King Arthur was, of course, Merlin's protégé and best friend. Recently, we discovered that Jethro de Loix, who is a fellow necromancer and a friend of ours, is the reincarnation of King Arthur. He is also the lost King of the Faeries."

Stella was rattling the words off in a quick-fire way that betrayed her nervousness and didn't allow for any interruption. Violet listened with half an ear. *A lisping voice.* It had triggered a memory. She knew a man with a lisping voice. It was the same man she had remembered in Paris. The angry man. He had a lisp.

The story of Nate seeking revenge troubled her, but the man with the lisp pricked at the edge of her consciousness, close to the surface. She felt she could almost reach out her hand and touch him.

As Stella continued with her stories of life in the palace and the exploits of her children, Violet tuned in with half an ear as she tried to capture that elusive memory. Who was this man? A man she was sure had played an important part in her life. A man Nate hated so much he wanted to kill him. A man whose identity those around her were determined to keep hidden.

Chapter 15

"Until recently, no one had really tried to draw any detailed maps of Otherworld." Cal stood at the desk in his study and pointed to the charts that were spread on its surface. "Then, my friend Lorcan Malone and his wife, Tanzi, traveled to Valhalla and brought back more detailed information about the islands beyond the territory that was charted. These are still not perfect, but they are a hell of a lot better than what we had before."

"Valhalla?" Nate raised his brows in surprise. "Isn't that where the gods live?"

"Valhalla is Odin's hall of fallen heroes." Cal indicated the farthest point on the map. "These are the Isles of the Aesir. They are the approach to Asgard. That is the home of the gods."

"You'll have to excuse my ignorance." Nate shook his head with an expression of bemusement. "It's not every day I find myself in a place occupied by gods, werewolves, faeries and heaven only knows how many other races."

"That's the reason for this geography lesson," Cal explained. "Otherworld is essentially a series of islands. As I said, until recently no one had attempted to chart them. This is still only a rough guide." He pointed to one of the biggest land masses on the map. "We are here. These are the Faerie Isles. The fae population is one of the largest and most powerful in Otherworld. Now that Moncoya is dead and Jethro is king, the whole political situation throughout Otherworld has become more stable. The other leaders are no longer looking over their shoulders, fearing an invasion." Cal moved his finger to the next group of islands. "This is the Vampire Archipelago."

Nate raised incredulous eyes to his friend's face. "You're serious, aren't you?"

"Deadly, and that's not a pun. Ruled over by Prince Tibor, one of the most powerful of the Otherworld rulers, the vampire dynasty is probably the most stable of all. Tibor does not allow for any criticism of his rule."

There was something chilling in Cal's words. Nate resisted a sudden impulse to look over his shoulder. "He sounds formidable."

"If you meet him while you are here, you will encounter nothing but courtesy and charm. It masks the fact that Tibor is a ruthless killer." Cal shrugged. "He's a vampire prince. Killing and being ruthless are what he does best." He was about to move on, but he paused. "On second thought, since you are mortal, it's probably best if we make sure you don't encounter him while you are here."

The words sent a shiver down Nate's spine. They were a timely reminder of the dangers he was facing here. "Thanks for the warning."

"Tibor may be the least of your worries." Cal's silver eyes shone bright on Nate's face. The sorcerer moved his finger to another, larger cluster of islands. "The sworn enemies of the vampires have always been the werewolves. These are their lands. There are hundreds of islands making up the territory known as the Wolf Nation. The two main islands are Reznati and Urlati. Reznati was the base of Anwyl. Urlati has always been Nevan's home. In recent years, the feud between the vampire and werewolf dynasties has lain dormant. That's because the werewolves have been fighting their own, internal battles."

"I know something of that struggle, remember? When he was inside my head, controlling my movements, Nevan wasn't the leader of the werewolves. He wanted Stella's heart because he believed it would give him the power he craved."

Cal nodded. "There was an ancient prophecy that whoever could claim the heart of the necromancer star would unite Otherworld. Some people, like Nevan, took it literally and believed it meant if they could rip her heart out of her body they would rule Otherworld. What it actually meant was that the person who won her love was destined to bring together the warring dynasties." Cal held his arms wide. "You're looking at him."

"So Nevan sent me to rip out her heart and he didn't even have his facts straight?" Nate asked, his voice filled with disbelief.

"At that time, Nevan would have done anything to topple his rival Anwyl. The dispute between them had been going on for many years at that time. I'm not sure even the two of them can recall what the trigger was. The werewolves were in chaos. When Nevan finally did defeat and kill Anwyl, many thought it marked the beginning of a new era of stability. Nevan has many of the same traits as Tibor. He is ruthless, but he is a strong leader." Cal ran a hand through his hair in frustration. "Instead, we have exactly the same situation going on between him and Roko. When

Nevan defeated Anwyl and took over as Wolf Leader, Roko formed a new resistance. It was low-key and posed no real problem for Nevan, being more about charitable aid than armed opposition. God knows what possessed Nevan to have his beta wolves drag Roko away from a party in the mortal realm and throw him into prison in Otherworld for what appeared to be no reason. He has made a minor enemy into a hero."

"I may be able to shed some light on that," Nate said. "I don't know all the details, but the night I met Violet, she was in a forest close to a werewolf party. She lost her memory during an attack by the feral werewolf I was hunting. Although she had no idea who she was, or where she came from, I thought it was safe to assume she had something to do with the party. I took her to the house with the intention of finding out if anyone there knew her. When we arrived, a man called Roko—who seemed very agitated—recognized her and approached us. That was how we knew her name was Violet. Before he could say or do anything else, a group of werewolves—the same ones who disrupted the Beast concert in Marseilles—burst in and attacked Roko and his friends. They dragged them away with them, saying they were taking them to their master."

"So Nevan's reason for locking Roko up was personal, not political. It was all about Violet. Roko was only imprisoned recently and for a short time, so that would fit with what you are saying. Nevan's beta wolves went to the mortal realm, where they must have been searching for Violet. They returned with Roko and his friends, throwing them into prison in the Wolf Nation without charge." Cal whistled. "Roko escaped and, now he is free, he has drummed up a huge amount of support for his cause. Werewolves are intensely loyal, and his followers are outraged at the unfair treatment he received."

Nate frowned, his concerns more personal. "Why was Violet in the mortal realm with Roko? Were they in a relationship?"

"Not that I'm aware. Before she disappeared, Violet was becoming quite outspoken against her father's methods. The reason I met Violet was that she was campaigning for the Alliance to help the refugees who had been displaced when her father defeated Anwyl." Nate remembered Violet's brief flash of remembrance about a man who was angry with her. "I expect that brought her into contact with Roko, since he held many of the same views as her about Nevan's autocratic style and was also involved in the relief effort."

Nate did his best to fight off the wave of jealousy and fear that was threatening to sweep over him. His job here was to return Violet to her own life, not to protect his own interests. He had to accept that he had no part in her future. There was a reason why she had been with Roko that night. If that reason did turn out to be a romantic one…well, that was Violet's business and no one else's. *Not even mine.*

Cal continued speaking, drawing Nate's attention away from the dark thoughts that were threatening his composure. "The reason I wanted to explain all of this to you is that it may pose a more immediate problem for you during your stay here in the palace. Part of my job as leader of the Alliance is to mediate in any disputes that may disrupt the peace between Otherworld and the mortal realm. This clash between Nevan and Roko is spilling over and causing problems between their followers in both worlds."

Nate frowned. "How does that affect me?"

"I have been trying—and, until recently, failing—to get Nevan and Roko to sit down together to see if we can reach an agreement on a way forward. They have finally agreed to a meeting. Both of them are arriving here in a few days for peace talks."

Although Stella explained that time was not measured in the same way in Otherworld as it was in the human world, Violet judged that a mortal week had passed since her arrival. A week in which she had grown steadily stronger.

This was the first day on which she had felt able to leave her room, and now she sat in a chair on the terrace that ran the length of the rear of the palace. A blanket covered her knees, even though the day was warm. Bright sunlight dappled the perfection of the lawn, and a light breeze stirred the heads of nearby multicolored roses, sending wafts of delicate perfume in Violet's direction.

Around her, the conversation ebbed and flowed. Cal had taken time out from affairs of state to join the family group, and he and Stella were accompanied by the Faerie King and Queen. Jethro was not what Violet had expected from faerie royalty. The man who had once been the legendary King Arthur certainly looked like he belonged to another era with his swept-back, wavy hair and hawk-like profile. He had a swash-buckling, dangerous air about him. In looks, his wife, Vashti, made up for her husband's lack of fae-ness. She was dainty and fair, although Violet got the impression that beneath her ethereal exterior she could be tough and uncompromising.

The group had been expanded by the arrival of Vashti's twin sister, Tanzi, and her husband, Lorcan. Stella explained that they had traveled from their home on the Isle of Spae for one of their regular visits. Children belonging to each couple tumbled on the grass. Violet and Nate had been welcomed into the noisy family group as if they were old friends. Violet was surprised at how comfortable she felt with these people. Since her memory had still not returned, she had nothing to compare it with, but she wondered if she had ever felt this at ease in any other company. Laughing at silly jokes, playing with the children, chatting about everyday things…it was all so easy and relaxed.

The children's backgrounds were complicated. Each was a mix of faerie, mortal and necromancer, with Cal and Stella's feisty daughter and rough-'n'-tumble twins having the most complex pedigree of them all. It didn't matter. They were all individuals, and the love that was lavished on them stirred a deep, previously untouched longing within Violet. *Our children would be half human, half wolf. They, too, would be loved for who they were.*

This is what I want. She reached for Nate's hand, and saw her own thoughts reflected in his eyes. It was so unfair that the future couldn't promise these simple pleasures for them. She didn't want riches or fame. Just laughter and hand-holding and companionship. Just Nate…and one day a family of their own.

She still hadn't broached the subject of what he was keeping from her. Perhaps it was cowardice that kept her from doing so. She preferred to think it was self-preservation. She had almost died, and she owed Nate her life. She trusted him with every fiber of her being. This last week had been about garnering her strength. And, maybe, just maybe, unraveling the threads of her lost memory to find a way back to who she really was. Because, if she could do that, wasn't it just possible she might find there was a glimmer of hope for her and Nate? She would do anything—go to the ends of this world and the next—if it meant they could be together.

Her ears tuned in to the remarkable stories of the couples around her. Of Cal and Stella, who had fought the mighty Moncoya in an epic battle to be together. Lorcan and Tanzi, who had faced the wrath not just of Moncoya, but also of Satan himself. And Jethro and Vashti, who had traveled to the legendary Isle of Avalon and faced the evil sorceress Morgan le Fay before discovering Jethro's true identity.

If they could do all of those things, can't we find our own way? She just needed to push aside the curtain that hid her past from view. To get to the life she wanted, she had to unearth the life she once had. And sitting here with a blanket over her knees was not the way to do it.

Although she hadn't shifted since her arrival in Otherworld, she had been conscious of the wolf inside her growing stronger. Senses she could only attribute to her inner shape-shifter were growing more pronounced. Every physical sense was enhanced. Colors appeared more vivid. Sounds were stronger and clearer. She could detect scents that normally passed her by. Her sense of taste was richer. Her skin was highly sensitive to the slightest stimulus. All of these things gave her a sharper awareness of what was going on around her. And a restlessness that wasn't going away.

When Stella announced that she was going inside to see to lunch, Violet leaned closer to Nate. "Can we take a walk?"

"Are you strong enough?"

"There's only one way to find out." Thrusting aside the restrictive blanket, she got to her feet. She was pleased to find there was no wobble in her legs, and although she didn't feel ready to run for miles the way she used to, she felt invigorated. She was still woefully thin, but she could almost feel the strength flowing back into her limbs.

The palace was in an idyllic setting. Having waved a farewell to the others, they set off across the lawn toward the lush formal gardens, where the scent of lemon and orange trees vied with the sharp tang of pine forests that covered the steeply sloping hillsides. In the distance was a vast shimmering lake and soaring cliffs that resembled the jagged teeth of an ancient slumbering dragon.

"I take it you want to head for the forest rather than the lake?" Nate quirked a brow at her, and Violet was jolted all over again by his good looks. How did he manage to make her heart somersault that way with just a smile? If only they had the luxury of growing old together, so she could find out if he could do that when he was gray-haired and that handsome face was lined.

"How did you know?"

"Lucky guess."

She laughed, catching hold of his hand and twining her fingers with his. *Don't take this from me.*

The forest was a cool, woody paradise, and Violet's first instinct was to slip off her lightweight sandals so she could feel the leafy carpet beneath her feet. Without knowing how she knew, she was conscious that forests had always been her favorite places. But there was something special about this one. It was an Otherworld forest. Everything about it was *more*. More sylvan. More pine-scented. More fern-veiled. More secretive.

Or is it just me? Am I growing more aware?

Excitement surged deep inside her, and she turned to look at Nate. "I think…" She was so overwhelmed, the rest of the words wouldn't come.

He caught hold of her other hand, turning her so she was facing him at arm's length. "Is this it? You feel ready to shift?"

His eyes were so full of joy for her that her own excitement almost reached stratospheric levels. Because, unlike in the mortal realm, she knew what to do. There was no hesitation. No thinking was needed. No mantra required. This was what she had wanted and needed for so long. A craving so intense it hurt.

Quickly stripping off her clothes, she closed her eyes and saw herself becoming a werewolf. Pictured the transformation of her body. It wasn't unfamiliar to her this time. She wasn't viewing it as an outsider. It was part of her. As natural as breathing. Shifting was just that. It needed only a minor change. It was altering her consciousness from her human to her animal. It was varying her view of the world so that she saw it through the eyes of a werewolf. So she was ready to experience the urges and instincts of her inner animal.

When the changes came, they were swift and subtle. A lengthening of her features. A relaxing of her muscles. A sense of relief as her body eased into the shape of her wolf.

Violet opened her eyes, blinking at Nate before dropping onto all fours. She prowled around him, nudging his thigh with her snout, before throwing back her head and giving a single, victorious howl.

Nate stared at the werewolf in amazement. Even though he had been expecting this, part of him had wondered how he would feel. He had tried to prepare himself for this moment. The moment when he first saw the woman he loved in her werewolf form. Would he be able to accept this change in her? Or would he find the difference too startling? Even, possibly, be repulsed?

Because I hate werewolves.

But Violet was a stunningly beautiful one. Her pelt was as thick and black as her human hair, and those intense blue eyes hadn't changed. Her body was lithe, hinting at a strength that must have been impressive prior to her illness. When she came to him and nudged him, he knew it was a message. She was asking for his approval. And there was no hardship about his actions as he tangled his hands in the thick, glossy pelt at her neck. When he crouched so he was on her level, she rubbed her face against his, and Nate wrapped his arms around her neck.

Not this werewolf. I don't hate this one. She was still Violet. Still his.

When he released her, the werewolf broke into a run, her long strides soon taking her out of his sight. Nate sat on a fallen tree stump and waited for her to return. Would she return? He sensed she would. They had a lot to talk about. Then would probably be the time to tell her the whole story.

He scrubbed a hand over his face. If the time had come for the truth, then the time for parting was close. He clasped his hands between his knees and bent his head over them. He had faced some tough challenges in his life, but this? When he thought she was dying, he had made a pact with himself. *Let her live and I'll be able to walk away from her with no regrets.* He had truly believed that knowing she was alive somewhere would make him happy. And on one level it did. This was better than a world with no Violet. When he was old and gray, the knowledge that his beautiful wolf was here in Otherworld, running through her beloved forests, would afford him some comfort.

But I want more. I want it all. I want my beautiful wolf at my side for all the days of my life. I don't want to be noble. I want to be selfish. I want Violet.

He had spent the last week desperately trying to think of a way to make it happen. Maybe if her memory returned, if she remembered how to shift, they could try again in the mortal realm? But when he recalled how ill she had been, he knew he would never ask her to risk that. And besides, she was werewolf nobility. Otherworld was her home. This was where she belonged.

And Nate had a life in the mortal realm. He was a celebrity. The thought still struck him as humorous. From feral werewolf to rock star. His life certainly wasn't boring. If he was offered the chance of a life with Violet here in Otherworld, he would miss some aspects of the mortal realm. Life on tour with Beast, the thrill of performing, his relationship with his bandmates and Ged. But would he exchange those things for a life with Violet? In a heartbeat.

Maybe he could go to Cal, make a case for this arrangement to be a permanent one? Ask his friend to work his magic so that Nate could stay in Otherworld forever? He dismissed that idea immediately. Asking the leader of the Otherworld Alliance to bend the rules for a friend wouldn't be fair. He knew Cal had already stretched his principles on Nate's behalf by letting him come here in the first place. Mortals were not allowed in Otherworld for a reason. The main one being that, for several of the races here, they were considered a snack.

All his soul searching had brought him to one conclusion. It was what he already knew. There was no alternative. Once Violet learned the truth—that she was the daughter of Nevan, the Wolf Leader—and Nate had returned her to her family, he would have to walk away from her. *'Tis better to have loved and lost than never to have loved at all.* When Alfred, Lord Tennyson wrote that famous line, he clearly had no idea what the fuck he was talking about.

For the longest time, Nate had believed he had no heart. He hadn't had any practice at getting it damaged and dented because he hadn't believed it was there. He had truly believed that, when Cal drove that silver dagger into his chest, the sorcerer had shriveled that part of him that was capable of love. How could he have known how wrong he was? His heart wasn't the wilted, dried-up piece of garbage he had believed it to be.

It had been frozen in time. His heart was just as big and strong as it had ever been; it had as much capacity for love as ever before. It was just as easily hurt. He had trained himself to believe he couldn't feel the joy of loving the way he loved Violet. Then she had burst upon him, searing her radiance and charm into his heart, soul and body. He had been as wrong as he could be about his ability to feel love. Now he had to accept he could also feel the awful, grinding pain of loss.

Cal's knife had left scars on Nate's heart. Walking away from Violet would smash it into tiny pieces. The scar tissue that remained would be a permanent, never-to-be-healed memory of their time together, like cracks in a china vase. Even though he now knew his heart could do its job, he also knew no one would ever fill the space that Violet had occupied. Love came in all shapes, sizes and color, but so did loss. The day would come when he would never again laugh as he watched her devour an enormous meal. He would never kiss her darling lips good-night. He would never see her mischievous smile or hear her laughter. And he knew that nobody else in either world could ever reproduce those precious moments or that one magical laugh.

For the sake of his heart, it was time for Nate to start practicing how to say goodbye.

Chapter 16

The sweet delight of running free through the forest refreshed her body as nothing else could. The trees enclosed her, sheathing her in their familiar, pine-scented fragrance. Her werewolf memory stirred. Swirling mists of thought came back to her. She recalled the first time she had shifted. She was a member of a pack. She had siblings. They had taken the place of the mother who had died just after Violet was born. These were less like coherent memories and more thoughts that flowed back to her along with the pounding of her paws.

From an early age, she had learned to cope as a human. More than cope. Her family had been destined for greatness. But, for a werewolf in human form, there was always a sense of being trapped. Of suppressing the most important part of herself. Violet was half wolf, half human. Both parts were equally important, and sometimes her wolf rebelled against the rules imposed by society. Over time she had learned to walk in skin, but she needed regular opportunities to run in fur. For her, it was a fundamental need, like eating or sleeping. Her wolf couldn't remain dormant, and that had been the problem in the mortal realm. Because of her memory loss, she hadn't remembered how to shift. Trap the wolf, and the human couldn't survive, either. That was what she assumed had happened, but maybe it was something more. An allergy to something in the mortal realm, or a virus. Whatever it was, returning to the mortal realm wasn't an option, in case it caused a relapse.

This was what her wolf self had craved. This freedom. The dank smell of the earth mingling with the aromatic scent of sap and mud. The faint sounds of movement in the undergrowth. The feel of the moss and dried leaves underfoot. The pinpricks of golden light drifting through the canopy of branches overhead. She grew stronger with each step as the woodland air rejuvenated her. Violet covered the miles swiftly, pausing only occasionally to drink from the clear waters of a stream. Eventually, flanks heaving and tongue lolling, she turned and retraced her tracks.

When she returned to where she had parted from Nate, he was seated on the stump of a fallen tree. Nate didn't hear her approach as she shifted back. He looked so lost and alone that she knew he must be thinking of her…and torturing himself. How had they come to this? From love and laughter to hurt and fear? She would give anything to wipe that frown from his brow. Violet watched him for a moment, her heart aching with so much love it felt like it was overflowing, as if all her feelings were streaming from her body and seeking his.

She might not have all of her memory, but she knew she had never known what real happiness was until Nate came into her life. Had never known it was possible to feel this way, to wake up each day with a smile simply because there was another person in the world she loved so completely. Because knowing Nate had brought her a contentment so great that, if it hadn't happened to her, she never would have believed it could exist.

Acting on impulse, she crossed the distance between them and dropped to her knees before him, grasping his clasped hands. "I'm here now. Let's not waste what time we have."

His eyes darkened as, with a groan of longing, he pulled her to him. As their lips met, Violet pushed his T-shirt up his chest and over his shoulders. His tongue parted her lips, invading her mouth with slow, deliberate strokes. Need ignited instantly between them. Nate's hands cupped her breasts, his thumbs tracing a pattern around her diamond-hard nipples as Violet pressed closer, her nails raking his shoulders.

Getting to his feet, he shrugged out of his clothing before pulling her down next to him on the carpet of leaves. His eyes devoured her, drinking in every detail of her body, before he lowered his head to cover the tip of her breast with his lips. Arching her back, Violet released a cry that trembled the canopy of leaves high above her. Nate suckled her deeply, as if he couldn't get enough of her, lashing her nipple ferociously before he moved on and gave its twin the same treatment. Then his lips were moving lower, his hands pulling her thighs apart, lifting her, spreading her wide open for him as his mouth covered the swollen flesh of her sex.

Fireworks went off inside Violet's head as his tongue rasped over the sensitized little pearl of her clitoris. She was already so close. So tightly wound that one more stroke would tip her over the edge. She gave a soft cry of frustration as Nate moved lower, licking along her slit before darting his tongue deep inside her. Violet lost herself in the rhythm he established, licking, circling and plunging. Over and over.

She locked her fingers in his hair, holding him to her, lifting her hips in time with the desperate riot of heat and sensation that Nate was blasting through her.

"Please, Nate," she moaned, twisting her head from side to side among the leaves. "I can't take much more."

Using his thumbs, he spread her outer lips farther apart, pressing his mouth closer against her. At the same time, his tongue increased in speed and pressure. Fire began to coil through her, starting deep in her core and flaring outward. When it came, her orgasm was pure, molten heat exploding through her. It sucked the air from her lungs and swept every trace of reality from her world, replacing it with intense, unthinking sensation. She convulsed beneath him, her whole body rippling and shattering with quakes as Nate continued lashing her with his tongue.

"You are mine." As the last violent shudders stilled, he moved into position over her. The look in his eyes was one of ownership as well as love as he took his weight on his elbows. Violet gasped as the head of his cock nudged against her still-clenching core.

"Always," she whispered in reply. "No matter what happens in the future, I will always belong to you."

She threw her head back, gazing at the dappled sky as he drove into her. Dear God, nothing had ever felt so good. She caught her breath at the tight, tingling sensation as he began to part her still-tender flesh. Nate raised her legs, hooking her knees over his arms as he lifted her to him. She opened to him, stretching tightly around his cock, gripping him as he worked inside her inch by throbbing inch.

"You're so perfect. So hot and tight." Nate's gaze moved to the point where he penetrated her.

"Please… I want… I *need* all of you."

He retreated marginally before working the tip back inside her. His neck was corded and taut as he watched his shaft sink inside her. Violet's internal muscles were clenched so tight around him that she could feel every vein and ridge, every detail of the velvety rod inside her.

Her hands were clawing at his shoulder as he began to pump, filling her further as she relaxed, allowing him to slide all the way in. She could tell Nate was fighting for control, his dark brown eyes blazing fiery need down at her, his hair flopping forward over his brow. As always, he called to something deep within her. Something primal and animal. Something that went beyond the physical sensations she felt and imprinted itself on her soul.

She barely had time to draw a deep breath before he began to slam into her. Violet's hips jerked in time with his thrusts. This was what she needed. Not to be treated with caution. She didn't want safe and gentle lovemaking. She wanted fast and furious. He was so hot, so deeply and firmly buried within her yielding flesh, that she would remember the feel of him forever.

Sensations built and layered so she couldn't tell where one feeling ended and another began. Pressure swelled from the point where their bodies connected, and she ground against him, desperate to increase it. Her breasts were cushioned against his rock-hard muscles, the friction of her nipples rubbing against his coarse chest hair causing a frenzy of sensory overload.

Nate slid smoothly into her tight entrance, retreating, then driving all the way back until he was buried to the hilt each time. Each stroke stirred her sensitive nerve endings to higher pleasure until she couldn't think of anything but the searing, agonizing ecstasy of him thrusting into her.

He was growling against her neck, his teeth nipping

at her shoulder. *This is how it would feel if we were both werewolves.* The thought slipped away as she writhed wildly beneath him. From nowhere the urge to sink her teeth into the juncture between his shoulder and neck—at the point that would mark him permanently as her mate—became overpowering. Even in her frenzy, Violet forced herself to fight it. *He is not a werewolf. He has not asked for my bite.*

Nate powered into her with a hunger like nothing she had ever dreamed of, branding her, scorching her, driving her to the outer limit of her endurance. Violet was gasping beneath him, her nails piercing his back as she tightened around him, the first spasms of her climax tipping her over the edge. Color and light filled her mind as she exploded. Everything inside her let go, spun out of control, triggered contraction after echoing contraction until she was spent and whimpering.

Distantly, she heard Nate's hoarse growl as he let go and surrendered to his own release. He pumped inside her harder, swelling again, surging above her one final time before shuddering and dropping his head to her shoulder.

Long, silent minutes later, Nate drew away from her and flopped onto his side. His breathing was still harsh when he finally spoke. "Violet, I wasn't thinking straight. I can't believe I didn't use a condom."

Violet's voice was almost regretful as she answered him. "Now I know for sure I'm a werewolf, it doesn't matter. My cycle is the same as a wolf's. I'm only fertile during the mating season."

Nate seemed to understand her feelings. This would be a disastrous time for her to get pregnant, but the reminder that it would never happen for them still hurt. These conversations and plans weren't theirs to have. He drew her into his arms, pressing a kiss to her temple. "Then I guess we should see what we can do about getting the leaves out of our hair before we find our clothes, get dressed and head back for lunch."

The white marble palace shimmered in the sunlight as they crossed the gardens hand in hand. Violet's strides matched Nate's. There was no question about it. Shifting had empowered her. Although she was thinner than before her illness, her eyes sparkled with their old love of life and her former vitality was back. There was a spring in her step, and she appeared almost fully restored to health.

I can't put this off any longer.

Nate paused, leading her to an ornate bench that was set to one side of the palace entrance.

Violet raised an inquiring brow. "Is this important? I'm hungry after all that activity." There was a naughty twinkle in her eye as she clasped Nate's thigh suggestively. "And I don't mean the running."

He drew a deep breath. "There's something I need to tell you."

Her smile vanished and her eyes became wary. "This sounds serious."

"It is…"

Before he could say any more, there was a commotion behind him as two men erupted from the main entrance to the palace. Nate recognized one of them immediately. It was Roko, the young, good-looking werewolf who had been at the party in Vermont the night Nate had rescued Violet.

The second man was tall and powerfully built, with jet-black hair swept back from a broad brow and the golden brown eyes of a thoroughbred wolf. His features were masterful, proud and uncompromising. Nate sensed, from the crawling feeling he got down his own spine, exactly who this man was. There could be no question about it. This had to be Nevan, Violet's father and the evil, murdering bastard who had used his strength of will against Nate when he had been at his most vulnerable.

"Violet?" Roko started toward them, his eyes narrowing as they dropped to take in her hand on Nate's thigh. "We saw you from the window."

Cal emerged from the building in the wake of the two men. His expression was apologetic as he looked from Violet to Nate. "I'm sorry. They weren't supposed to arrive until tomorrow. There was a mix-up over the time of our meeting. I sent one of my clerks to find you and warn you. Clearly he missed you."

"Could someone please tell me what's going on?" Violet's voice, while it was confused, held a note of annoyance. "Who are these people?"

"This is no time for games, my daughter."

Nevan's voice drained the energy from Nate's body, replacing it with memories of confusion and fear. It was the voice that had once invaded his head. The voice that still haunted his nightmares. That cold, calculating voice with just a hint of a lisp. That was how he'd known who Nevan was. Six years ago, when he'd described the voice to Cal, when he'd explained who was urging him to find Stella and tear out her heart, Nate had mentioned the lisp. Cal had told him back then that Nevan, who was then the werewolf rebel leader, had that distinctive sibilant slide. That was when Nate had sworn to kill this man.

Violet's gasp brought Nate's focus back to her. She was all that mattered. Her eyes were fixed on Nevan. "You are my father?"

"Violet has lost her memory," Nate explained.

Nevan's eyes flickered over him without interest. "Whoever you are, I do not remember asking for your contribution. You will move away from my daughter."

Nate felt his temper flare. Before he could respond, Violet gripped his hand. "I will decide if that is to happen." She turned her head to look at Nate. "And it isn't."

Nevan's lips thinned. "When I give an order, I expect instant obedience."

"Perhaps we should all go inside?" Cal intervened smoothly. "I have a room set aside for the negotiations we had planned, and I can have lunch sent in."

Nevan made a protesting sound, but Violet forestalled him by getting to her feet. "Thank you. I'd like that." Outwardly, she was perfectly calm. Nate was the only person who knew, by the tight grip she maintained on his hand, that it was a facade.

Cal led them inside. He entered a small conference room with a central table set up in preparation for a formal meeting. Cal took a seat at the head of the table, and Violet slid into the chair on his left. Since she still had hold of Nate's hand, he moved into place next to her. Nevan took the seat opposite. It was clear from his manner that Roko did not feel comfortable sitting next to his sworn enemy. After a moment's hesitation, the younger werewolf moved into position opposite Cal at the foot of the table. When two faerie waiters brought in a buffet lunch and arranged the plates of food in the center of the table, it started to feel like a very uncomfortable dinner party.

The waiters had left, and Cal took charge of the proceedings. "Since Violet has no memory, I will undertake some introductions for her benefit." He went around the table in turn. "Nevan is the Wolf Leader and he is your father. You are his youngest child. You have two brothers and two sisters. Roko is the leader of the opposition in the Wolf Nation. They have both come here because there is considerable unrest among the werewolves and I was hoping that we could begin negotiations to bring it to an end."

Cal turned to Nevan. "From your perspective, you must be wondering why Violet has been staying here without your knowledge. She was in the mortal realm and was rescued from an attack by a feral werewolf, during which she lost her memory. While traveling in the mortal realm, she became seriously ill. She was brought here to the palace to recuperate. The plan was to return her to her family once she was strong enough. This is Nate Zilar, the mortal who rescued her from the feral werewolf and who brought her to Otherworld in time to save her life." Cal's gaze was fixed on Nevan's, clearly conveying a message. "We all owe him a debt of thanks for saving her, not once, but twice."

Nevan cast a look in Nate's direction. Nate tried to categorize the look in those eyes that were not only unlike Violet's in color, but which also lacked the warmth and sparkle of his daughter's. Was it hatred he saw? Anger? Possibly even the threat of retribution? Nevan's gaze certainly didn't contain any gratitude. "Since Violet is now returned to her family, this mortal may go."

"Nate is not leaving." Violet's anger was tangible, snapping through the air as she spoke.

"There is no place for a stranger in this conversation." Nevan's voice was equally heated.

"Violet, it's not often I agree with your father—" Roko spoke for the first time since they had entered the room "—but he is right. This mortal may have assisted you, but his usefulness is at an end."

"Your opinion on my daughter's welfare is neither required nor welcome." Nevan's lips drew back as he addressed Roko.

"I have many more opinions about your family, most of them gleaned during my stay in the cellars beneath your home. Would you like me to air them now?" Roko pressed his palms flat on the table and sprang to his feet, every part of his body tense and prepared for a challenge. "I think the leader of the Alliance would be interested to hear the details."

"May I remind you of our agreement that this meeting would be conducted in a nonthreatening manner?" Cal's calm tones cut across the sizzling atmosphere. While his intervention may not have diffused the tension, it did provide a timely reminder that the palace was not the place for a wolf fight.

Violet stood. Her voice was steady as she spoke directly to Nevan. "I'll take your word for it that you are my father. I don't know what the purpose of this meeting is if what you want me to do is sit in silence and listen while you toss orders around and snarl. I know you have other business to discuss, so if you have nothing else to say to me, I'd rather be elsewhere."

Nevan's eyes narrowed as he stared at Nate. "Are you responsible for brainwashing my daughter?"

"Brainwashing." Violet, who had been on her way to the door, halted in her tracks, repeating the word slowly. She turned to stare at Nate, who was just behind her, her eyes widening in horror. Her complexion blanched several shades as she looked from him to Nevan and back again.

"Stella said the voice you heard inside your head six years ago—the one that compelled you to find her and rip her heart from her body—had a lisp." Violet raised a shaking hand to her throat. "It was him, wasn't it? The werewolf who bullied and tormented you, the person you never forgot, the person you swore you would one day take revenge against…that person was my father."

Chapter 17

Violet wasn't sure where she was going; she only knew she had to get out of that room with its crackling atmosphere of anger and oppression. Once she ran out of the palace, she kept on running until the edge of the cliff stopped her from going any farther.

The view across the bay was blurred by the tears in her eyes. It was a metaphor for her memory, but she felt something stirring. It wasn't anything precise. More feelings than actual recollections. She knew Nevan's autocratic behavior just now had been typical of his approach to her throughout her life. The mounting frustration and annoyance she had felt at his refusal to listen to her—to even acknowledge that she might have an opinion about her own life—were so familiar she sensed they were a regular feature of every encounter she had ever had with her father.

A movement behind her made her turn her head, but

Nate's arms were wrapped around her waist before she could fully face him. She gripped his wrists tightly, leaning back and using his warmth and strength to anchor herself.

"I should have told you." His voice was anguished. "But I was scared of what harm it might do when you were still so weak."

Violet choked on a sound that was somewhere between a laugh and a sob. "I think I'd have been happy never to have known the truth of my identity. If you and I could have gone away somewhere together and I had never found out." She turned in his arms, resting her forehead against his chest. "That makes me a coward, doesn't it?"

"After what I just saw, I'd say it means you have a healthy self-defense mechanism."

She sniffed back another sob, lifting her head. "I'm a werewolf. I guess self-protection is part of my DNA. But so is the protection of my species." Her eyes were troubled as she gazed up at him. "You have sworn to kill my father, Nate. Is that vow still in place?"

"I won't do anything that harms you."

"That's not quite an answer." Peeping over his shoulder, she frowned. "Oh, hell."

Stepping out of the circle of Nate's arms, but remaining close to him, she turned to face Roko. He was striding toward them, a frown marring his features. "Violet, I understand that your father's conduct may have angered you, but walking out on me—and with another man—is childish and beneath you."

"Why?" Unlike her feelings about Nevan, her sensory memory of this man was nonexistent. He stirred no feelings in her, meant nothing to her, left her cold and unmoved.

"Because of our relationship." He took a step closer, stopping short when Violet held up a hand to forestall him. "You must remember. We were in the mortal realm together because we love each other."

Violet scanned his face. His handsome features projected an image of hurt. With a flash of intuition, she knew it was a mask with nothing behind it. His facial expressions were the practiced artistry of a professional politician. He was lying because it suited him to do so.

"That isn't true."

Roko's veneer slipped slightly. A brief flash of impatience showed through. "Your memory—"

"I don't need my memory to tell me my feelings. I know I don't love you. I never have."

He shook his head sadly. "When you recover from this amnesia, you will remember why you were in the mortal realm." His eyes traveled over Nate with an air of superiority. "Why you chose me. Meanwhile, Merlin Caledonius has requested that you return to the palace. He has asked me to give you his guarantee that further conversations will be conducted in a reasonable manner."

"Maybe you should hear the rest of what Nevan has to say," Nate said quietly.

He was right, of course. She couldn't stay here at the palace forever, no matter how much she might want to. Shutting herself away from reality wasn't an option. She had a life, even if it might not be the one she wanted. Now she had a duty to find out all she could about it before doing what she could to pick up the shattered pieces of the past. Only then would she be able to set her feet on the road to any kind of future.

"I will be there in a few minutes."

Roko gave a curt nod before turning away and striding back in the direction of the palace. Violet watched him go, trying to figure out his place in her life. Why had she been in the mortal realm with him? What did he mean to her? When she looked up, Nate's eyes were fixed on her face. It was obvious that he was following the train of her thoughts.

"You *were* with him." His tone was carefully neutral.

"I don't care what he said." She tilted her chin stubbornly. "I have never been in love until I met you."

His smile, the one that always knocked her sideways with love and lust in equal measures, dawned. "I can see how that would be. How you would bypass the handsome, young werewolf with the movie-star looks in favor of the cynical, care-worn wolf hunter."

Violet moved closer, pressing herself up against him. "I have a confession to make."

"You do?" Nate's voice was husky as he gripped her hips.

"I'm just a groupie at heart…with a thing for the bass guitarist." She pressed a kiss on his lips before breaking away with a sigh. "I guess we should go back."

"Is it such a good idea for me to be there?" Nate asked as they walked between the formal gardens and the lake. "My presence seems to inflame the situation."

"I want you with me." How could she explain that the only thing getting her through this nightmare was his closeness? Somehow, his quiet strength could communicate itself to her, even when he didn't speak. If that was withdrawn, she felt as if her world would implode.

"Then that's all that matters."

When they reached the conference room, Nevan, Roko and Cal were waiting in the places they had occupied when they left. Violet and Nate resumed their seats. Violet realized with surprise that she was starving. She must be on the road to recovery if, even at a time of such stress, food was uppermost in her mind. As Cal started talking, she reached for a plate and piled it high with cold meat.

"Nevan has agreed that our conversation should focus on your return to the Wolf Nation."

"That sounds like a good idea."

She met Nevan's eyes and wondered what her memories of this man would be. Had they ever laughed together? Done father-daughter things together? She thought back to the scene earlier today, and pictured Cal, Jethro and Lorcan with their children. Had this man ever looked at her with the same love in his eyes? Listened to her with the same attention? Played with her as though he didn't have anything else in his life that mattered? Why did she sense that wasn't the case? Instead, she felt there were soul-deep divisions between them, fundamental differences that might never be bridged.

"Since I have no memory, before we discuss anything else, perhaps you could help me out by telling me why I chose to go to the mortal realm?"

Roko made a protesting sound. "I have already explained—"

Nevan ignored him. "You were angry with me over some trivial matter. I forget what it was. You always were hotheaded. Running away from home was your way of punishing me for what you saw as my inflexibility."

Violet frowned. That explanation didn't sound any more realistic than Roko's. It made her sound like a rebellious child. One man was telling her she had traveled to the mortal realm because she was in love with him, the other was saying she was a spoiled brat. *Maybe the truth falls somewhere between the two, but I don't like the versions of myself I am being offered.* Somehow, she just didn't feel either was the case. Frustratingly, she sensed the real reason she had been in the mortal realm was being hidden from her both by her wayward memory and by these men who wanted to claim her for their own purposes.

When she didn't respond, Nevan proceeded to discuss his plans for returning home. "I will be leaving early tomorrow morning." Clearly he didn't believe he needed to set aside much time for his discussions with Roko. Did that mean diplomacy and the peace talks about the future of the Wolf Nation were unimportant to him? "That will give you time to prepare."

Violet paused in the act of raising a chicken leg to her mouth. Prepare? She realized Nevan's gaze was on Nate and that there was a hint of triumph in his eyes. "We'll be ready."

"We?" Nevan's head swung around to her so fast he must have cricked his neck.

She nodded. "Nate and I will be ready with you."

Her father's lip curled. "It will not be possible for a mortal to enter werewolf territory."

"Then I'll stay here." Violet turned to look at Cal, willing him to support her. "That will be okay, won't it?"

He nodded, his silver eyes alight with sympathy and something more. It might have been admiration. "Of course. You are welcome to remain here at the palace as long as you need to."

"This is nonsense. Your home is with your own kind, with the werewolves," Nevan growled.

"I agree. But unless Nate comes with me, I'm not going anywhere." Violet gave her father a regretful smile.

"I could not guarantee his safety in the Wolf Nation." Nevan was reduced to blustering. "Once my pack gets the aroma of a mortal in their midst…" He shrugged in a gesture of helplessness.

"Perhaps I could offer a reassurance on that score?" Cal, ever the diplomat, intervened. "Nate is here under my protection. In other words, he is here under my spell. He doesn't have the aura of a mortal. You will know that already, having been in his company for an extended period of time." He glanced from Nevan to Roko. Violet was relieved Cal didn't go further and reveal Nate's werewolf hunting activities. To do so in this company would be to ensure his instant death.

It was Roko who gave a reluctant nod. He appeared subdued. Unnaturally so. Violet wondered if he had been warned to behave himself by Cal. "It's true. I do not scent anything mortal about him."

"That spell will continue to protect him when he travels to the Wolf Nation." Violet was surprised to see a change in Cal's expression. The charming smile vanished to be replaced by a hard, implacable determination. This was a man she wouldn't cross. This was a man who had maintained his grip on both worlds for centuries, not only with his spectacular magical prowess but also with his strength of will. It was obvious from her father's altered attitude that he was not prepared to oppose Cal in this mood. "Just so we are clear…nothing will happen to Nate while he is in Otherworld. That is my decree. I hope it is understood?"

Nevan cleared his throat. "Understood."

Cal's smile reappeared. "Then that's settled. Violet and Nate will travel with you to the Wolf Nation tomorrow morning."

Roko gave a grudging murmur of assent. Violet turned her head to look at Nevan. Briefly, she was caught in a blaze of fury from his eyes so strong it caused her to recoil. Then his eyelids lowered and the look was hidden. Shaken, she turned to Nate to see if he had noticed, but he was looking at Cal. When she glanced Nevan's way again, his expression was neutral. Shaking her head, Violet chastised herself for her foolishness.

No memory, but too much imagination. Just one more problem to add to a growing list, Violet, my girl.

* * *

"Just as I extracted a promise from Nevan that you would be safe with him, I need a similar guarantee from you." Cal drew Nate to one side just before he prepared to descend the cliff to the waiting boat.

"You think I'm going to push him overboard at the first opportunity?"

Cal didn't smile at Nate's attempt at humor. "I know your desire for vengeance has been the driving force in your life for the last six years. Every time we've met, you have done your best to persuade me to let you come to Otherworld so you can kill Nevan. Now you are here, and he is within your sights, I need your assurance that it won't happen. Just as I need to know that, as a werewolf hunter, you will be okay with this trip to the Wolf Nation."

Nate looked across to where Violet was attempting to make awkward conversation with her father. Beyond the cliff edge, the water was a deep blue dappled with diamond patterns of brilliant sunlight. A light breeze stirred the air, sending a crisp, clean tang of salt and seaweed in a nostalgic assault on his nostrils. It reminded him of childhood outings, of sandcastles and ice cream. It was a perfect summer morning, just about as far from feral werewolves, ruined dreams and threats of vengeance as it was possible to get.

Cal said Nate had Nevan in his sights. It was true. But as he looked over at where the Wolf Leader stood, Nate barely saw the man who had tortured and tormented him, the man who in many ways had ruled his life for so long. Because what he also had in his sights was an image of perfection. It wasn't possible for Nate to look at anything, or anyone, else for long when Violet was near. She was the sole focus of his attention. She was everything. Pain, suffering, vengeance…all those things faded into insignificance compared with what he felt for her.

"I'd never do anything that would hurt her." He wasn't aware he had spoken aloud until Cal's hand came down on his shoulder.

"That's good enough for me." There was a world of understanding in the silver eyes that had seen everything over the many centuries of the sorcerer's life. "I wish I could promise you a different ending."

Nate grasped his hand. "If you think of something while I'm away, let me know. Immortality, disguise me as a non-feral werewolf, overthrow Nevan…anything."

Cal nodded, his serious expression signifying there was nothing he could do. Nate guessed there were rules about how far he could go to help a friend. "You'll be the first to hear."

Nate joined Violet and Nevan. Violet's expression of relief told him all he needed to know about how her efforts at making conversation with her father had gone. With a final wave to Cal, Nate began his descent to the beach. Although there appeared to be a sheer drop down to the tiny bay below the cliffs, there was a series of steep steps cut into the rock. Nevan led the way and Nate went next, turning regularly to check if Violet needed assistance. Although she clambered down nimbly, her father seemed to have forgotten that she had recently been seriously ill and might need help. Nate sent a frown in Nevan's direction at such unfeeling conduct, but it went unnoticed.

Minutes later, their feet crunched onto the sandy beach. A dinghy was pulled up onto the shore, and a young man scrambled to attention when he saw Nevan approaching. There was a larger vessel bobbing on the waves in the deeper water and, raising a hand to shield his eyes from the bright sunlight, Nate saw it was a motorized sailboat.

"Where is Roko?" Nate asked as the young man helped Nevan into the dinghy.

Nevan gave him a dismissive glance. "His method of transport is his own affair. I am not concerned with the movements of my enemies."

"I take it the peace talks were not productive?" Nate placed his hands on Violet's waist and lifted her into the dinghy before climbing in beside her.

"I may be forced to tolerate your presence, but I do not have to discuss werewolf business with you." Nevan turned his gaze to the open water as his servant set the dinghy skimming across the waves.

Violet tucked her hand into Nate's and mouthed the word *touchy* at him. Her spirits didn't seem to have been damaged by Nevan's coldness. She had taken it in stride, and Nate wondered if there was a part of her, even if it was buried deep in her subconscious, that knew this was all she could ever expect from her father.

Nate didn't have much experience of sea travel, but, as he stepped from the dinghy onto the larger vessel, he appreciated that this was a luxurious boat. The living areas were paneled in light wood, and the upholstery looked expensive. Stepping into a saloon with a cushioned bench settee and a central table, he glanced around at the other accommodations. Beyond the saloon there was a spacious aft cabin with a double berth, storage and a bathroom. Behind him was a smaller cabin, with one single bunk.

Without speaking to anyone, Nevan stalked off to the larger cabin, shutting the door behind him.

"I guess that puts an end to any protracted conversation about who is sleeping where." Nate carried his and Violet's bags through to the tiny cabin. "At least I won't lose you in here."

"How long will it take us to reach the Wolf Nation?"

Violet asked the man who had brought them across in the dinghy.

"Two days." He blushed, casting a furtive glance in the direction of the closed cabin door. "I'm glad to have this chance to thank you, my lady."

Violet regarded him warily. "You are?"

"Yes." He kept his voice to a whisper. "My father was one of Anwyl's supporters. He was killed when your father took over and, like all families who were loyal to the former leader, we were thrown out of our home. My mother was ill and frail. I thought she would die. Then, on one of your weekly visits to the refugee camp, you noticed her plight. You not only got her medical care, you also found me this job." He cast another look in the direction of Nevan's cabin. "The Wolf Leader still doesn't know my background."

Violet stared at him in silence for several seconds before answering. When she spoke, her voice was shaky. "I remember. You are Emil." She turned her head to Nate, her eyes shining. "I can remember something at last." She placed her hand on Emil's arm. "How is your mother?"

His eyes brightened with tears. "Even though she is still in the refugee camp, she is well, my lady. She speaks of you often."

Observing the exchange, Nate noticed something new in Violet's demeanor. He had always known she had reserves of inner strength, but now he got a sense of inner responsibility from her, as well. He recognized that she had felt it was her duty to help Emil about his mother, and that she saw supporting those less fortunate as part of her role. Somehow he didn't think that obligation to others had been inherited from her father. On the contrary, he got the feeling that Nevan would do his best to thwart any attempt his daughter might make to assist those people who had been displaced when he took over as leader of the werewolves. Standing up for her principles in the face of Nevan's opposition must have taken courage and determination, and he saw Violet square her shoulders as some appreciation of what she was up against started to come back to her.

Nate began to realize there might be a lot more to Violet's story than that of the spoiled, rebellious werewolf leader's daughter who had traveled to the mortal realm to defy and annoy her father. That was the impression Nevan might want them to get, but it didn't fit with what Emil was saying. She was rebellious, that much was true. If she was assisting the people who had been harmed by her father's actions, then she was hardly behaving a way that Nevan would consider dutiful. Spoiled? Emil had spoken of one of her weekly visits to the refugee camp. That meant she visited regularly. That, coupled with her behavior toward him and his mother, was hardly that of an overindulged young woman.

No, Nevan had been less than truthful when he spoke of the reason for her defiance, Nate decided. But what he hoped to gain from it was unclear. He must know Violet would regain her memory sooner or later and that she would recall her past commitments. Unless he really was so arrogant he believed that, between now and then, he could bring enough pressure to bear on her that he could change her mind?

From the renewed sparkle in Violet's eyes, Nate doubted that would be the case. *And he has me to contend with if he makes the attempt.* Either way, he suspected his visit to the Wolf Nation was likely to be an interesting one. Add Roko, the jealous would-be lover into the mix…

The boat gave a forward surge as Emil started the engines and their journey began.

Chapter 18

They had navigated a series of smaller islands, but now Emil called them over and pointed out the distant outline of a larger land mass. "That is Urlati, one of the two main islands of the Wolf Nation."

Violet stared at it, trying to find something familiar in its shape.

"I don't think I'm cut out for a life on the ocean waves." Nate stretched his long limbs. "I might be going ever so slightly stir-crazy."

"You spend most of your time on a cramped tour bus," Violet pointed out. "How is this different?"

He leaned over the deck rail and gazed into the churning water. "I can't decide to get off this boat and walk around the way I can with the bus. And while having you as my roommate in exchange for Khan or Torque definitely has its compensations, I'm sure that cabin was intended for a five-year-old."

Throughout the two days of the journey, Nevan had remained in his cabin, eating the meals Emil prepared alone and not surfacing to speak to anyone. While part of her was relieved that she didn't have to interact with this person who was essentially a stranger to her, it seemed an odd way to behave when he had just been reunited with his daughter. It made Violet slightly fearful to think about what she would uncover when she finally got to know the man who had provided 50 percent of her DNA.

Ever since Emil had spoken to her about his mother, odd snippets of her past life had drifted back to her. They were mostly connected to the things Emil had talked of. She saw images of Anwyl's supporters being driven from their homes by her father's beta wolves, groups of those same black werewolves who had attacked the party in Vermont and stormed the stage at the Beast concert in Marseilles. She even recalled going to Nevan and protesting, pleading with him to be merciful in victory.

Her mind took her back to the refugee camp, to the unimaginable suffering she had witnessed there. She saw packs of displaced werewolves huddled together, lost and confused, their lives torn apart because of a power struggle that had nothing to do with them. Men, women and children robbed of their basic human rights and their fundamental werewolf dignity. She remembered making a promise that one member of her family at least would not turn a blind eye to their suffering. *My lady.* It was what Emil had called her, and she heard the words ringing in her mind, accompanied by hands lifted in supplication and tears of gratitude. And overlying it all was a sense of fear, of wanting to do more, needing to find a way to make things better.

Why and how that vow had taken her to the mortal realm she had no idea, but she felt her presence there had something to do with the charitable work she had undertaken on behalf of those refugees. It was almost as frustrating to have half memories as it was to have none.

Nate seemed to pick up on her thoughts as he nodded across the expanse of water at the looming island of Urlati. She had told him about her flashbacks, so he knew her memory was trying to resurface. "Do you remember it at all?"

Violet stared at the shimmering outline. Was it because she wanted to feel something, or was there really a tug of emotion deep within her? Whatever it was, the tiniest flicker of warmth stirred in the recesses of her memory. A faint nostalgia. She tried to clutch at it. Yes, this place meant something to her. Urlati was her home, the land of her birth. She had been raised here. Her family and friends lived here. The more she chased the feelings, the further they danced out of her grasp.

"I'm not sure." It was a disappointed sigh.

He slid an arm around her shoulders. "You're getting there. It will all come back to you in time."

Nevan came on deck as Emil brought the boat alongside a harbor wall. When they alighted and stepped ashore, they were in a scenic village, and Violet could see Nate staring around him in surprise. She guessed he was thinking that this was not the picture conjured up by the words *Wolf Nation*.

"Did you imagine it would be a dark, apocalyptic place filled with warring packs of snarling werewolves?"

"I don't know what I imagined," he said as they followed a narrow lane toward rolling hills. "But I don't think it was anything like this."

Because she had no recollection of her homeland, Violet wasn't sure what she had expected. During the short time she had spent in the mortal realm, she had become accustomed to the fast pace of life there. Crowds of people had packed into huge stadiums, where noise, light and color had been the dominant features, to see Beast. She had stayed in large, luxurious hotels in densely populated cities. They had traveled in a huge tour bus along vast, congested freeways. Ged had used the internet to communicate, and the band members had been amazed at Violet's lack of knowledge of social media. With no memory to draw on, she had been unsure whether her ignorance was due to lack of experience or amnesia.

The faerie palace had represented a very different pace of life. Instantly, everything had slowed down. There had been no crowds, no vehicles, no cell phones or internet. Stella, whose job in the mortal realm had been to design digital games, had confessed to Violet that she had initially found the contrast bewildering. Violet had experienced no such difficulty in adjusting. She had not missed the trappings of technology that went along with the mortal realm. She hadn't realized that the noise, bustle and constant motion bothered her until they were gone. Once they were, she had breathed a sigh of relief.

The Wolf Nation echoed the peace of the Faerie Isles and took it a step further. As Emil led them away from the harbor, Violet drank in the simplicity of her surroundings. The sylvan setting of rolling pastures and wild woodland was only occasionally broken by small clusters of dwellings. Something stirred in the recesses of her memory. Some residual sadness. She cast a sidelong glance at Nevan. Her father was a violent man. She recalled that, as she was growing up, her overriding feeling toward him had been anger at his insistence on dragging the werewolves into a prolonged and bloody civil war. She also knew that questioning him had always been futile.

"Wolves are pack animals. We fight for our own fami-

lies. It is not in our nature to follow the cause of another."
She spoke the words out loud, knowing she had said them
to Nevan before. Many times.

He turned his head sharply, glaring at her. "Why do you
say that? Why now, when the war is over?"

"Because it still matters. The fight between you and
Anwyl tore our dynasty apart. Now you are proposing to
do it all again by taking this feud against Roko to the same
lengths." She waved a hand around her. "These lands are
mostly composed of these tiny villages. Individual packs.
The reason our population is so large is that our lands are
huge and there are so many of these small hamlets. Plus,
there is a huge werewolf community in the mortal realm.
You draw your reluctant army from each of these small
areas of paradise. And when you won, you weren't mag-
nanimous in victory. You burned the homes of the losing
side to the ground. You wiped out entire packs and left the
wives and children of the losers homeless."

Violet was aware of Nate listening intently to what she
was saying, his expression shocked and disgusted at what
he was hearing. The contrast between the beauty of the
scene and the ugliness of her words could not be more
marked.

"Your spell in the mortal realm hasn't changed you.
You still know nothing of politics," Nevan growled. "*My
reluctant army?* How can there be such a thing?"

"Because you rely on the single most important trait
a werewolf has." Violet's voice was sad. "These people
leave their homes to fight for a cause out of loyalty. They
are forced to take sides and are punished when they do."

Although what she was saying needed no illustration,
they crested a slight hill and before them the waste and
destruction she was describing could clearly be seen. In
the valley below a series of small villages lay in ruins,

the buildings nothing more than burned-out shells. Violet paused, feeling bitter tears sting her eyes.

"I remember this place." She groped for Nate's hand. "Oh, I was never allowed to come here because, even though it was on Urlati, this was Anwyl's territory and I was Nevan the Rebel's daughter. But the villagers were known for their generosity. They tended the sick and injured, gave shelter to travelers from other lands and cared for orphans from other packs. When Anwyl was defeated, my father had them all put to death."

"I suppose you think you could do better than I?" Nevan snarled.

Still gripping Nate's hand, Violet faced him bravely. "I know I could not do worse."

Nate stood at the window of the attic room he had been allocated and gazed out over the darkening landscape, his mind attempting to make sense of everything he had heard since he arrived on Wolf Nation soil.

This beautiful mansion reminded him of a stately home he had once visited in the mortal realm. It was like stepping back in time. Or maybe stepping into the pages of a Gothic novel. Tucked under a hill, surrounded by towering sentinel trees, this could be Sleeping Beauty's bower, untouched by time. The exterior of the house was adorned with decorative, fairy-tale features. It had high, arched windows, pinnacles and finials, gables and a forest of chimneys. Known as the Voda Kuca—the Leader's House—it was the perfect secret hideaway.

From the moment he stepped foot over this threshold, he had experienced the strangest, unshakable sensation. He felt like he had come home.

Of course, Nevan had wasted no time in relegating him to this poky room under the eaves. Nate's lips had twitched in amusement as Emil led him along a series of increasingly narrow corridors. The message was clear. Nate's presence may have been forced upon him by Cal, but Nevan had a point to make. *I am banished to the servants' quarters.* Violet had protested, but Nate had silenced her with a shake of her head. *Save your energy for other battles.* He had a feeling she was going to need it.

The conflicting emotions this place aroused in him were shocking and exciting at the same time. How could he feel like this was somewhere he was meant to be? This was the Wolf Leader's stronghold. It should be the last place on earth Nate felt comfortable. He wondered if it was because this was Violet's home. Was he drawn to this place because she was *his* home? Although that was true, it was more than that. Yes, he would feel comfortable wherever Violet was. If he could be with her, his surroundings wouldn't matter. He would make his home in a tent, in a cave or in the open under the stars. But this house *mattered*. It drew him in, wrapped itself around him, called to something deep within him. And it wasn't just the house. Although it was strongest here, it was the land itself.

Could I, the man who hates werewolves, have found myself in sympathy with the Wolf Nation?

The question raised a whole world of possibilities, ones that meant Nate had to open his mind. He had to rethink the last six years of his life. It was a scary thought. He was just getting used to the idea that Cal had not completely destroyed the wolf in him. The silver dagger that had pierced his heart hadn't driven out all of his werewolf urges. So much had happened since he had allowed himself to accept that likelihood that Nate hadn't had time to fully examine it. He knew he liked one part of it very much. The part that drew him to Violet. The part that made them soul mates.

Was the residual wolf within him drawn to this land

of werewolves? That could be one explanation for why he felt this way. But he knew there was more to it. He had to face up to something more fundamental than that. Something that made him question his own motivation over the last six years. Ever since the night he had been attacked by a feral werewolf, he had been living apart from the world, touched by only two things...his hatred for Nevan and his ambition to rid the world of feral werewolves. He had believed those two emotions added up to a hatred of all wolves.

Listening to Violet confront Nevan today, hearing the passion in her voice as she denounced her father's behavior and described his atrocities, Nate had been seized with admiration. And more. He had experienced a deep and profound yearning to help, to be a part of the solution. When Violet had responded to Nevan's taunt that she couldn't do worse than he had, Nate had wanted to stand shoulder to shoulder with her and say, "Together we can put this right." He, the man who had believed he hated werewolves, burned with a fierce desire to help them. He wanted to rebuild this dynasty, to restore its lost pride and nobility.

It was similar to his wish to hunt down and kill feral werewolves, even though they were a danger and a curse. Nate had never hated the rogue werewolves he hunted on Cal's behalf. He pitied them. Having been through that transformation himself, he understood their suffering. He knew death was preferable to prolonging their agony.

So here he was, six years on from that strange turning point in his life, standing at a new crossroads. He was in love with a werewolf. Through her, he was learning to accept that a large part of his own psyche was still wolflike. And this new discovery that his sympathies lay with the werewolves was not repulsive to him. On the contrary, he found it exciting and tempting. Which meant he had to

ask himself whether he had ever hated *all* werewolves...
or whether he had misread and misdirected his hatred for
Nevan.

He forced himself to face the truth. He had projected all
the fear and loathing he had felt for that insidious, lisping
voice that had penetrated his mind and driven him to murder onto a whole species instead of accepting it for what it
was...a justifiable hostility toward Nevan.

Nevan. Nate's lip curled in contempt when he thought of
Violet's father. Those six years of hatred didn't feel wasted.
The man who had invaded his head and urged him to kill
an innocent woman had not improved upon closer acquain-
tance. Nevan was every bit the cold, manipulative bully
Nate had believed he would be. The only thing that had
changed was that Nate was unable to put his vow to kill
the Wolf Leader into practice. The thought brought with it
a pang of regret. If ever the world would be a better place
for one man's removal, that man was Nevan. But Nevan
was Violet's father, and even though it appeared there was
no love lost between them, Nate would not be the person
who murdered him. When they parted, that would not be
her memory of him. And he had made a promise to Cal,
his friend, his mentor and the man who had saved his life.

Nate was still mulling over the problem of Nevan and
the damage he had caused to his daughter and to the werewolf dynasty when a brief knock on the door was followed by Violet's arrival. She cast a quick glance around
the room.

"It is *slightly* larger than the cabin on the boat." Although she smiled, Nate saw the troubled look in the depths
of her eyes.

"Let me guess what has brought that frown to your
face. Your father?" He held out his arms, and she walked
into them with a sigh.

"I'm beginning to think I don't want my memory back if he is part of it."

"What has he done this time?"

"Apart from relegating you to this broom cupboard?" Violet rested her cheek against Nate's chest. "When I tried to ask about my brothers and sisters, he initially refused to speak of them. Eventually, after I persisted, I got a brief account. It turns out none of them have anything to do with him. My sisters both have mates and families of their own. They live on other islands in the Wolf Nation and never visit with my father. One brother lives in the mortal realm, and my father banished the other one, Bartol. He hasn't seen or spoken to either for years. He wouldn't tell me why." Her sigh reverberated through her slender body. "When I had the audacity to ask him about my mother, he strode away from me and slammed the door of what Emil tells me is his study."

Nate took her hand, leading her to the narrow bed and drawing her down to sit next to him on its edge. "And you still don't remember any of it?"

Violet shook her head. "My only memories are of the political strife that has torn this place apart. My family, this land, this house—" there was confusion on her face as she looked up at him "—it still means nothing to me. The only recollection I have of my father is of the damage he has done to our dynasty. Surely it should be the other way around? My memories of my home and my family should be my strongest ones."

"Not if your father is an evil bastard." The words had left his lips before Nate could stop them.

Violet's expression grew even more anxious. "It must be so hard for you to be here. I almost forgot that you have more reason than anyone to hate him."

"And I find a new reason to hate him every time I see his behavior toward you," Nate said.

"Stella told me you swore you would one day take revenge for what he did to you." There was a worried frown furrowing Violet's brow as she gazed at him. "It is his brutality that concerns me. Answering that with more violence is not the solution."

He kissed the line that drew her brows together. "For your sake, I will not harm him."

Violet relaxed against him. "It feels like I'm close to knowing who I am, but my father won't help me. Instead, he puts up more barriers. It's so frustrating. One thing that puzzles me more than any other is why I was in the mortal realm."

"Then we need to talk to Roko again to find the answer to that question."

Her lip curled. "So he can tell more lies about how much I love him?"

Nate laughed. "Maybe we can persuade him to tell the truth."

Violet appeared unconvinced. "How will we find him? My father is hardly likely to disclose the whereabouts of the rebel leader, even supposing he knows."

"I wasn't proposing to ask your father." Nate rose and held out his hand, pulling her to her feet. "I have a feeling Emil may know more about the resistance than he would like anyone else to know."

Chapter 19

The Voda Kuca was a large house, and a team of servants ensured its smooth operation. Emil's role seemed to be that of general maintenance. Early the next morning, Violet found him raking leaves in the gardens. When she explained that she wanted to speak to Roko, Emil dropped his rake and stared at her openmouthed.

Casting fearful glances around him, he twisted his hands together. "He is the resistance leader. I am dutiful to your father, my lady. Why would you ask me such a thing?"

Violet placed her hand on his arm. "Emil, this is not a trap to discover where your loyalties lie. I simply want to know if you can get a message to Roko for me."

Emil licked his lips nervously. "Let us go into the clearing."

He led her away from the trees and shrubs, where someone might hide and overhear their conversation, and toward a small field. On the way, Violet noticed a small, igloo-shaped building at the edge of an ornate lake. Its double doors were firmly secured with a huge, serviceable padlock.

"What is that?" she asked, as they passed the strange building. "I'm sorry, but, even though this is my home, I have no memory of it, and that place looks strange."

"It's the icehouse," Emil explained. "Most of the structure is underground. It is no longer used, but its purpose was once for the storage of ice and the preservation of meat."

He led Violet into the middle of the field, where he was sure they couldn't be overheard.

"When Anwyl was defeated, your father crushed his supporters. There was no hope of them rising again," Emil said. "But there was residual anger because of the way he treated us."

"I know that." It was one of the few memories Violet did have. One that hurt her most. "I wish it could have been different."

"Although Roko tried to rouse Anwyl's followers to support him, he was never successful. Not until your father imprisoned him without reason. That changed the tide of support in Roko's favor." Emil cast a thoughtful glance Violet's way as though wondering how much to tell her. "There was something else that swayed Anwyl's supporters to rise up again and swear allegiance to Roko."

"What was that?" It must have been something very powerful, Violet decided, to incite that downtrodden, beleaguered group to action.

"You, my lady."

"Me?" Violet was aware that the word came out as an undignified squeak.

Emil nodded. "When Roko escaped from prison, he rallied his followers. He accused your father of sending his beta werewolves into the mortal realm to beat him and drag him back here to captivity. He also said you were on his side in the fight against your father, and that your father was so enraged by your defection that he had threatened to banish you. You have saved many of Anwyl's followers and made even more lives better through your actions, my lady. They supported Roko because of you."

Violet took a moment to allow the full force of what he was saying to sink in. Anger at Roko's duplicity soon gave way to dismay at the prospect of the task that lay ahead of her. The thought that she had unwittingly become the reason why her dynasty might be once again plunged into a bloody civil war was too awful to contemplate. She had to unravel this deceit before it led to even greater harm. The only way she could think of to do that was to get Roko to withdraw his self-serving remarks about her. It was even more important than ever that she should talk to him.

"And you, Emil? Did you become one of Roko's supporters?"

He shook his head so vehemently she didn't doubt his honesty. "No, my lady. But I do have friends in the resistance." He gulped in a deep breath. "I can get a message to Roko if you wish."

"Thank you. Just tell him I wish to speak to him." She started to walk back to the house and then turned back. "And Emil...please tell him I need it to be as soon as possible."

When she returned to the house it was quiet, but, as she set her foot on the first stair in preparation to go up to Nate's room, a door to her right opened. It was the room Nevan used as his study.

"You are out and about early this morning." Was she imagining the look of suspicion in her father's eyes because she felt guilty? But surely if he wouldn't provide her with the information she needed, he should expect her to seek it elsewhere. Violet wasn't entirely convinced that her loyalties should lie with this man, even though he was her father.

"You would know better than I do whether I am usually an early riser." She paused, still with her foot on the stair. "I can't remember."

He inclined his head as though acknowledging the truth of her statement, but changed the subject. "Now that you are home, you will oblige me by dressing in a manner more suited to my daughter. These clothes—" he indicated her jeans and hooded sweatshirt "—are not becoming to your status."

"Was there ever a time when I obediently did as you asked?"

He seemed taken aback at the question. "What do you mean?"

"I'm going to wear what I want to wear regardless of your wishes. But you seem to think you can tell me to change my clothes and I'll do it. So, I'm asking a serious question. Was there ever a time when I would have done that?" He remained silent, and she decided to push the question further. "Did my mother do everything you asked her to?"

The frown that descended on his features was truly terrifying, and after staring at her for a few seconds without replying, he turned back into the room, slamming the door so hard behind him that a nearby picture frame rattled against the wall.

I guess I can add my mother to the list of taboo subjects. With a sigh, she continued up the stairs.

"Where is the refugee camp?" Nate wasn't sure why it should matter so much, but the need to know more had taken a strong grip in his mind.

Violet, who was lying next to him in his narrow bed, turned her head to look at his face. "I don't know. I can remember going there, but not where it is. Why?"

"Would it upset you too much to return?"

She gave it some thought before shaking her head. "I think it would be a good idea. It might help me to remember."

Nate knew she was still intensely frustrated by her elusive memory. Bits of it had returned, but other parts remained stubbornly beyond her reach. It was as if her mind was teasing her, revealing tantalizing glimpses of her past life, while keeping the bigger picture hidden away. Nate knew how much Violet was enjoying some aspects of being back in her home environment. The ability to shift when she chose had brought a renewed strength and vitality to her body.

Every night, when darkness claimed the forest, Violet would take to the woods. Unlike feral werewolves, other wolves weren't influenced by the phases of the moon, but they were at their strongest when it was full. Fascinated, Nate had gotten into the habit of accompanying her on her nightly expeditions. He loved to watch her face as she shifted. The intensity and enjoyment of her expression was beyond compare. Her wolf was incredible, a beautiful, magical creature. The sights and sounds of the forest as he waited for her to return from her run became familiar and comforting, like an old friend he sought for comfort. And there was another feeling he got as he watched Violet in her natural environment. He felt envy. He wanted to join her. He'd have given anything, in the instant she shifted, to experience that same euphoria, to break into a run with her, to become a creature of the night alongside his beloved wolf.

They had been at her home for three days and had seen

very little of Nevan during that time. The Wolf Leader seemed preoccupied with the rebellion and was in almost constant meetings with his beta werewolves. Dario, the werewolf Nate had fought and defeated at the hotel in Barcelona, was a regular visitor. He still limped slightly from the injury Nate had inflicted with the knife. Although he cast some dark looks in Nate's direction, he appeared to be under orders to keep his distance. It seemed Cal's warning had a far-reaching impact.

Emil, their only source of information, had told them that Roko's followers were causing problems on a small group of outlying islands known as the Kurjak. These sparsely inhabited isles were strategic because of their location. No one could leave the main islands without passing through the waters of the Kurjak. If Roko could take control of them, he would trap Nevan on Urlati. The Wolf Leader would be rendered powerless, imprisoned on his home island.

Nevan, having fought for so long to take power from Anwyl, now faced the prospect of seeing it slide out of his grasp as Roko—a younger, wilier opponent with a large following—used unexpected tactics against him. Nevan wanted a face-to-face fight, but Roko wasn't prepared to give him what he wanted. The rebel leader employed guerrilla techniques, haranguing Nevan's pack, then backing off before the Wolf Leader could organize reprisals. With so much to occupy his mind and his time, Nevan gave the impression of barely noticing Violet and Nate.

Emil, having realized that he could trust Nate and Violet not to inform against him, had overcome some of his nervousness around them. After they had finished dinner that evening, Nate asked Emil to join them in the library. The young werewolf looked slightly wary, but obeyed the summons without question.

"We want to go to the refugee camp." Nate got straight to the point. "But we don't know where it is."

"It is on the island of Vukod. It is the northernmost of the isles of the Wolf Nation. When Anwyl's followers were displaced, they left their homes in droves. Nevan tried to drive them away from the Wolf Nation altogether, but there was nowhere for them to go. The Alliance intervened and Merlin Caledonius declared it a crisis. They forbade Nevan from forcing them out to sea. The next lands are the Vampire Archipelago, and there would be unimaginable bloodshed if werewolves attempted to land there. Having no other choice, the refugees settled on Vukod."

Violet looked horrified. "But they had no food, shelter or clothing...nothing to meet their basic needs."

Emil's eyes were warm as he looked at her. "Not until you stepped in to help, my lady."

"Can you take us to Vukod?" Nate asked.

Emil appeared to be fighting an internal battle. "It would mean risking the wrath of the Wolf Leader."

"Leave him to me." Nate's voice was grim. "If he finds out, I'll tell him I forced you to take us. He can direct his wrath at me."

He didn't add that he would welcome a confrontation with Nevan. Everything the Wolf Leader did demonstrated his unsuitability for the role of leader of all wolves. Nate would enjoy telling him so.

"Very well." Emil nodded decisively. "It will mean leaving early in the morning and returning late."

"We'll be ready," Nate assured him.

When Emil had gone, Violet sank into one of the wing-backed chairs that flanked the huge fireplace. "*How* did I do these things? I know I would have wanted to reach out to those poor refugees who were stranded on Vukod. But you've seen what my father is like. I couldn't have gone behind his back and organized a relief effort on my own. I must have had help."

Before Nate could answer her, his attention was drawn to a slight tapping noise on the window. When he looked up, Emil was standing outside looking in. Nate made a move toward the window, but Emil held up a hand, jerking his head in a gesture that clearly meant he wanted them to join him outside. When they didn't move quickly enough, he impatiently repeated the action.

"He was only here a minute ago. What the hell is he playing at?" Nate muttered. He was feeling the same level of frustration as Violet and was certainly in no mood for riddles. "Let's go and find out what's going on."

They exited the house through the front door and made their way around to the side of the building where the library window overlooked a pretty rose garden. There was no sign of Emil, and Nate was about to exclaim in annoyance when a soft whistle from a clump of trees attracted his attention.

"Is this Emil's idea of a joke?" he muttered, starting toward the noise.

"Emil doesn't strike me as the sort of person to play games with us," Violet said.

She was right, of course. Nate decided he was allowing his annoyance at the lack of progress with Nevan to color his judgment of Emil. So far, the young werewolf had proved loyal and trustworthy. He had no reason to suspect his behavior on this occasion was frivolous. When they reached the thicket, Emil was waiting for them. His usual air of nervousness had increased to the point where he was dancing from foot to foot with restless energy.

"Do you still wish to meet with the rebel leader?" Emil asked Violet.

"Yes, of course I do."

"Then I am to take you to him."

* * *

Emil led them to a disused hamlet about half a mile from the Voda Kuca. When they arrived, a group of young werewolves were guarding the entrance to the ruined settlement. Violet recognized some of them from the party at the house in Vermont.

She and Nate were led inside a run-down cottage, where Roko was waiting for them.

"Do you need me to stay?" The werewolf who had escorted them hovered at the entrance.

"Wait outside, Teo." She remembered Roko had used that name when speaking to one of the werewolves at the party.

Roko gestured for them to be seated on the wooden bench that ran along one wall. He rested his hip on the rickety remains of a table.

"Thank you for seeing us. I know it is dangerous for you to be here." They had discussed in advance the best approach to take to this meeting. Nate's opinion had been that Violet should do the talking. Her tone? *Keep it conciliatory.* She kept Nate's words in mind now. No matter how angry she was at Roko for the messages he had given to Anwyl's supporters, it wouldn't do to alienate him before she had gotten the answers she required.

"The message I received made it sound like you needed to speak to me urgently." She wasn't sure from the look on Roko's face whether he was prepared to act without hostility in return. "In fact, it sounded a lot like a summons."

Violet suppressed the spark of annoyance his tone ignited. "I've been hearing about the refugees on Vukod. I know I was involved in helping them before I left to go to the mortal realm. Since my memory hasn't fully returned, I was hoping you might be able to tell me the reason—the real reason—why I was in the mortal realm with you."

Roko regarded her for a moment or two, his expression speculative. Then, giving a curt nod, he seemed to reach a decision. "Your father had threatened to banish you if you didn't stop providing help to the camp on Vukod. You refused, and I offered my help. I have friends in the mortal realm who were fund-raising for the relief effort. You came with me so that we could meet with them and gather even more support. That never happened, mainly because we had your father's beta werewolves on our tail from the moment we stepped through the portal."

Violet wrinkled her brow in an effort to remember. "How do you and I know each other?"

"We were both involved in the effort to help the refugees. But—" Roko cast a dark look in Nate's direction "—while I may have exaggerated when I said we were in love, I like to think that was the way things were headed between us eventually."

Violet, conscious of the coiled tension in Nate's body, decided to change the subject. "What is happening now to help the people on Vukod?"

"The resistance does as much as we can. Once Nevan is defeated, it will be a different matter. Then they can return to their homes, and the rebuilding work will begin."

"You really think you can defeat my father?" Violet asked.

"I don't think it, I know it." Roko's lips drew back in a snarl. "And if you knew what I had seen when I was imprisoned in the cellars beneath the Voda Kuca, you would be cheering the resistance on to victory."

"You spoke of that once before. You said what you saw in the cellars gave you an opinion about my family. What was it?"

Roko shook his head. "I made a promise never to speak of it, even though, should it be known, it might shake the foundations of Nevan's power. If you want to know more, you must ask Nevan. Although I doubt he will be willing to tell you. He has kept his secret for all your life, Violet. He will not be ready to share it now."

The words sent a chill sweeping through Violet's body. They could have been bluster, designed to intimidate the daughter of his enemy. But she knew that wasn't the case. She knew Roko was telling the truth. Nevan was a man with a secret so dark it was emblazoned on his soul. That secret had something to do with Violet, and the answer lay in the cellars beneath the Voda Kuca. Had she spent her whole life living a lie? Living, sleeping, eating, laughing, all the time blissfully unaware that her childhood home was balanced on top of a powder keg?

Roko rose. "I must go. Urlati is too dangerous for me to linger here."

"Is there any way this fighting can end?" Nate spoke for the first time since they had entered the cottage. "Any way the people of the Wolf Nation can live in peace?"

Roko paused. "Yes, there is a way. Nevan was the one who began this feud with Anwyl. Before that, the were-wolves were a peaceful dynasty. When he dies, that peace will return. Until then, the blood will continue to flow."

"We have to find out what is in the cellars."

Violet shivered so violently the tremors ran through Nate's body, as well. "I'm scared to go down there." Her voice was an agonized whisper.

"Until we do, you will always be plagued by doubts. We'll never know if what he said was just bravado on Roko's part, just an attempt to scare you into believing your father is worse than he is, or whether there really is some dark family secret he is keeping hidden from the world."

"From *me*. You heard what Roko said. He has kept this

secret all my life. My father may be hiding it from the world, but whatever this is, it is about me."

Nate gripped her upper arms, holding her slightly away from him so that he could look down at her. There were dark shadows in the glorious blue depths of her eyes, and her face was pale. He was starting to worry that bringing her home to the Wolf Nation might have been the wrong decision. Although she was physically stronger, her emotions were in turmoil. One thing was clear. She needed him now more than ever.

He drew her close, trying to impart some of his own strength to her. Gradually, as he held her in his arms, her trembling ceased and she lifted her head to kiss him, tangling her tongue with his. Nate swept over her mouth demandingly, kissing her with an instant heat and hunger that had her moaning and arching into his body.

"Make it go away." Violet whispered the words into his mouth. "At least for now, make me forget it all."

Knowing that the bed in his little attic room was small and hard, Nate carried her to the only other item of furniture, a large velvet chair close to the window. Kneeling before her, he removed her clothing, placing each item aside and kissing her exposed flesh until Violet was squirming with pleasure. His hands cupped her breasts, and his gaze fixed on hers as his tongue slowly flicked over one nipple and then the other. Violet's head tipped against the chair back as she buried her hands in his hair. He drew one nipple fully into his mouth, rasping the little bud with his teeth and tickling it with his tongue.

He lifted his head and gazed at her face. "Does that feel good?"

"So good." Her reply came on a gasp.

Nate lifted her legs, spreading them wide, pulling her to the edge of the chair and feasting on her with his eyes as she lay back, exposed to his gaze. His hand smoothed up the inside of her thigh until he stroked inside her narrow slit, coating his finger with her juices.

"Touch your breasts." His voice was hoarse as he released his straining erection from his jeans.

"I…" Violet blushed, her expression dazed and embarrassed.

"I want to see you play with yourself when I'm inside you." Nate pressed the tip of his cock to her swollen folds. "Let me see that, Violet. Please."

She raised her hands from his hair to cup the full mounds, grazing her nipples with her thumbs and gripping her lower lip with her teeth. Her gaze lowered, her eyes widening as she watched him press into her. He drew his steel-hard flesh out of her, and she cried out in protest before he eased back, stretching her as he sank deeper. Velvet heat gripped him. A strangled moan escaped Nate's lips as he watched her stretch around him. It was the most erotic thing he had ever seen, watching his cock enter her as she caressed her breasts and lifted her hips to meet him. Inch by inch he impaled her, pumping his engorged flesh as growls of need rumbled deep in his chest. It was a pleasure so intense it was close to madness.

He took one of her hands, placing her middle finger on her clitoris. "Touch yourself here, as well. Play with your nipples with one hand while you rub yourself with the other."

Violet made a soft whimpering sound. Using her finger to stroke the tiny bud, she kept her mesmerized gaze on the point where his cock was embedded inside her. Nate drew back, spearing into her, watching her face as she pushed herself higher and higher. Electricity chased up his spine, tingling all the way up and into his scalp. His erection was burning, throbbing. He could feel the deep, coiling sensation beginning to build inside him. His whole body tightened as he picked up the pace.

Violet writhed wildly against him, thrusting in time with his masterful strokes. He felt her give way, her cries becoming screams as the final strands of her control snapped and she succumbed to a hot, hungry climax.

It drove Nate over the edge. Too much tightness, too much heat, too much throbbing, clenching need around him. His own cry mingled with her screams, his scalding release jerking high inside her as he thrust one final time before collapsing forward, resting his head against her shoulder.

When Nate's strength returned, he lifted Violet in his arms and carried her to the narrow bed, reflecting that, since their arrival in Otherworld, uncomfortable beds had become a regular feature. He was surprised Nevan hadn't interfered in their sleeping arrangements, but once they had arrived at the Voda Kuca, the Wolf Leader had immersed himself so deeply in his own affairs he appeared not to notice what was going on. Either that, or Cal's warning went deeper than Nate had originally thought.

Pulling the bedclothes over Violet, he removed his clothes before joining her.

Her chuckle was sleepy. "That's the sort of memory loss I like. So I forget everything except you."

He held her close. "Get some sleep. We have an early start tomorrow."

Chapter 20

The desolate encampment on Vukod had an eerie feel to it in the early morning light. A faint mist rose above the settlement, and a chill breeze swept off the ocean as Emil pulled their dinghy up onto the beach and led them along a winding path.

As they approached the first of a cluster of wooden huts, they encountered a group of children jumping in and out of the puddles left by a recent thunderstorm. Their feet were bare, but they wore warm sweaters and rolled-up sweatpants, and they appeared well nourished. They paused in their game to watch the visitors as they passed. One of them, a girl who was bolder than the others, darted forward and clasped Violet's hand, walking alongside her.

"My lady." The child's eyes were bright as she smiled up at Violet.

The gesture and the look in the girl's eyes jolted something in Violet's chest. It was as if something broke loose inside her with a lurch.

"Oh, I remember this." She stopped in her tracks and turned her head to look at Nate. "I remember what it was like before we built the huts. And you—" she stooped to catch hold of the child's other hand "—I remember you. You are Mila."

The little girl laughed delightedly and dashed on ahead, calling out as she ran. "My lady is here! She has come back."

There was a bustle of activity among the meager huts as Mila scampered between them. People came outside to see what the commotion was about and remained in front of their stark dwellings when they saw Violet. As she walked among them, catching glimpses of faces she knew, it felt like walls inside her head were tumbling down. She recalled the heartbreaking horror of this place when these people first arrived.

"Roko was useful," she explained to Nate as they proceeded along the narrow track that led them into the center of the camp. As she progressed, people called out to Violet, and she responded to many of them by name. "I asked him for help, and he mobilized his supporters to build these huts. We traveled around the other islands together, appealing for donations of food and clothing. Wolves are pack animals. Even my father's supporters could not bear to hear of other werewolves suffering in this way. Although they gave secretly, they were generous in their donations."

When they reached the center of the camp, Emil left them to go and see his mother while Violet made her way toward one of the huts. An elderly man was seated on a stool beside the door, and his eyes crinkled into a smile when he saw her.

"So you came back?"

"I never meant to stay away." She bent to hug him.

When she straightened, she held out her hand to Nate, drawing him forward. "This is my friend Marko. There is nothing he doesn't know about werewolf healing. We are very lucky to have him here in the camp."

Nate looked around him at the sparse living conditions. "Do you feel lucky to be here?"

"I am lucky to be alive," Marko said. "If it was up to Nevan, I would have died on a boat, adrift in the middle of the ocean." His calm tone took any drama out of the words, yet made the reality of them starker. "Or the instant I set my foot on vampire soil."

Violet sat on the scrubby grass next to Marko's stool, and Nate joined her. "How are things here?" Violet waved a hand to indicate their surroundings.

"Much as they were when you left. There are the illnesses you would expect from these conditions. Our biggest enemy is boredom. We are werewolves, so we need to run free, and we need fresh meat. There are too many people on one small island, and we have hunted the local wildlife almost to extinction. We supplement our diet with berries, fruits and vegetables. It keeps us alive, but malnutrition is a concern, particularly among the children. Fortunately, rivers and streams are plentiful on this island, so bathing, sanitation and fresh drinking water are not a problem." Marko's face was grave. "You want my honest opinion? I think we'll struggle when winter comes."

"Then we must put an end to this and return these people to their own islands so we can begin rebuilding their homes before winter." The quiet determination in Nate's voice surprised Violet. He sounded like a man who was making plans for the future. The problem was, he had no future here in the Wolf Nation.

"There is only one way to finish this. Since it involves ending the existing regime, I can't see it happening before the colder weather arrives." Marko's words were an echo of what Roko had said the day before.

Violet looked up as Emil approached them with a woman at his side. Violet recognized her instantly, and her heart did a glad little flip at the sensation. *My memory is returning at last.*

"Valentina." She got to her feet, holding out her hand to Emil's mother.

Valentina gripped Violet's hand in both of hers. "My lady, I wanted to thank you again for everything you have done for us." She gazed up at Violet with an almost worshipful look in her eyes. "Your mother would be proud to know that you have grown up to be as good and kind as she was."

"You knew my mother?" Violet felt a surge of excitement. Perhaps she would finally get some answers about the woman who had given birth to her.

"I met her a few times. Dorotea was very beautiful. You look just like her. Except for your eyes." Valentina shook her head. "Do you know how rare it is for a werewolf to have blue eyes?"

"I never thought about it," Violet said. "I always thought—" *Did I always think? Was this a memory resurfacing?* "—that, because my father has brown eyes, my mother's must have been blue, and that I inherited them from her."

Valentina shook her head. "In all my long life, I have only ever seen one other wolf with blue eyes. He had violet eyes exactly like yours." She turned to Marko. "Do you remember?"

Marko nodded. "I remember."

Violet's heart began to thud. "Who was it?"

"It was Anwyl."

* * *

Violet had been subdued on the return journey from Vukod to Urlati. They had prepared a story to tell Nevan about why they had been missing all day, making up an excuse about sightseeing around the islands, but Nate guessed the Wolf Leader would barely have noticed their absence.

When they reached the little harbor, Violet thanked Emil absentmindedly for his help and took Nate's hand. Instead of returning directly to the Voda Kuca, they walked along the shoreline, looking out at the darkening ocean.

"Just because you and Anwyl share the same eye color, it doesn't mean anything," Nate said.

"No." Violet kept her eyes on the water.

"Coincidences like that happen all the time in genetics."

"Yes." Her gaze remained fixed.

"There could be a hundred scientific explanations."

"I know." She still didn't look at him.

He tried a different tactic. "What are you thinking?"

She sighed, turning to face him. "That Anwyl was my father. I feel it." She pressed her fist to the center of her chest. "Here. And I can feel a lot more than that. I can feel the responsibility for what happened to my people pressing down on me. I'm the cause of the war between Nevan and Anwyl. I am the reason why those people we saw today have been treated so badly."

"You can't think like that. Nevan's actions are his responsibility and no one else's. Certainly not yours. Although, if Anwyl is your father, it would explain a lot," Nate said. "Cal said no one really knew where the sudden animosity between Nevan and Anwyl came from."

"It explains *everything*. You've seen how Nevan is with me. He's not a father to me. There's no love there."

"But if you are not Nevan's daughter, why does he keep

up the pretense? Why not simply tell the truth about who you are? Dismiss you from his life?" Nate asked.

"Pride. My mother was his wife. If he disowned me, he would have to admit that Dorotea cheated on him with Anwyl. You've seen what Nevan is like. He would never do that, would never publicly say his wife preferred another man." Violet raised a hand to her mouth. "My God, Nate. My mother died soon after I was born. You don't think…?"

"That Nevan killed her?" He considered it. "If it was any other man, I would say no. But this is Nevan. I've lived with that bastard inside my head, urging me to kill a woman he'd never met because he believed her heart could bring him power. I'd say there's a good chance he could have killed Dorotea if he knew she'd cheated on him. You know what this means?"

Violet nodded. "We have to find out what secrets Nevan is hiding in the cellars beneath the Voda Kuca. I know I was scared at what we might unearth, but my fears are nothing compared to the need to discover the truth."

"Are you ready to go now?"

She forced a smile. "As long as you are with me, I'm ready for anything."

As they reached the door of the Voda Kuca, the weather changed. From nowhere, the wind began to howl. In the darkening skies overhead, clouds began to boil and swirl in competing shades of black and gray as the elements spewed their rage upon the island. Brutal rain slashed at the ground with stinging force, lightning speared the trees and the tempest reached screaming pitch. It was as though nature was hurling a warning at them for what was to come.

As they stepped inside the house, they were already soaked and shivering from the onslaught of the sudden storm. Water saturated their hair and plastered their clothing to their skin. Even so, Nate felt a curious heat radiating through him, a nervous energy that buzzed along his nerve endings. This was a turning point. Everything told him it was so. He knew Violet felt the same certainty. Her eyes were huge, her lips parted, her chest rising and falling as her breath came fast and hard.

"I don't know where the cellars are." Violet's whisper seemed louder than a shout in the silence of the entrance hall.

"I'm guessing there will be an entrance around here somewhere," Nate said. "But if Roko is right and there is some dark, underground secret, I don't imagine getting in will be easy."

He moved toward the first of the doors that lined the hall, but Violet paused, her expression intent. It was as if his words had triggered something in her mind.

"Underground." She said the word slowly.

"That's right. We have to find out if one of these doors leads us down into the cellar."

Violet shook her head. "We don't need to look here. I know where the entrance is."

"How do you know? Has your memory come back?" Nate returned to her side. Violet was shivering now, but he wasn't sure whether the cause was her wet clothing or the excitement that had her in its grip.

"No. But when I was talking to Emil in the grounds the other day, we passed a funny little building. When I asked him what it was, he told me it was an icehouse. He said it was no longer used. He also said that most of the structure was underground."

"It sounds promising, but what makes you think the entrance is there?" Nate asked.

Her eyes shone brilliant blue with excitement. "Why else would a disused icehouse have a huge padlock on its doors?"

* * *

By the time they had changed into dry clothing and found Emil, Violet's anticipation and impatience levels were almost off the scale. Added together with her nervousness, the storm of emotions coursing through her was greater than the tempest outside. She felt as if some of the lightning had entered her body, sending electricity coursing through her bloodstream.

Emil cautiously agreed to their request and some time later knocked on the door of Nate's attic bedroom. When Nate answered, the young werewolf sidled inside and handed over a bolt cutter and a flashlight.

"If anyone knew—"

"They won't." Nate cut him off before he could say any more. "If anyone discovers we have these items, we will say we took them without your permission."

Emil nodded gratefully. "The Wolf Leader has gone to a meeting with a group of his followers on the other side of the island. He is not due back for several hours." As he was about to leave, he turned back. "Good luck."

"Thank you." Violet felt the mood shift and become unexpectedly solemn, almost as if Emil was about to take an oath in their honor. "We will always remember your loyalty."

Emil nodded as though her words satisfied a need within him, and left.

Nate handed her the flashlight. "Ready?"

In response, Violet pulled the hood of her waterproof jacket up over her hair. "Let's do this." As she said the words, she realized her nervousness was gone. In its place was anticipation. Finally, she might get some answers, not just to the missing pieces of her lost memory, but to the mystery of who she really was.

Although it took only minutes to reach the icehouse,

the weather was conspiring to drive them back. Thunder crashed overhead with such violence it shook the ground beneath their feet, and lightning lit the sky with the same pyrotechnic creativity as the wildest of Beast's concerts. The driving rain churned the pretty gardens and green fields to mud and drove into their faces with gleeful fury until they were blinded by its force.

When they reached the icehouse, Violet held the flashlight so Nate could use the bolt cutter on the padlock. He fumbled several times in the icy onslaught but finally managed to cut the lock loose. When he cast it aside and tucked the bolt cutter into the waistband of his jeans, the ancient wooden doors swung inward with a protesting groan that could be heard even above the fury of the elements.

Violet stared into the gaping blackness as her heartbeat pounded out a warning. The scent rising from within was of mold and age. It held a hint of rotten fruit and crushed rose petals, but there was something more, something feral lurking beneath the musty, damp-air smell. It was the stench of secrets.

"Be careful." Nate raised his voice above the howling wind. He took the flashlight from her and directed the beam onto the icehouse steps. "It's wet and mossy down there."

They left the storm-drenched grounds and entered the icehouse. Quiet descended, shutting out the sound of the storm and causing Violet to cast a longing look over her shoulder. The known or the unknown? The fury of the raging tempest outside, or the unearthly silence of the descent into the darkness ahead of them? Before she could answer her own question, Nate had set his foot on the first step.

Using his right hand to guide him along the jagged wall, he held the flashlight out in front of him with his left. Beneath their feet the rocky steps were uneven and slimy.

Water ran down the walls and dripped onto their heads. From below a faint scurrying sound signaled a sign of life, although Violet doubted it was the source of the secret they sought. Her sensitive ears told her the icehouse was likely to be home to numerous rodents as well as any mysteries Nevan might be hiding.

Their descent was slow. Several times, Violet felt her feet begin to slide on the treacherous surface of the steps. Each time, she just managed to right herself and stay upright. When they reached the bottom, Nate shined his flashlight around. They were in a low-ceilinged, circular room. The rocky walls of this chamber were green with slime. Violet guessed that this must have been where the ice was stored. The chill that seeped through her skin and into her bones seemed to confirm it.

"Look." Nate's voice had an eerie echo as he pointed.

There was an archway in the wall opposite. When they made their way through it, they found themselves in a narrow tunnel. Nate made his way cautiously along it, staying just ahead of Violet. In parts, the roof was so low he had to duck his head. It twisted and turned, sometimes leading them down, now and then appearing to take them up. At one point, Violet stumbled on the slimy slabs, falling onto one knee and crying out.

Nate turned to her, catching hold of her by her upper arm and hauling her to her feet. "Are you hurt?"

"No." Her shaky laugh echoed off the walls of the tunnel. "I shouted because I thought I was going to land flat on my face."

"Who is there?" They both froze as a woman's voice, faint but unmistakable, called out to them.

The sound had come from farther along the tunnel, in the direction they had been moving. A crawling sense of anticipation tracked up and down Violet's spine as they continued on their way.

"Is that you, Dario?" The voice was closer now. "Have you brought the medicine I asked for at last?"

The tunnel twisted sharply to the left, then, in the beam thrown out by the flashlight, Violet saw it widen. Hurrying now, they reached a point where the tunnel they were in crossed another, forming a T shape. The second tunnel was wider and higher. Along one wall a series of lanterns was strung at shoulder height, giving off a soft, golden glow. They stepped into this tunnel, and Violet drew in a shocked breath as she recognized what its function was. Along the opposite side of the lanterns the space was divided into a series of small cells, each of which had iron bars across the front. They were in a prison. This must be the place where Roko had been held captive during his imprisonment.

A woman stood up against the bars of one cell, gripping them with her hands. When she saw Nate and Violet, she gave a startled cry and lifted one hand to cover her mouth. Violet felt the impact of the other woman's shock ricochet through her own body. Putting back the hood of her waterproof jacket, she stepped up to the cell.

Tears filled her eyes as she held out a hand. "Mother?"

Chapter 21

If Nate had passed Dorotea on a crowded street, he'd have known she was Violet's mother. The likeness between the two women was remarkable. Apart from her dark brown eyes and the touch of gray in the hair at her temples, she might have been Violet's sister.

When Violet pushed back the hood of her jacket and stepped forward to take her mother's hand, Dorotea initially appeared frozen in place. She gazed at Violet as though she believed she might be hallucinating. Then huge, swollen tears began to roll down her cheeks as her whole body began to shake.

"Violetta. My child." She grasped Violet's hands through the bars, smothering them with kisses. "He told me you were dead."

As the impact of what she was saying hit home, Nate felt his hatred toward Nevan ratchet up even further. How could such evil exist? The Wolf Leader had kept his wife locked up beneath the floor of his family home for all these years. And for what? Her crime—her lapse—had been to fall in love with another man. For that Nevan had deprived Violet of a mother's love and Dorotea of her daughter's life…and of any life of her own. Of all the reasons Nate had to loathe and despise the werewolf leader, this new discovery about the depths of his villainy had just rocketed up to the top of the list.

As the two women did their best to embrace through the bars of the cell, Nate drew the bolt cutter from the waistband of his jeans. He wasn't sure how much use the tool would be. These iron rods were more substantial than the padlock that had secured the icehouse door, but he got to work anyway, levering the cutting edge of the tool against one of the rails.

Dorotea, catching sight of what he was doing, cast a scared glance along the tunnel in the opposite direction from that from which Nate and Violet had come. "You must go. He will be here very soon."

"Who will?" Violet asked.

"Dario." Dorotea's voice held both fear and revulsion as she said the name. "He is the one who guards us."

Nate paused in his task. As he feared, the bolt cutter had barely scratched the bar. "Us?"

Dorotea pointed to the cell next to hers. "Bartol is your brother," she told Violet, her eyes filling with fresh tears. "Ever since Nevan imprisoned him here, his health has been declining. Now I fear he may be dying. I have told Dario he needs medicine or professional care, but he refuses to do anything."

Nate placed an arm around Violet as she stepped to one side to view the pitiful figure lying on the narrow bunk inside the next cell. Slumped under a blanket, Bartol appeared to be unconscious.

Although Nate knew that time was not the same concept here in Otherworld that it was in the mortal realm, if Dorotea had been imprisoned since the discovery of her infidelity, she had been here since around Violet's birth. Even without an accurate measurement of time, that was a lengthy captivity.

"Do you remember Bartol?" he asked Violet.

"Only vaguely. The last time I saw him, I was a very young child." From those words, Nate surmised that Bartol's imprisonment must also have been a long one. "Nevan told me he had banished Bartol." Violet's shoulders shook as she spoke. "I remember now that when I refused to stop helping the refugees, he threatened to exile me the same way he had done to my brother. I thought he meant he would send me away. But it was this. This is his idea of banishment."

"Bartol found out I was imprisoned here, and he tried to free me. Nevan discovered his intention before Bartol could release me." Dorotea covered her face with her hands. "I will never forget the look on Nevan's face, or the hateful sound of his laughter. He said if Bartol was so fond of me, we could spend all eternity together. Nevan had Dario beat him and throw him into the next cell." Her voice grew stronger. "You must leave here before they do the same to you."

"It is too late for that." A mocking voice came from the shadowy part of the tunnel beyond Nate's view. Dario limped into view, a smug smile twisting his lips. "But I did enjoy the touching family reunion."

Nate stepped forward, blocking Dario's access to Violet. "I beat you once, man against wolf. What makes you think the rematch will be different?"

"Because you don't have your friends with you this

time—" Dario's smile deepened and became nastier "—but I do."

Nevan stepped out of the gloom to stand alongside Dario. Ranged behind him were the other four men who had accompanied Dario to Vermont, Marseilles and Barcelona. The men who had shifted to become huge, destructive werewolves.

This wasn't going to end well, but Nate decided he was going down fighting. Swinging the bolt cutter with both hands, he caught Dario a crushing blow across the side of the head with the heavy metal tool. A look of surprise crossed the other man's face, and blood splattered Nate's hands before Dario hit the floor in a crumpled heap. It was the cue for the other men to attack. Shifting into werewolf form, they circled Nate with bared teeth and pinned-back ears.

"The leader of the Alliance warned you not to hurt him." Violet's voice, high-pitched and panicky, echoed off the tunnel walls. "Merlin Caledonius will not tolerate it if you harm his friend."

Nevan spat out a curse. "She is right. That half-breed sorcerer has guaranteed his pet mortal will be protected throughout his time in Otherworld. Capture him, but leave him unharmed."

Snarling their disappointment, the werewolves shifted back. Determined not to give in without a fight, Nate lashed out left and right with the bolt cutter, even managing to open the tool and inflict damage on his opponents by slicing into their hands as they tried to grab him. Howls and profanities filled the air.

"Take that fucking weapon off him." Nevan's furious shout rose about the sounds of the fight. "He is only a mortal."

Eventually, the four men cornered Nate and overpowered him, pinning him to the floor with his wrists behind his back. Nevan stepped up close to him, a smile that didn't reach his eyes just touching the corners of his lips. "Since your sorcerer friend is so fond of you, I will be happy to return you to him. Always supposing you survive the journey, of course. I can't be held responsible for any accidents that may befall the boat that carries you, can I?"

Nate jerked against the strong arms that held him, but it was useless. "I don't care what you do to me, as long as you let Violet go."

Nevan laughed, a harsh, unpleasant sound. "You speak as though she means something to me. She never did. The daughter of my worst enemy and his whore? Why should I care about her?" He turned to Dario, who had regained consciousness and was staggering to his feet. "Put the girl in the cell next to her mother." He laughed again. "Quite the family gathering we have down here now."

As he was pulled along the tunnel away from the cells, Nate dragged his feet, turning his head frantically in an attempt to look over his shoulder. "I'll come back for you, Violet. Somehow, I'll get back here and free you."

"I wouldn't get your hopes up too high," Nevan said. "I really don't think you will."

Nate caused Nevan's beta werewolves so many problems that, in the end, they tied him up before dumping him on the deck of the boat on which he and Violet had traveled with Nevan from the Faerie Isles. As he flailed wildly in their grasp, landing punches and kicks indiscriminately, he sensed the restraint it was taking them to follow Nevan's orders and keep from beating him senseless.

Good. I hope the stress gives one of you a fucking coronary.

When, after about half an hour, they eventually had him

under control, Dario, one side of his face a bloody mess, opened the cover on the engine and ripped out a handful of wires. Kneeling on the deck, he held the tangled mass close to Nate's face with a grin. "Let's see how far you get without these."

Nate didn't have a clear view of what was going on around him, but he saw Nevan shove Emil onto the boat.

"Start it up," the Wolf Leader growled at the young werewolf.

Emil licked his lips and, with shaking hands, started the engine. His expression became even more fearful when he heard the groaning and clunking noises it made. "There is something wrong with it."

Dario laughed and threw the wires he had torn out into the water. "You don't say."

Nevan and his beta werewolves stepped onto the harbor wall. "If the engine doesn't work, you'll have to use the sails."

"We'll never make it to the Faerie Isles under sail," Emil said. "Some of the waters we have to pass through are treacherous even in calm weather. Today there is another storm brewing."

"At least you can say you died trying." Their laughter combined with the chugging sound of the engine as the boat began to move.

The vessel limped out of the bay in a cloud of gray smoke that streamed from the engine. Although Nate was no sailor, he could tell by the screeching noises that there was something very wrong. It was also evident from the pitch and roll of the boat that the sea, even in the sheltered harbor, was choppy. Once they were out of sight of land and he was sure they could no longer be seen by Nevan, Emil shut the engine off and untied Nate.

Nate rubbed his cramped wrists and ankles. "Is there

anything you can do to fix the engine?" Even as he asked the question, he knew it was futile.

Emil slumped onto the wooden boards of the deck in an attitude of defeat. "It's damaged beyond repair."

"Why did Nevan involve you in this?" Nate asked. "Did he find out you had helped us?"

Emil shook his head. "I don't think so. He remembered that it was my lady who got me the job. He said he wanted no more reminders of her in his house."

The words struck fear into Nate's heart. Could he rely on Nevan keeping Violet alive, even as a captive? He had to act, and do it fast. But how? The sea was whipping up into a frenzy. The boat was already being tossed around like a toy on white-tipped waves, while darkening clouds threatened worse weather to come. "So we need to use the sails?"

Emil gave him a pitying look. "I already explained we will never make it to the Faerie Isles under sail."

"I'm not suggesting we try." Nate rose and reached down a hand and pulled the young werewolf to his feet. "We only need to go as far as Reznati."

"Reznati?" Emil was blinking at him in wonder.

"Have I got the name wrong? The island where the resistance is based? I need to find Roko."

Emil nodded slowly, his expression changing to one of fascinated wonder. "That is Reznati."

Nate viewed the sky. "I saw it on a map once, and it didn't appear too far away, but these conditions don't look good. Can you take us there?"

Without warning, Emil erupted into action. "We need to start the engine back up briefly so we can keep the boat facing into the wind as we hoist the sail. You will have to take the wheel while I hoist the sails." The switch from frightened boy to experienced sailor within seconds was astounding, but Nate wasn't complaining.

Holding the boat steady against the heaving waves and blustering wind was no easy task. Nate's muscles were soon aching as he battled the wheel, conscious as he did so of Emil struggling to get the mainsail in place. Once that was done, Nate could see him raising a smaller, triangular sail. Something in the recesses of his memory told him it was called a jib. Since he had no idea about sailing, he was glad to be traveling with someone who knew what he was doing.

His mind insisted on returning to Violet trapped in that cell, and he forced himself to focus. He could be of use to her only if he kept going and didn't stop to think. Allowing his mind to freeze while negative thoughts of fear, anger and revenge took over wasn't helpful. Those feelings hadn't gone away, but he would deal with them later, when Violet was safe. Because he had to make sure Violet *was* safe. Anything else was unthinkable. He would do all he could to make it so. Sail on a damaged boat in a looming storm. Seek out Roko, a man who hated him, and place his life in the hands of the resistance and ask for their help. Return to Urlati, and deal with Nevan...even if it meant breaking his vow and killing the bastard. If the truth was told, turning his back on a promise and killing Nevan was looking very tempting right now. It was about the only thing keeping him from tipping back his head and howling at the churning sky.

And if that is yet more confirmation that I'm a wolf in human clothing...well, I'll take that.

Once Emil got the sails in place, he returned to shut down the beleaguered engine. Nate was happy to be relegated to the position of first mate, following the younger man's instructions as the boat took off, climbing the waves, reaching the crests and swooping down the other sides. From then on, they were on a constant roller-coaster ride. Foam sprayed around them, limiting visibility, while water poured over the deck, threatening to sweep them off their feet. The constant plunging-and-jerking movement was disorienting, and keeping the boat on course while the elements attempted to throw it around was exhausting.

Although the journey should have been a short one, they were blown wildly off course and had to keep fighting to get back on track. Nate had no idea how many hours later it was when they finally sailed into the harbor at Reznati. He had reached the stage of fatigue where he was aware of what was going on around him, but his body was stretched so tight with weariness that his whole focus was on remaining upright. The journey had drained every ounce of his energy, yet somewhere at the back of his tired mind a tiny hint of exhilaration was starting to flicker into life.

They had done it. Against all the odds, they had made it to land. Now all he had to do was persuade Roko to help him instead of killing him.

Although she and Dorotea couldn't see each other in their side-by-side cells, if they sat with their backs against the bars and slid their hands outside, they could just touch fingertips. They sat that way for hours. Even though it was impossible to judge the time of day in the depths of the tunnel, Violet knew night had fallen. Her wolf, so recently rediscovered, told her it was so by surging against the constraints of her mortal body, demanding release.

She had a horrible feeling that Bartol was suffering from the same debilitating illness that had struck her in the mortal realm. Perhaps his own wolf, trapped by these confining walls, was unable to find release and was dying, taking his human self along with it. But, if that was the case, why did Dorotea appear healthy?

"I wondered about that," Dorotea said when Violet explained her theory to her. "I am older than you and Bartol, and my inner wolf is not as active. When I shift, I do not require as much exercise. I still shift regularly in this small cell, and I do find it restrictive, but it keeps my werewolf satisfied. It wasn't enough for Bartol."

Violet conceded that it was a possibility. If so, it didn't bode well for her future. She had recovered so recently from her illness that she was sure a stay of any length in this cell would cause her to quickly relapse. There was no point mentioning that to her mother. Having one child wasting away down here was bad enough. She didn't need to contemplate the prospect of it happening to a second.

"The man who was with you… I could tell he loves you very much."

"His name is Nate." Violet's breath hitched. "We love each other."

"He said he would come back for you."

Violet summoned up the image of Nate's face as Nevan's beta wolves dragged him away. The anguish and determination on his beloved features would be forever imprinted on her mind. "It isn't that easy," she explained. "His survival in Otherworld is fragile now that he is away from his friend Cal. He is a mortal."

"I don't understand." Violet could hear the confusion in Dorotea's voice. "He *felt* like a werewolf."

"It's a long story." She told her mother all of it. From the feral werewolf attack to their arrival in the Wolf Nation. "Nate isn't a werewolf, but he is my mate."

"He sounds like a fine man. I wish I could have spent time getting to know him." Violet didn't like the finality her mother's words hinted at. "There was another man imprisoned here for a short time. His name was Roko. He spoke of you with great fondness, too."

The mention of Roko's name triggered something that had been bothering Violet. "How did he manage to escape, yet he left you and Bartol here?"

"I don't know how it happened. He was here one day and gone the next, which makes me wonder if he may have bribed Dario." It sounded like Dorotea had given the matter some thought. "There is no other way out of these cells. Believe me, I have tried everything over the years."

"Roko said you swore him to secrecy."

"I knew he was determined to leave here and take up arms against Nevan. I thought if he used my story to drum up support for the resistance, it would damage my family. I didn't know you were alive, of course, but I thought of the gossip that would ensue and how it would affect my other children." There was a note of pride in Dorotea's voice. "And I didn't want to be the woman whose infidelity was the cause of a civil war. Anwyl and I fell in love. We didn't plan it, and we didn't intend to hurt anyone, least of all Nevan. I won't have our love for each other used to promote someone else's ideals."

Violet didn't want to hurt her mother by telling her then that her infidelity *had* been the cause of a civil war. One so long and violent it had torn the Wolf Nation apart. If Dorotea ever got out of her prison, she would have to know the truth, but for now she may as well remain in ignorance.

"Tell me about Anwyl." Violet had never been close to Nevan. She couldn't help wondering how her life might have been if she had known the man who was really her father.

Dorotea's voice softened. "My life with Nevan wasn't happy. Oh, there were happy moments within it. My greatest pleasure was my children, and, although Nevan could be demanding, I never saw his cruel streak until later in our marriage."

"So until your affair with Anwyl, he had no thoughts of rebellion?" Violet had only ever known Nevan as the angry, driven man who, throughout her life, had wanted to destroy Anwyl and to take over as Wolf Leader.

"No. We were an ordinary family. Nevan was success-ful and we had a comfortable life, but when I met Anwyl my whole life changed. For the first time, I knew what love was." Violet thought of her own feelings toward Nate and understood exactly what her mother meant. "When Nevan found out, he was wild with rage."

"How did he find out?"

"When I discovered I was pregnant with you, I knew you were Anwyl's child. I told Nevan the truth. He waited until you were born and then locked me up down here. He took great delight in telling me that the whole world, including Anwyl, thought I had died from the complica-tions of childbirth."

"Weren't you able to get word to Anwyl during your pregnancy? Couldn't the two of you have gone away to-gether?"

"He was away in the mortal realm dealing with prob-lems there throughout that time. He left just before I found out I was pregnant and I never saw him again. But, even if he had known, he would have faced a difficult choice. He, too, was married with children of his own."

"So through all the years he and Nevan were fighting, Anwyl never knew you were alive." Violet shook her head at the tragedy of the story. Nevan had kept three people who should have known and loved each other apart all those years. Four people, if Bartol was included. Through his anger and selfishness, her family had been deprived of so much.

"Dario told me Anwyl had been killed when Nevan took over as Wolf Leader. Is that true, or was he lying to torture me?" There was a note of hope in Dorotea's voice and it broke Violet's heart to be forced to quash it.

"I'm sorry, but it's true."

Dorotea grew upset and Violet did her best to comfort her, even though this relationship was so new to them both and they were only just learning how to know each other. After a while her mother became tired and bade Violet good-night. By the light of the wall lanterns, Violet could see the narrow bunk in her cell and a metal bucket in the corner. She grimaced. It was no good. Nature was calling, and she was forced to use the bucket to empty her bladder. There was a bowl of water in the other corner, and she splashed her face. Practical notions occupied her mind as she removed her sneakers, jeans and sweatshirt in preparation to try to get some sleep. Dorotea had appeared clean, so there must be some way to do more than just wash her hands and face, and her mother's clothing wasn't worn, so somewhere along the way she must have been provided with new items.

She lay down on the bunk clad only in a T-shirt and her underwear and closed her eyes. Sleep refused to come. Her memory had returned in full now, and thoughts of her strange, loveless childhood occupied her mind. She wondered now if one of the reasons why her memory had taken so long to return was that there wasn't anything she *wanted* to remember. She knew now it was because she had received more affection and warmth from the refugees on Vukod than she ever had from the man who had called himself her father. Perhaps subconsciously, her mind had been busy trying to create new memories with Nate because, for the first time in her life, she had found love and happiness.

Her thoughts were interrupted by the sound of a key grating in the lock. She looked up in surprise as Dario entered the cell, locking the door behind him and leaning his broad shoulders against the bars. Her heart sank as she read his intention in his eyes.

"It will be nice to sink into fresh, young flesh for a change." His gaze made her skin crawl as it wandered over her body. "Your mother is a good-looking woman, but she grew tired of fighting me years ago. I feel sure you will provide me with more of a challenge."

"You bastard." Violet slid off the bed and backed up toward the rear of the cell, the implication of his words hitting her. "You have been abusing my mother and now you want to boast about it?"

He followed her. "No. Now I want to do the same to you."

With her back to the wall, Violet had nowhere to go. As Dario loomed over her, she focused on not letting this happen without a fight. Ducking under his arm, she grabbed the metal bucket and hurled it at him, flinging the contents in his face. He howled with rage, rubbing his eyes and lunging for her. Violet brought her foot up between his legs. He grunted out a curse and went down on his knees, clutching his groin with both hands. Violet shifted and sprang on top of him, forcing him onto his back and holding him there as she sank her talons into his chest.

She had never killed a mortal or another wolf, but she didn't hesitate now. She didn't dare give Dario time to shift. As soon as her canines lengthened, she struck without hesitation, tearing deep into the flesh of his throat. The warm, coppery flavor of his blood filled her mouth, dripping onto the fur of her chest as the man beneath her struggled and thrashed. Violet shook her head back and forth repeatedly until she heard the final telltale crack of Dario's neck breaking.

Chapter 22

"I have no problem with a plan to rescue Violet. Just explain to me again why I need to include you. Why shouldn't I just do away with the opposition and kill you now?" Roko asked.

"Because you are a decent—" Nate paused. What was the right phrase? *Human being?* But he wasn't. *Werewolf?* Right now he wasn't in wolf form. "—person. I'm not your enemy. Nevan is. We're on the same side here."

"We might be on the same side, but a mortal would slow the mission down." At least the resistance leader was no longer talking about killing him.

"Take me as bait. I'll deflect Nevan's attention away from the real operation while you rescue Violet and her mother and brother."

Nate realized he was starting to sound desperate. *I don't care. I am desperate.* He would get down on his hands and knees and beg Roko if that was what it took to get the other man to do as he asked. He was prepared to do anything to get Violet out of that cell.

They were in a house that was a smaller version of the Voda Kuca. Nate was slowly realizing that werewolves were not very imaginative. They were loyal and reliable, fiercely devoted to their mates, their pack and a cause in which they believed, but creativity wasn't their strong-point. During his brief time in the Wolf Nation, he'd seen that caution applied to the way they dressed, their homes and, to an extent, the way they thought. Werewolves had an architectural style that worked, and they stuck to it. Nate, who was highly artistic, found it strange.

Roko was unusual in that he was prepared to deviate from the tried-and-tested werewolf rules of engagement. It was why Nevan found him a frustrating opponent and one of the reasons the resistance was winning the latest round of skirmishes. He considered Nate's suggestion with interest.

"You think you can distract Nevan long enough for me and a group of my men to get into the Voda Kuca?"

"I'm prepared to give it my best shot." Nate felt a glimmer of hope as Roko's expression switched from speculative to conniving. He decided to push further. "As long as we leave right now."

Roko started to laugh. "For someone who is at a complete disadvantage, you are very demanding."

Nate waited, forcing himself to resist the urge to keep up the pressure. He could see Roko was tempted. He knew the other man would not easily pass up the opportunity to get inside the Voda Kuca and face his enemy. Right at that moment, Nate wasn't interested in Roko's ambitions or emotions. *Get me back to Urlati, back to Violet.* That was all he cared about. Later? Once she was safe, he would help clean up any mess the resistance's actions left behind.

"Okay." Roko nodded decisively. He signaled to his second-in-command. "Teo, get the boats ready. We are going to pay Nevan a little visit."

There was a flurry of action, during which Nate turned to Emil. "You do not have to be part of this. This is not your fight. Stay here on Reznati."

Emil looked hurt. "Nevan made it my fight. And this is for my lady. Of course I wish to be part of it."

Nate dropped a hand onto the young werewolf's shoulder. "I should have known you would."

As they made their way to the harbor, Nate was relieved to see that the skies had cleared and the wind had dropped. Although he'd have willingly undertaken another white-knuckle ocean crossing, he was glad he didn't have to.

There were about twenty resistance fighters manning five small sailboats. Nate and Emil joined Roko in the first of these. As they sailed out of the harbor, Nate was aware of Roko studying him with curiosity. He turned to face the other man. "Go on. Ask the question that is burning you up inside."

Roko shrugged. "None of my business."

"Please yourself." Nate started to turn away.

"Okay." The word burst from Roko's lips. "What happens next? You can't stay in Otherworld, so what becomes of the great love affair?"

"It ends." He had said those words often enough inside his head, but saying them out loud burned his throat.

"How can you do that?" Roko shook his head. "If you love her, how can you just walk away from her?"

Nate had been over and over this so many times it hurt his head to think of it. "I don't have a choice."

"Why the hell not?" Roko's face expressed amazement. "I may have seen you as a rival at first, but I've moved on from that now. I can see she never loved me, but if she had,

I'd have done anything to keep her. She does love you. I don't understand why she would choose a mortal, but even more than that I don't understand you. What sort of sick human pride would keep you from accepting the chance of a future with her?"

Something within Nate faltered at the words. Roko seemed to be saying there was a way forward. A chance at a future for him and Violet. Nate believed he had thought of everything. Considered all the options. Had he closed his mind to something blindingly obvious? When Roko spoke of his human pride, it hinted at one thing.

Nate had been bitten by a werewolf once. It had been a life-changing experience, resulting in the worst time of his life. Had he deliberately shut out the possibility of letting Violet bite him because of that? He almost laughed out loud. She was his mate. His *life*. Without her he was nothing. He was a werewolf in everything except name. The prospect of Violet sinking her canines into him during sex didn't scare or repulse him. It filled him with wild, shuddering excitement…

He staggered as the boat bumped against the harbor wall. Roko's voice interrupted his thoughts. "We are here."

"Violet?" Disturbed by the noise, Dorotea sounded nervous. "Are you all right?"

"I'm fine. Don't worry." Violet tried to keep the wobble out of her voice. It was difficult when she was trembling all over.

She had shifted back once she was sure Dario was dead. Now she eased to her feet and stood over him, running a shaky hand over her mouth. The taste of blood was thick and bitter in her mouth, and she spat it onto the floor of the cell. *I'm a werewolf. Since when did I become squeamish about blood? That would be around the time I first killed a man*. Violet had never seen herself as a killer, but she couldn't regret his death, not after what she had learned about his abuse of her mother, and his deliberate cruelty toward her and Bartol.

Stripping off the tattered and bloodied remnants of her T-shirt, she used the water in the bowl to clean the blood from her face and chest. Feeling calmer, she slid her sweatshirt, jeans and sneakers back on. Dario had left the keys in the cell door, and she stepped around his body to unlock it.

The door swung open, and Violet breathed a deep sigh of relief. It was only the first step on the road to escape, but it felt good. The key to her cell was on a ring with several others, all of which looked the same. She guessed they opened the doors to the other cells.

Dorotea's eyes widened in amazement when Violet approached her with the keys in her hand. "How did you get out?"

"Dario tried to attack me."

As Violet fumbled with several different keys and eventually found the one to unlock the cell door, Dorotea wrung her hands. "I should have warned you about him. He is an evil man."

Violet gave her a brief hug before drawing her through the open door. "He won't ever bother you again."

Dorotea was almost hesitant as she stepped from her cell into the tunnel. Violet supposed that was what decades of captivity would do to someone. Her mother had become institutionalized, conditioned to view life in that cramped room as normality.

Despite the need for haste, Violet gazed at Dorotea in astonishment. Waves of emotion rippled through her as she drank in the features that were so like her own. The features of a woman she had believed was dead. Shock didn't come close to explaining how it felt to know she was alive.

I have a mother. It was a wonderful feeling, but the warmth those words brought were wrapped up in sadness at all the things they had lost. All the first times, the confidences, the everyday things they would never get to share.

No matter what came next for them, the catching up, the ways they would find to develop closeness—and Violet had no doubt that, if they got out of this, they *would* find a way—their future would always be tainted by the separation they had endured. It was another reason to resent the way Nevan had reacted to his wife's infidelity.

Dorotea's eyes widened in alarm as she glimpsed Dario's body on the floor of Violet's cell. She gave a fearful little moan. "What now?"

"Now we get away." Violet kept her voice brisk and determined, injecting it with a confidence she wasn't sure she felt.

"Nevan will never let us escape."

Those words gave Violet the boost she needed. "Let him try to stop us."

"What about Bartol?" Dorotea moved to stand beside her son's cell. Gripping the bars, she pressed her face up against them, her expression despairing.

Violet paused. It was a good question. They couldn't leave Bartol here to die or to be the subject of Nevan's revenge. He would slow them down, but there was no choice. "Bartol comes with us."

She unlocked the door of her brother's cell. Between them, the two women hoisted Bartol's pitifully thin figure to his feet. By draping his arms around their shoulders and placing one of their own arms each around his waist, they were able to drag him along between them. It would be a slow process, but the three of them would be just about able to move along the tunnel that way.

"We have to go the way Nate and I came," Violet said.

"Toward the icehouse. If we go in the other direction, we will end up in the Voda Kuca and risk encountering Nevan."

When Nate had fought Dario and the other beta werewolves in the tunnel, he had dropped the flashlight. It had rolled and lay abandoned now against the tunnel wall. Violet stooped to pick it up, hoping it was undamaged. Luckily it was, and holding it in front of her with her free hand, she lit their way as, supporting the unconscious Bartol between them, they made cautious progress along the rocky corridor.

By the time they reached the circular storage chamber, Violet's shoulders felt like they were on fire. Sweat was rolling off her body and running down her face, and she was breathing harder than after her longest run. Reminding herself that she had just recovered from a life-threatening illness, she paused.

"Let's take a rest."

Dorotea seemed glad of the suggestion. She, too, was panting from her exertions. They carefully propped Bartol in a seated position against one of the walls. His head flopped onto his chest and, even by the limited light thrown out by the flashlight, Violet could see that he was deathly pale. She didn't want to worry Dorotea, but she hoped their efforts hadn't been in vain. Her fear was that Bartol might not survive their attempt to get him to freedom.

Violet and Dorotea sat on either side of him, instinctively supporting him and attempting to comfort him with their presence. As soon as she had time to think, Violet's thoughts swerved in Nate's direction. Where was he? Was he injured? Was he still alive? He had to be. The idea of a world without Nate in it was unbearable. Even if she never saw him again, she had to believe he was okay. She had to be able to picture him in the mortal realm, playing his guitar, refereeing squabbles between Khan and Diablo, thinking of her as she would be thinking of him, wishing their story could have had a different ending.

Nevan had implied he would stage an accident during Nate's return to the Faerie Isles, but Nate was here in Otherworld under Cal's protection. Violet had to place her trust in Cal. And in Nate. He was a survivor. A slight smile touched her lips as she pictured how his biography would look. Now *that* would be a celebrity story worth telling. Somehow she doubted Ged would allow the true story of Beast and its individual members to be told. The fans would only ever get to hear the sanitized version.

One day, perhaps, she would have the courage to ask Cal how it turned out for Nate. She knew she would never hear that he had moved on and found someone else. They were bound together for life. Just because they couldn't be together physically, it didn't mean they would move on and find other partners. Love like theirs didn't work that way. But she liked to think that in the future she would be strong enough to ask how he was doing without her heart splintering into a thousand pieces. One day.

When her breathing had returned to normal, she stood. "We should get Bartol into the fresh air."

Navigating those narrow, slippery steps wasn't going to be easy. In the end, Violet went up the stairs backward, supporting Bartol under his arms while Dorotea took his feet. They had to pause on each step while Violet found a secure footing, but, after long, agonizing minutes, they eventually surfaced through the icehouse doors and onto the field.

Violet had known all along that her only plan was to get this far. Now she had to think of a way to get them past the Voda Kuca and down to the harbor. The only way she could think of getting to safety was to get into a boat and to get away from Urlati. It wasn't fully formed, but maybe if she could get them to Vukod, Marko might be able to help Bartol. It was all she had right now, and it was better than waiting around until Nevan found them.

From where she stood, she could see the Voda Kuca in the moonlight. It should be still and silent. Although the occupants of the house were werewolves and would be drawn to the moonlight, that time of night when they would shift for pleasure was gone. Dawn was approaching. Yet something was going on at the house.

Dorotea followed her gaze. "What is happening?"

In the shifting shadows cast by the clouds obscuring the moon, Violet could just make out a group of figures stealthily approaching the rear of the house. "I'm not sure."

"Your dashing hero has decided to stage a rescue." Nevan's voice behind her startled a cry from Violet as she swung around to face him. "I think we should go and let him know he's too late, don't you?"

The plan was simple. Nate would walk in through the front door of the Voda Kuca and challenge Nevan to a fight. Meanwhile, Roko and his resistance fighters would sneak around to the rear and stage a surprise attack before the beta werewolves had time to figure out what was happening.

It was a straightforward operation, one that relied on a basic component. For it to work, Nevan had to be in the Voda Kuca when Nate got there.

When Nate walked back into the Voda Kuca, heart racing, breath coming in short, fast pants, primed and ready for the looming confrontation, the house was empty. He felt it as soon as he walked through the door. Silence greeted him. The lights were on—all of them—but no one was home. It was a cliché that summed up the way his brain was refusing to process what he was seeing.

A sense of powerlessness overwhelmed him. To have reached this point, to have everything in place, and to find his chance at saving Violet snatched away... *No.* He took a huge breath. *Think. Nevan couldn't have known we were coming. Something must have happened.*

As he tried to make sense of what was happening, a sound from the doorway behind him made him turn with a sense of dread. Nevan, his hand encircling Violet's upper arm, shoved her over the doorstep in front of him. Behind him a group of beta werewolves, larger than any Nate had seen before, followed. One of them dragged Dorotea with him, while another carried Bartol's unconscious form.

"Looking for someone?" Nevan snarled.

Violet's eyes flew to Nate's face, and despite the circumstances, he saw the flare of joy that lit them. It matched his own.

"I remember everything about my life now," she called out to him. "And I would like to forget it all, Nate. Everything...except you."

When they had dragged him away from her in that tunnel and Nate had sworn to come back, a part of him had feared it might never happen. Even when he had been fighting to make it so, had taken that fucking awful sailboat ride to hell, had gone prepared to beg and plead with Roko, somewhere deep inside, there had been a feeling of dread, a horrible, clawing notion that their time together was up.

Maybe that was how it had been meant to be. Maybe being back here now defied all the odds. All he knew was this was their second chance, and they were taking it. Seizing it with both hands and clinging to it for all they were worth. It didn't matter how many beta werewolves Nevan had lined up behind him, how the odds stacked against them. This time they were walking out of this together. He and Violet, hand in hand. For good. Or he would die trying.

"Yes. I was looking for you." He stepped forward to face Nevan. "Are you going to hide behind two women and a sick man or fight me face-to-face?"

The growl that left Nevan's throat told Nate his words had touched a nerve. *Good.* Flinging Violet from him, Nevan covered the distance between them, his lips drawing back to show his teeth. Nate tensed, preparing for the other man to shift.

Before anything happened, Dorotea's gentle voice reached their ears. "Our son is dying, Nevan."

Something flickered in the depths of Nevan's eyes. Briefly, Nate caught a glimpse of the man the Wolf Leader had once been. He saw decency, love and dignity. He saw the pain of loss. The man Nevan had been before his wife's betrayal destroyed him. Then the shutters came down again.

"You did this to him." Nevan threw the words at Dorotea without looking at her.

"Don't let Bartol die because of your hatred for me." Dorotea's voice was soft and persuasive. "Remember how delighted we were when he was born?"

"Get her out of here." Nevan snapped the words over his shoulder at his beta werewolves, but Nate could tell he was shaken.

When Nevan shifted, Nate was prepared for the fight of his life. As Nevan in wolf form circled him, he crouched low, finding the wolf instincts inside himself. He recalled his fight against Dario. Lethal teeth and claws were his enemy's strength. He had to do all he could to keep them from slashing into the vulnerable parts of his body.

As Nevan lunged, Nate grabbed the huge werewolf by

the throat. Nevan had the advantage of speed and strength, and he forced Nate down onto his back. It took every ounce of strength Nate had in his arms to maintain his hold on the snarling werewolf. Nevan's jaws snapped inches from his face. Nate smelled his fetid breath and read triumph in the golden depths of the werewolf's eyes. Teeth and claws. He didn't have the same weapons as Nevan, but he had the element of surprise. Using every reserve of energy he had, he scrambled out from under Nevan, reversing their positions and pinning him facedown under him. Avoiding the snapping jaws, he grabbed one of Nevan's ears and sank his teeth into fur and gristle.

His mortal rebelled at the idea of fighting this way, but the wolf within him took over. Shaking his head back and forth, he tore into the tender flesh while holding his opponent down. Nevan howled with unbridled fury and bucked beneath him. Nate knew he wasn't going to be able to hold him for long. Sweet, coppery blood filled his mouth and his teeth ripped through the flesh of Nevan's ear with a snapping sound as if he was biting into a carrot. When he let go, he spat a chunk of Nevan's ear onto the floor.

Fuck. All I've done is enrage him further.

Nate braced himself for the next onslaught. Before Nevan could hurl himself on him, there was a flurry of activity from the rear of the house as Roko and his resistance fighters burst in through the back door. And that was when all hell broke loose.

The hall of the Voda Kuca resembled a war zone as Nevan's black beta werewolves launched themselves at the resistance fighters. Roko gave the order for his followers to shift, and carnage ensued. Clawing, biting and tearing, each side inflicted terrible wounds on their opponent before tossing them aside and moving on to the next. Within minutes the beautiful mosaic tiled floor was slippery with blood and littered with bodies of dead and dying werewolves.

Nate glanced around him and found Emil. "Get the women and Bartol out of here."

"I'm not going anywhere." Violet raised her voice above the fury as she slid her hand into his. "My place is at your side."

Emil moved quickly, carrying Bartol up the stairs and escorting Dorotea with him. As Nate tried to size up the best way to deal with the out-of-control situation, Nevan closed in on Roko, his teeth bared. Both men were in human form as they faced each other.

"You dared to enter my home?"

"It's over, old man. You have spent too long fighting personal battles and not enough time taking care of the needs of the werewolf dynasty—"

Before Roko could finish speaking, Nevan shifted. His talons slashed into Roko's unprotected stomach. Attacking him before he had a chance to shift was a cowardly and unwolflike move. Shock registered on Roko's handsome face as he dropped to his knees, clutching his stomach. Werewolves didn't do devious, and Nevan had caught him unawares. Showing no mercy, Nevan went in for the kill. Violet turned her face to Nate's neck, unable to watch.

A howl rent the air as Teo, Roko's right-hand man, threw himself on Nevan, dragging the Wolf Leader away from Roko's body. When he saw what Nevan had done, the young werewolf turned on Nevan, his lips drawn back in a snarl. Nate, reading his intention, had no time to get to him before Teo attacked. Nate had never seen ferocity like it. Teo ripped his opponent apart. Blood sprayed in an arc from Nevan's severed arteries. Within seconds, Nevan lay dead on the floor, his throat ripped out as Teo stood over him, wiping the blood from his mouth.

"Enough!" Nate took the stairs two at time, pausing on the half landing to look down.

Would they listen to him? Would they recognize his authority? Could he do anything to stop this senseless slaughter? All he knew was he had to try. This was his pack. He belonged here. For the first time he was willing to acknowledge it, not just to himself, but publicly. He wasn't prepared to let them keep tearing each other apart.

"Your leaders are both dead." He was pleased his voice held steady and showed none of the shock and horror he felt. Violet came to stand beside him, and he took her hand. Her touch steadied his resolve further. "This ends now."

No one moved. At least they weren't charging up the stairs ready to tear his head off. He drew a breath. *Think.* Deal with the practical aspects. Get them moving away from each other. The dead and dying would have to be dealt with. He knew from experience that werewolves were not truly dead unless they were staked and decapitated. These unfortunate souls might be horribly injured and appear to have ceased breathing, but they would be left maimed and incapacitated unless that final kindness was performed. This would be the test of whether he was in control here.

"Teo, organize a group of men and begin the cleanup operation. These bodies will have to be disposed of according to werewolf law."

Nate kept his eyes fixed on Teo's, assessing the other man's response. After a slight hesitation, Teo nodded. The fire went out of his eyes, and his shoulders slumped into an aspect of compliance.

"There is also Dario's body in the cells," Violet said. "We must take care of them all."

Nate spared a moment to look at her in surprise and admiration. She had overpowered Dario? That was a story for another day, but his beautiful werewolf would never cease to amaze him.

Emil had reappeared after seeing Dorotea and Bartol safely to one of the bedrooms. Violet turned to him. "Take a boat to Vukod and bring Marko and your mother back here to care for Bartol. In a day or two, we can begin the task of returning the refugees to their homes."

As she spoke, Nate felt the atmosphere in the room shift. He was prepared to take charge if he could, but Violet was seen as Nevan's daughter and, unlike him, she was a werewolf. This was a hierarchical society, one that recognized the dominance of the alpha male. Would they accept the leadership of a non-wolf alpha and his alpha female? With her hand in his, he felt it might just be possible. He looked back at the remaining werewolves in the hall. They had all shifted back now and were gazing up at Nate and Violet. One by one—whether they were supporters of Nevan or of Roko—they dropped to one knee and placed their right hand over their heart in a signal of allegiance. With a feeling of shock and appreciation, Nate realized the gesture was directed toward the two of them.

Chapter 23

Violet arched her back at the delicious invasion of Nate's erection. Her muscles tightened around his thick, hot shaft as he plunged deep inside her. She lost her breath along with the ability to think coherently. Tilting her hips, she gazed up at the canopy of trees through half-closed eyes as he commenced a steady, pistoning rhythm.

His cock was like a brand of fire, imprinting itself in the depths of her body. As he took her to new heights, the pressure built and tightened. She was already so close. Her body was one long tremor after another, her muscles convulsing, preparing for the rising orgasm to rip her apart.

Nate pulled back, keeping her hovering on the brink of climax, and Violet made a soft mewling sound of frustration.

"Bite me." He threw back his head, the tendons in his neck corded. He pressed his fingers to the spot where his neck and shoulder met. The special place where a bite would mark him as her mate forever. Where the piercing of her teeth would transform him into a werewolf. "Here."

She opened her eyes fully as he thrust into her again, hard and deep. There was no question about what he was asking. No need for words or discussion. No asking "Are you sure?" or "Shall we talk about this?" Everything she wanted to know was there in his eyes. Her muscles began to tighten and throb around him, and her canines lengthened as she shifted. Her body convulsed as her orgasm neared. As she sank her teeth into his flesh and tasted his beloved blood, fire and energy engulfed her. It wrapped itself around her, in her, coursing through her, exploding over her.

Nate cried out as she impaled him with her bite and his own release overcame him. He drove into her, on and on. Wildly, mindlessly, flesh pounding into flesh, keeping the sensations washing over her until she released him and his body came to a shuddering standstill. Even then, her muscles continued to spasm around him in a series of delicious aftershocks.

"So how fast do these things work?" Nate lay back on the grass, pulling her down on top of him as she shifted back into human form again. Two days had passed since the dramatic scenes in the hall of the Voda Kuca, and this was the first occasion they had managed to snatch any time alone. "How soon before I can run faster than you through the forest?"

"I don't know. I've never bitten anyone before." Violet leaned closer and flicked her tongue over the wound she had made in his neck. "Felt good, though."

"Am I supposed to bite you in return?"

Violet sprang to her feet. "You'll have to catch me first."

She took off at speed, laughing as Nate's startled cry followed her. Dropping onto all fours, she shifted as she ran. A noise beside her made her turn her head, and there, running alongside her, was the most magnificent male wolf she had ever seen. Violet threw back her head and gave a single, triumphant howl.

I know you.

The male howled in return, acknowledging her cry, his victorious growl echoing through the woodland.

Side by side, the two wolves ran through the forest, moving fluidly in time with each other. The male was much larger and stronger than the female. His brown fur was lighter than her black pelt; his brown eyes glowed gold compared with her unusual blue ones. Beside his powerful, muscular frame, she appeared slender. Deep in the woodland, he paused, his body language inviting her to come to him. The female knew her place. Crouching low, she rubbed her face against his muzzle. The male stood proud, graciously permitting this gesture of subservience.

They moved together and apart repeatedly, in a timeless ritual, a mating dance. When they came together for the final time, the female rolled onto her back, trusting him, presenting her unprotected belly to him. Her mate stood over her, baring his teeth as if he was considering ripping out her tender throat. Instead, he rested his jaw against her chest, pressing lightly to reinforce his dominance. When he released her, he nudged his nose down her body, marking her with his own essence. A low, rumbling growl rose in his throat, a sound that might have been anticipation.

He caught the loose fur at her neck between his teeth, and the female froze. Bringing his body over hers, the male sank his teeth into her flesh, and she submitted to him with a soft howl of surrender. Her mate had claimed her, marked her as his own, just as she had taken him earlier. They were bonded together at last, never to be parted. Now, and forever.

"I'm not sure I believe in fate." Nate turned away from his contemplation of the view from the window of the study in the Voda Kuca as he spoke. He was still finding it hard to think of it as his study rather than Nevan's. He supposed familiarity was something that would come with time.

"Fate sure as hell seems to believe in you," Cal responded with a fervor only someone who had known Nate throughout the last six tormented years could summon.

They were words to make anyone stop and think. They certainly made Nate pause and look back on his life since he had been attacked by a feral werewolf on that fateful night.

His life seemed to have been a series of interlinked turning points, each of them building on the other to lead him to where he was now.

Would he have been able to appreciate what it meant to be Wolf Leader if he had never been feral? There had been no opposition to Teo's emotional proposal that Nate should take over that role. On the contrary, once it was known that he had Violet at his side, there was universal approval.

Would he have been able to bring the strength and compassion needed to unite the troubled werewolves of the Wolf Nation, if he had no understanding of what had torn them apart? He had been human for most of his life, so he brought a very different perspective to the role, but he loved a werewolf, one who knew more about how to mend the hurt this dynasty had suffered than anyone.

Getting to this point in his life had built him up and torn him down so many times, he had developed an inner resilience he had hardly known was there until he had to call on it to rescue Violet and call a halt to this civil war.

Could he say this had been meant to be? He thought that might be going too far. All he knew was that he was uniquely equipped to fulfil the task he had been given, and he intended to do it to the best of his ability.

And being a werewolf? A full-blown, non-feral werewolf? For the first time in six years he finally felt he belonged. Even with Beast, that had never happened. Ged had tried to rescue him, but he had never been able to find a home for him within the group. Because Nate had been unique and there hadn't been anywhere he belonged... until now.

When Nate found that place deep inside himself—the one Cal's silver dagger had been unable to destroy—and shifted, his heart filled with joy. He had never questioned his decision or known a moment's regret. This was his home.

"Do you need any help from the Alliance with the refugee crisis?" Cal's question brought him back to the present.

"The refugees are all back on their home island of Reznati. That was our first job when we took over. Everyone from both of the former factions supported us and helped in the task. But rebuilding their communities will be long and slow. When the celebrations are over, I'll take you to see what needs to be done."

"Talking of celebrations..." Cal drained his glass, and nodded toward the door. "I think it's time."

Nate grinned. "I have never been more ready for anything in my life."

Everyone agreed that the wedding was beautiful. The bride looked lovely, the groom's face shone with pride and they were the perfect couple. The only slight hitch occurred when the twins, Jethro and Arthur, who had been given the task of bearing the rings, came to blows in the middle of the ceremony and had to be escorted outside by their embarrassed mother. Stella was full of apologies later.

Violet's sisters, Gabriela and Marina, were there with their families, together with her other brother, Franko. Bartol's strength was returning, and he had been well enough to stand throughout the ceremony. The family reunion was as touching to see as the love between the newlyweds.

Violet wore a full-length, white lace gown. There had been much debate about how to find the right garment at short notice. In the attic of the Voda Kuca, Dorotea still had the dress she had worn for her marriage to Nevan, but they were united in their agreement that it would be a bad omen for her daughter to wear that. In the end, the Faerie Queen, Vashti, stepped in to help. She had dresses for every occasion. Violet and Dorotea had spent a pleasurable and luxurious few days at the faerie palace, getting to know each other and gasping over the delights of her wardrobe. Once Violet had found the perfect gown, a flowing one fit for a fairy-tale bride—ordered by Vashti for a formal function and never worn—skillful faerie dressmakers had undertaken the necessary alterations.

The werewolf guests were delighted at the amount of raw meat provided for the wedding feast, while the faeries and mortals among the party heaved a sigh of relief to discover that there were alternative items on the menu.

Cal, who had performed the ceremony, gave a short speech. He talked about the obstacles his friends Nate and Violet had overcome to reach this day, his pride in their achievements and his hopes for the future of the werewolf dynasty under a new, compassionate leadership.

"I once feared that the werewolf dynasty was a story of nobility lost. Now I have hopes it will be a tale of nobility restored." He raised his glass. "I ask you to join me in a toast to my friend Nate, the new Wolf Leader."

"Not so fast." Nate got to his feet, drawing Violet up with him. "There are two Wolf Leaders from now on. We will bring about the changes needed and we'll do it together. Side by side."

Dorotea's voice rang out before Cal could speak again. "To Nathan and Violetta."

A huge cheer rang out as everyone raised their glasses and Nate swept Violet into a kiss that went on for a very long time. When he raised his head, her eyes were brimming with so much love he felt light-headed.

"I have a wedding present for you."

She chuckled naughtily. "You are supposed to wait until we are alone. It gets embarrassing for the guests if you don't."

"You are a very badly behaved woman," he said, pretending to be shocked.

She nodded. "And you love it."

"I do." He kissed her again. "Come with me."

Grabbing her hand, he led her out toward the gardens. Violet gathered up her long skirts and hurried to keep pace with his long strides. The guests followed, curious at the strange behavior of a bride and groom who ran out on their own wedding feast and into the night.

"Where are we going?" Violet asked.

"You'll see."

Nate propelled her along with him until they reached the edge of the clearing. Once there, he stopped and, with a gesture curiously like a conjurer about to perform a magic trick, raised his arm. Instantly, the field burst into life. Spotlights lit up the sky and focused on a makeshift stage. A familiar, frenetic cacophony of noise filled the air. Violet turned to Nate with wide eyes.

"How did you get them here?"

"It took a bit of organization, but it wouldn't be a werewolf wedding without a bit of Beast."

Letting go of her hand, he bounded onto the stage, fist-bumping his bandmates as he went. Torque handed Nate his guitar. Waiting until their bass guitarist was in foot-stomping, back-arching position, Khan lifted his mic stand and let loose with a soulful, sky-rending screech. The wedding guests, released from their stunned immobility, broke into a frenzy of cheering.

"This one is for the bride."

As the strains of her favorite Beast number filled the air, Violet felt her heart swell. On the stage, she watched her husband, the man who had brought love into her empty life and restored the dignity of her people. Behind her, the Voda Kuca, her beautiful home, was waiting for them to fill it with life in the future.

As the new, joint Wolf Leaders, she and Nate would promote tolerance and openness, starting with her recent announcement that she was Anwyl's daughter. This had caused shock, but also some rejoicing throughout the Wolf Nation. Violet had also sent a message to her half-siblings, Anwyl's children from his marriage, who had fled their homeland years ago, telling them that they would be welcome to return.

Ged joined her, kissing her on the cheek. "What do you think the chances are of Beast doing a tour of Otherworld?"

Violet looked around her. At the Faerie King and Queen, who were dancing with their children in their arms. At Merlin Caledonius, the greatest sorcerer the world had ever known, who was belting out the words of the song at the top of his voice as he serenaded his wife. At her newfound family who were imitating Khan and using their fingers on either side of their heads in the sign of the beast. At Marko and Valentina, who, ignoring the tempo of the music, were performing an old-fashioned waltz on the grass.

"Pretty good from what I can see."

Ged laughed, holding out his hands, and they danced together for the last few minutes of the number. Once Nate had finished playing the first song, he handed his guitar to Finglas and came back to Violet, sweeping her into his arms. "Do you think our guests would notice if we slipped away?"

She laughed up at him. "Was this all a diversionary tactic?"

"You know me too well," he said, as he led her back toward the house. "Much as I love our friends and family, I can't wait to create more unforgettable moments with you, my beautiful wolf."

* * * * *

MILLS & BOON®

n o c t u r n e™

AN EXHILARATING UNDERWORLD OF DARK DESIRES

A sneak peek at next month's titles...

In stores from 9th March 2017:

- **Angel Unleashed** – Linda Thomas-Sundstrom
- **The Immortal's Unrequited Bride** – Kelli Ireland

Just can't wait?
Buy our books online before they hit the shops!
www.millsandboon.co.uk

Also available as eBooks.

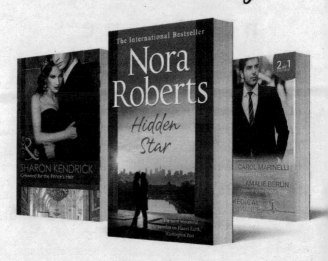

Join Britain's BIGGEST Romance Book Club

- **EXCLUSIVE offers** every month

- **FREE delivery direct** to your door

- **NEVER MISS a title**

- **EARN Bonus Book** points

Call Customer Services
0844 844 1358*

or visit
hillsandboon.co.uk/subscriptions